THE TIME DANCER

Books by Zelda Leah Gatuskin

Spiral Map of Time Trilogy
THE TIME DANCER
THE TWO MAGICIANS
THE TEN YEARS

Fiction
CASTLE LARK
WHERE THE SKY USED TO BE
DIGITAL FACE

Creative Non-fiction
ANCESTRAL NOTES
TIME AND TEMPERATURE
IF I COULD CONVINCE YOU OF ONLY ONE THING

Poetry
BUT WHO'S COUNTING?

Art
ZELDA'S COSMIC COLORING BOOK

THE TIME DANCER

A Novel of Gypsy Magic

Zelda Leah Gatuskin

Spiral Map of Time Trilogy Book 1

Printed in the United States of America
        First Printing, 1991
        Second Printing, 2019
        ISBN-10: 0-938513-12-5
        ISBN-13: 978-0-938513-12-4
        Library of Congress Catalog #91-72033

                AMADOR PUBLISHERS, LLC
                Albuquerque, New Mexico U.S.A.
                    www.amadorbooks.com

for my family

The 22 Keys of the Tarot

0	The Fool
I	The Magician
II	The High Priestess
III	The Empress
IV	The Emperor
V	The Heirophant
VI	The Lovers
VII	The Chariot
VIII	Strength
IX	The Hermit
X	The Wheel of Fortune
XI	Justice
XII	The Hanged Man
XIII	Death
XIV	Temperance
XV	The Devil
XVI	The Blasted Tower
XVII	The Star
XVIII	The Moon
XIX	The Sun
XX	Judgment
XXI	The World

Prologue

"George! George! George Drumm, where are you!?"

"George! Come on! We're going to be late!"

The voices of the young men rang through the late afternoon mist but the George in question did not reply.

"Oh, for crying out loud!" Wilbur muttered, plopping down on one of many low stone walls that criss-crossed the rolling fields.

"What are we going to do?" Artie asked, coming up behind him.

"Find another fiddler—fast."

"And where do you propose we go looking for a fiddler this late in the day, and who do you suppose we'll find who can play with us at the wedding this very night? And even if we find someone, the Corys will have our heads if we show up without George Drumm. He's the reason they hired us, and they won't take anyone else . . ."

"All right, all right, Artie! What do you suggest we do?"

"I don't know, just keep looking and waiting, I guess. He'll show up sooner or later, he always does. Maybe he's down by the old cairns. How about you go back to your mum's house to see if he's shown up for practice, and I'll jog down to the cairns and then meet you back there."

"Well, be quick about it. *We* need to rehearse even if his highness doesn't. Sure, he always shows up for the jobs—and to collect his pay—but what about us? He gets away with murder, he does! Never practices, never spends a minute getting organized. Just shows up and plays and plays whatever he will—with us following along behind as best we can—and everyone loves him. They can't get enough. And if there's ever a wrong note or something a wee bit off, it's *us* they blame! Oh, Mister Drumm can do no wrong, he can. 'Too

1

bad about the lads,' they'll say, 'too bad George can't find some musicians who are his equal,' they'll say. But *I* say, you won't find *me* still living with me mum when I'm thirty-odd years old, or missing practices, or getting lost in the moors for days on end. No sir! I'll be married to the prettiest daughter of the richest family on the island before I'm twenty-five—and there won't be a soul would accuse me of playing badly on my flute *then*!"

Wilbur found he had made this speech to himself. Artie was already well down the path toward the ancient burial heaps.

"They're looking for you, Mister."

George pushed his hat back from his face and opened one eye, groaning. The bent old woman shaking her cane at him was as strange as the dream visions still lingering in his awareness. He sat upright and yawned, trying not to appear too interested in this self-appointed alarm clock. He had seen her before, from a distance. She too wandered the moors and the rocky coasts of the island. From his favorite vantage point atop the Corbel Shernyie, George would sometimes watch her hunched silhouette creeping along in the distance, stooping now and again to pick something up from the ground and place it in a large straw basket.

"What've you been collecting?" George noticed the basket now. It was resting at her feet, covered with a linen cloth.

"None of your business," she said mischievously, in a brittle voice. "Why don't you want your friends to find you?"

George could hear Artie's calls in the distance, first growing louder and nearer and then becoming faint again. George guessed that Artie had turned in the wrong direction and gone down through McGiver's Lea. He was glad, wanting to talk more to this strange woman.

"They'll find me in good time. I like it here. Tell me, do you know anything about the people who left these drawings on the rocks?" George pointed to the spot where he had been resting. Intricate patterns had been laboriously incised in the hard stone. The design that most intrigued George was the double "s"-shaped spiral. It was so perfectly proportioned. He would sometimes sit at home and try to draw this spiral himself, but he could never get it just right. No matter how he tried, he could not draw all of the coils the same distance apart, nor make the two halves of the "s" of equal size.

His teachers at school had been the first to show him the glyphs, taking him and his classmates to the cairns and lecturing them on the images, which they said ranged from two to ten thousand years old. Twenty years later, George was still fascinated by this, and he returned again and again to marvel at how the ancient craftsmen had wrought such perfect geometry in stone.

The crone stepped over and looked at the spiral upon which George had been resting his head as he slept. Then she looked into George's eyes, squinting as if looking for something at a great distance. Finally, satisfied by what she saw, the woman spoke in her shrill, quavering voice:

"Folk have been passing across these islands for all of Time. The sea brings them, and the harsh sea gales often blow them away again. See how many different marks there are here? They have been left by many different peoples at many different times. See the square wave pattern above you there? That is the symbol for the Piper People. You are of these people, George Drumm, as am I, as are most of us living here today."

"Then this one is from a time even before the Piper People came." George tried to get the crone to talk about the spiral. She was giving him the same lesson his teachers had so many years ago. He did not have time to listen to her explain how each wave of migrants to the island had found the cairns with the mysterious markings and piled on new stones, cut with fresh designs, so as to leave their own message for the spirits and for the future. Every school child knew that one could trace the history of the island by studying the piles of stone. As one followed the images from the top of the pile to the bottom, one followed a time-line back to a long forgotten past. While much had been discovered about the Piper People from their relatively recent markings, until now George had found no one who could tell him about the perfect spirals and the other exquisite circular shapes which appeared on the earliest layers of so many of the cairns.

The crone traced the path of the spiral with the end of her cane. Her bony hand shook slightly and she hummed to herself. When she spoke again her voice sounded different—no longer strained and squeezed with age, but breathy and low. George shivered. For the first time felt a bit fearful in the woman's presence. It was as if the words came out of the Past and were spoken by the wind through her aged lips.

"The Wanderer People cross all of the lands of the world with the greatest ease, for they travel on the waves of Magic. Time and Distance are no obstacles to them. The Spiral is their map and the Circle is their time piece. And the Figure Eight, should you ever discover it, is the symbol they use to mark their paths. If you find a sideways Figure Eight, you will be able to follow the path; but if you find an upright Figure Eight, there will be no way for you to follow, for it means that the Wanderer has set out across Time—and only one who knows the secrets can travel that path."

"You mean they still exist, these Wanderers? Why have I not heard of them? Why have they not come back to our island in nine thousand years?"

"They are now as they were then. If they are not here, then they are somewhere else. Have they not come back in all this time, or have they simply hidden their recent messages to each other and the spirits with great care? Perhaps if one is old and unafraid and wise in the ways of Nature and wanders the empty places, one might still meet a Wanderer on Sumweir Island." The woman's eyes twinkled knowingly at George, whose mouth was beginning to drop open. "But you won't find a Wanderer residing on the island, only passing through. The climate here has grown harsh and cold since the time of these spirals, and the Wanderers much prefer lands full of sunshine. Have you not heard of a people called the Gypsies who live in great traveling bands far, far to the East, beyond the Dromandy

Mountains? And there is another tribe called the Ethalees, with black complexions, who live in the southern deserts of the Great Continent. To find the Wanderers, one need only wander oneself, for by doing so you will become one with them, and then—*they* will find *you*."

"Why are you telling me all this?" George's skin was prickling.

"Because you asked," she said, her voice once more crackling with age. "And besides, if you do not show up to play at the wedding tonight, you had better take to the road! Old Mister Cory will have your head! Hee hee, hee hee . . ."

The crone's cackle blended with the mixed calling and panting of Artie, who had circled around and was approaching the cairn from the opposite direction.

"Oh, heaven help me!" George cried, noticing by the darkening sky that he was quite late. "Over here, Artie, over here! C'mon, let's go!" He snatched his fiddle from the ground and jammed his hat down on his head before running to intercept Artie. "Good bye, Ma'am—and thank you!" he called over his shoulder. But his words were lost in the wind, and the old woman was nowhere in sight.

The wedding of John and Martha Cory's youngest daughter Shawna was not soon forgotten. In the first place, the bride was most uncooperative. Always a spoiled girl, she refused to don her wedding dress until her husband-to-be was summoned to speak to her regarding events at his bachelor's party the night before. It was uncustomary—some would even say tempting ill fate—for the bride and groom to meet prior to the ceremony on the day of the wedding, but with the guests already assembling and the bride threatening to call things off there was nothing else to be done.

An unruffled Hubert Quiggley spoke soothingly to Shawna through the door of her bedroom. John and Martha paced the hallway downstairs and tried not to listen. After what seemed an eternity, Hugh galloped down the stairs and with a breezy "See you at church!" was out the door. No sooner had the latch clicked behind him than Shawna appeared at the top of the stairs, exquisite in

Martha's mother's satin gown. "Well let's be off then, shall we?" she said contritely, sniffling just the tiniest bit.

The upshot of all this was that when the trio of musicians arrived breathlessly at the Guild Hall fully expecting to be met by a furious John Cory and a pack of disgruntled guests, they found the hall empty. The tables at the far end of the room were laid with plates and silver and linen and crystal, great platters of untouched food, unopened bottles of champagne and ale. Chairs were set up neatly against the walls, leaving the middle of the floor open for dancing. A platform had been arranged for the musicians. They put down their instruments and wandered off to the large pantry, where they found several of the servers and butlers who had been hired for the occasion playing cards.

"Bride had cold feet," one of the tuxedoed men said, "tho' from what I hear, it's the groom who should worry. Ah well," he checked his pocket watch, "I imagine the deed is done now. They sent a lad over a bit ago to tell us the ceremony was finally starting."

Artie, Wilbur and George could not believe their luck. They rushed back to their platform and tuned their instruments. George explained some ideas he'd had while out on the moors and led Artie and Wilbur through a couple of new melodies. When they heard the voices of the first guests approaching, they stopped playing and put bored expressions on their faces.

Mrs. Cory was one of the first to arrive at the Hall. She rushed to George, bubbling over with apologies.

" . . . Of course after putting everyone through all that, we want the party to be extra special, and it may go quite late, but we will naturally make it worth your while . . ."

"Not to worry, Ma'am," George broke in graciously, "these things happen. Really, it's our pleasure. This is what now, the third daughter of yours we've helped to marry? Why we're almost family by now, so please don't trouble yourself over us."

"Third and last, praise the lord! You're a sweet boy, George. Now why didn't I get *you* for a son-in-law? You had three tries!"

As Mrs. Cory bustled off, George turned to Wilbur and Artie who were trying to suppress their guffaws. Was this the same Mrs. Cory who had once made it quite clear that a mere musician would be no match for any of her girls?

The hall was filling up with a well-dressed but surly crowd. Anticipating the Cory's generous spread, they had all skipped dinner. What they had not anticipated was the two-hour delay at the church, and the folks streaming past the musicians were hungry and irritable. George's mother slowed for a moment and made a face. "You lads have your work cut out for you," she hissed on her way by.

But the musicians were in fine spirits as George artfully led them through gentle renditions of some old ballads and love songs. The familiarity of the tunes and the soothing way they were played, as well as the long awaited food and drink, were soon restoring the wedding guests to good humor. By the time all had eaten their fill and no more brothers and best men remained to toast the newlyweds, the trio was picking up the pace with lively two-steps and reels.

As the floor filled with dancers, George gave a nod to the others, and they finally began to play full out. George always teased Artie that he danced with his squeeze box instead of playing it, and on this night he was outdoing himself. Wilbur, switching between an assortment of pipes and flutes as the music moved him, looked like a juggler. And with George fiddling so fast that it seemed possible he could actually become airborne, the group resembled a three-ring circus as much as a musical trio. Their excitement infected the crowd, and more and more people rose to dance.

George watched the pulsating throng and thought of the old woman—for a moment he thought he saw her. But the harder he stared into the crowd, the less he could make out. The dancers became a blur, a swirl—a spiral! Unaware of what he was doing, George let a reel he was playing turn into one of his own tunes. Artie and Wilbur, remembering the music from their brief practice, followed along with ease. They did not even notice when they had gone through all of the changes George had taught them and were playing completely new patterns. For the first time, they felt what George felt when he played: the music flowed in them and out of them, no thought was necessary—whatever came out would be right, would be perfect.

Even after the bride and groom had been seen off in a shower of rice, the party went on. Everyone remarked on the performance of George and "his boys." Soon, the ill-tempered bride and long delayed wedding were of secondary interest. It was the music that was truly notable. Women and men who had not danced in years took off their shoes and demonstrated their old style jigs for any who would watch. Long, long into the night the music and dancing continued.

One by one, exhaustion overtook the dancers and they limped home. John Cory stuffed a handful of notes into each musician's vest pocket, tipped his hat, and led a rosy-cheeked Martha Cory out. Finally, only George's mother remained, dozing in her chair by the musicians' platform. The men wiped their brows and put away their instruments.

"Wake up, Mum," George said, and she sat straight up with a start. "I have something to tell you all," he said as he stood on the platform, about to deliver a speech. "I'm leaving the island. Artie, Wilbur, you're fine musicians; I know you'll find another fiddler, one who's better behaved than me no doubt. Mum—what can I say? I hope you can understand . . ."

George's mother had begun to weep. They were all somewhat drunk. No one said anything for a long time. Finally Artie gave George a hug and went out. Wilbur shook George's hand and tried to say something but all that came out was "righto." He slung his bag over his shoulder and ran out to catch Artie. George walked his mother home. They went inside and George began to pack a few things; he would not sleep another night in the house in which he'd been born. Mrs. Drumm sat in her favorite chair and watched and listened to George's preparations, weeping softly.

"Take care of yourself, Mum." George bent and kissed her on the forehead.

"You're a good boy, George," she finally said. I've been lucky to have you with me as long as I've had. Blessed. I heard the voice of the Lord in your music tonight, son. And the wee spirits, too. Make sure to carry your fiddle with you always, my boy, and you will carry your special blessing and always be safe. This is why I can let you go without fear. Oh, but I will miss you terribly, son."

"Let us believe we will meet again," George said, believing not at all. "I love you, Mum." And with that he went out.

George did not rest until he had reached the cliffs overlooking the jagged southern coast of the island. He sat on the moss and watched the sun rise. When it was light enough to make out the sea below, George stood stiffly and bent to pick up a rock to throw. He had stood on this same spot many times in his boyhood and thrown rocks at the water. He wondered now how there could be any rocks left on this spot, for he was not the only youth to test his arm against the wind. George scanned the ground for just the right sized stone and settled for one which was larger than he would have liked. Picking it up, he was surprised by how heavy it felt, although it was only the size of a child's fist. George brushed away the loose dirt to see what kind of rock he had found. He discovered a mark: a figure eight scratched into the stone's one flat side. At once he put the stone back on the ground exactly as he had found it, fitting it into the impression left behind in the damp soil. With the rock in this position, the figure eight was lying on its side. One loop pointed back to town, the other to the treacherous path which wound down to the coast.

George picked up the stone once more and, after a long stern look, rapped himself on the forehead with it. "Ouch! Well I guess I'm not dreaming!"

He started to put the stone in his pocket but changed his mind and returned it once more to its original position. Then George jogged over to the path and began to skitter down to the sea.

Chapter 1

"I have never seen Audy react so strongly to any guest of mine," the Gypsy said, casting a curious look at the cat. Audy had leapt to the back of the over-stuffed chair to which the Gypsy had directed her visitor and was now purring loudly at the man's large, freckled ear.

"Just a way I have with animals, I guess," the man answered. And he settled back into the chair completely undisturbed by the cat's claws kneading his woolen shirt. "But say!" his eyes opened wide as if something had just dawned on him. "You're not thinking this is a bad omen for me, are ya? This being a black cat and all." He sat forward and twisted around to glare at the animal, which was settling itself as if for a nap. It winked disinterestedly from the top of the back of the upholstered chair.

"You say you have a special way with all animals?" the Gypsy asked as she studied her client. She stepped around to her own chair, across the round table from him, and watched him carefully as she snatched a square of purple silk out of the air and draped it across the table in a single motion. The man was dumbfounded and could not answer. He now appeared quite uncomfortable. Afraid to take his eyes away either from the Gypsy or the cat, he sat awkwardly twisted on the edge of his chair, shifting his eyes first back to the cat and then forward to the Gypsy.

"I wouldn't worry about the cat, then," the Gypsy said, as if her question had been answered. Indeed, the fellow seemed odd enough to be in touch with the animal world in a way she might not understand yet. He was physically rugged, unshaven, and smelled of the outdoors. Not at first glance the type who would seek out a fortune teller, but this business with Audy made her wonder—was the

11

man here *because* of the cat? Audy now appeared to have fallen
asleep and, at the Gypsy's reassurance, the man settled back into the
chair, still watching her movements alertly. "Do you wish to tell me
your name?" she asked.

"No, ma'am," he answered simply.

"Very well." The Gypsy began shuffling a deck of large colorful
cards. She knew of the superstition about names in these parts, and
had to respect the spiritual sophistication of her otherwise pragmatic
neighbors. The name. That by which we know ourselves. These folk
knew instinctively that a name spoken can summon the spirit of the
named, for good or ill; and a name written was weighty with the
power of symbols and numbers. "You do not trust me with your own
name," she mused aloud, still shuffling. The man seemed hypnotized
by the snap of the cards, the deftness of the Gypsy's brown fingers
as she fanned the cards across the purple cloth, scooped them up
again and shuffled some more. "But you are prepared to trust me
with all of the names I hold here. Each card of the Tarot has a name,
has many names. Do you not fear my calling of these names?"

"That is what I came here for," the man said bravely. He pulled
some silver from his pocket and threw it on the table in front of the
Gypsy. She smiled and passed the cards across the table.

"Very well, then."

Now the client shuffled the cards by carefully cutting and
re-stacking the deck. His method was to cut the deck into four or six
piles and then to pick the piles up in seemingly random order and
then start again. The cat, watching out of one half-open eye, began
to growl, and the Gypsy—who would normally attribute the man's
technique to lack of physical coordination—felt uneasy. 'Does Audy
like this person or not?' she wondered. 'What will these cards
reveal?'

As if on cue, and ignoring the cat completely, the client passed
the cards back to the Gypsy. She cut the deck one last time while
watching her guest closely. Did his expression change, or was it her
imagination? If this was an amatuer, his stacked deck would now be

ruined by her single cut of the cards. On the other hand, someone like Malcom—the Master Seer—could arrange the deck so that it would always reveal his intended spread, no matter how tampered with by an uncooperative hand. The Gypsy continued to peer at her client, who writhed under her glare.

Perhaps she was foolish to take such pains with this poor fellow, but Audy seemed to be warning her about something, and she had a great dislike of her card readings being manipulated in any way. She turned her attention to the cat, who was slithering down to the arm of the chair as if to get a better look at the cards. In contrast to his original friendly behavior, Audy now flinched when the man tried to pat him.

The Gypsy began to lay out the cards, face down, one by one from the top of the deck. She used only the top five cards. This would also perplex a novice who thought to stack the deck for a traditional six- or ten-card spread. But the client was more absorbed in the cat, who was reluctantly permitting the man to pet him.

The Gypsy touched the first card saying, as she had so many times—and each time being a revelation both for her and the person to whom she spoke—"This card represents you and your quest. Every person who comes to me to have the cards read is on a quest. You are many selves, but because you come to the cards as one on a quest, this seeking self is here revealed."

She turned the card over from right to left. "The Fool," she said seriously.

The cat and the man had reached a truce. Audy continued to perch on the arm of the chair and appeared to sleep. The "Fool," as the Gypsy would now think of him for lack of another name, held his hands quietly in his lap and was attending to the cards again, awaiting the Gypsy's explanation.

"The Fool is a traveler. He moves through the deck un-numbered and so with no permanent place. See how he carries his belongings over his shoulder?"

The client shifted in his chair, nudging the sack under the table with his toe, aware that the reading was already proving prophetic. He had arrived at the Gypsy's door with a few meager belongings on his back, as if ready to set out on a journey. After agreeing to read his cards, the Gypsy had walked ahead of him into her dark drawing room and busied herself opening the drapes. He did not think she'd noticed his bag either at the door or as he'd slid it under the table, but now it was he who wondered if she had tampered with the deck.

"The Fool is always seeking wisdom and enlightenment and yet is always an innocent. He is a fool because that which he seeks so determinedly along his arduous road can only be found in quietude within himself. But The Fool cannot cease his journey because he not only seeks, he flees. He flees his fate, which is for him as it is for us all: Death. Look, here is Death represented by the dog yapping at the Fool's heels. The Fool runs and runs but can never lose the yapping dog. Yet to *confront* the inevitability of Death and the knowledge that there are realities beyond the flesh and matter of this living world is to be enlightened. The Fool is made more a fool by running from that which he seeks, and for seeking that which he carries with him. The Fool's road is a circle."

The Gypsy made the last statement almost as an afterthought and then appeared to go into a trance. In fact, she was thinking about how very many of the readings she had given with the Tarot began with The Fool. Did this imply that those who sought to know themselves and their fortunes through her cards were fools? Probably so. She focused her dark eyes back on her client.

"The next three cards represent your Past, Present, and Future with respect to your quest."

The man gazed at the cards and the Gypsy's hands on the table. He did not look into her eyes. The cat's ears twitched, but Audy also kept his eyes lowered. The Gypsy turned over the first of the three cards.

"Five of Swords." The illustration on the card was menacing. A ruined building was depicted in the lower half of the card amidst wind-bent wild grasses and a tumultuous sky. The sky disappeared upward into blackness, and in the upper portion of the card five brilliant swords plunged downward like a curtain being lowered. This painting did not cover the entire card but was enclosed by a border: a black line and a yellow line separated the image from a white margin. In each of the four corners of this margin was a small yellow and black arrow. Centered within the top margin was the number V and centered within the bottom margin was the finely lettered word "Defeat."

The Gypsy took a deep breath and exhaled slowly. She reached into the card with her eyes, even as her client did, searching for its deepest meaning. She had to trust that once she could interpret the card correctly herself, she would also be able to reveal that interpretation to the client no matter how negative or foreboding. She had learned that whenever she started to panic about how to explain a "bad" card to someone, it was because her original judgement was too superficial. She had to go deeper to find the truth. Once she had found it, the truth always told itself.

"The suit of Swords represents the power of Air, which is able to enter all places, and Thought. Because it is the suit of Doom, it is also the suit of Glory. The appearance of the Five of Swords as representing your Past suggests that you have been challenged by dangers and hostile forces, either from within or from without, and that these have taken their toll on you. The number Five represents trials, hardships and dire events. It is not an inappropriate number to find at the outset of a serious journey. It tells me that whatever it is you seek is not trivial, and the hardships in attaining it should not be underestimated. The card reads *Defeat* but, as it appears as a Past influence, do not be overly concerned. Interpret it as a warning and not a prophecy. Your quest is dangerous and the hardships of the Past are not to be forgotten. This card says: You were once weakened and vulnerable, be careful."

Now it was the Gypsy who could not look across the table. She knew if she did she would recognize the expression on the client's face. He would be peering at her, wondering how she *knew*—how she could know so much about *him*, his *past*. What else could she tell about him? In fact she knew nothing at all about him, or any stranger who had sat before her like this. She knew only the cards. She read the cards. Through her, the cards spoke. How did the cards know? For that she had no answer, and neither had the Master Seer had an answer nor, she was sure, his teacher before him.

The Gypsy turned over the card she had indicated represented the man's Present and again felt uneasy. Shaken briefly from her concentration on the reading by her own emotions, she snuck a look at Audy and tried not to be too curious about the details of this particular client's life. Audy yawned, and the Gypsy thought she saw the thinnest slit of an eye peek at her, but then the cat was quiet again and apparently asleep. The "Fool" himself seemed to be sinking through the chair, as if he wished to hide from the Gypsy's truths. He was beginning to suspect her of being a mind reader as well as a fortune teller.

"Seven of Swords," she said. The entire image was of a door barred by seven swords. Like the other card, it was bordered with yellow and black, and had the arrows in the corners with the number VII written in the top margin. The lettering across the bottom margin read: "Futility."

"Seven is the number of the occult. Occult secrets are not readily revealed. He or she who seeks to open the door will be challenged." The Gypsy did not elaborate. Taking the message of this card to heart, appearing as it did in the Present, she now wanted to get on with the reading and be done as quickly as possible. She was glad she had only dealt five cards, and she hoped that the next and fourth card would not be another in the suit of Swords, though her fingers tingled with premonition as she turned it over.

"Nine of Swords," she said, and tried not to show the fear which suddenly engulfed her.

The client leaned over to get a better look at the image of the nine swords whose hilts radiated outward from the place where their points converged in entry of a dripping heart. The card was labeled

"Cruelty." The Gypsy noticed the man's breathing quicken. The cat stood and stretched and was about to jump nonchalantly to the floor when the man—the "Fool"—reached out one huge hand and petted Audy so firmly he was forced back into a crouch on the arm of the chair.

"Stop that!" the Gypsy said sharply, standing up, poised for—what? Audy hissed. The "Fool" now had both hands on Audy and looked shocked at the cat's behavior, almost hurt.

"STOP THAT!" the Gypsy said again, her voice becoming shrill. She pushed her chair back as if she would run around the table and wrestle Audy from the man, who now held the cat firmly despite its hissing and struggling.

"The last card, turn the last card!" shouted the "Fool" in a voice so commanding and so familiar that it froze the Gypsy where she stood. And in that brief moment the man reached under the table, grabbed his canvas sack in one hand and shoved the wailing cat into it with the other. The Gypsy stood helpless, paralyzed with fear and anger as the stranger snatched the fifth card of the reading from the table and strode out with Audy squirming and hissing inside his sack.

Only later, when the Gypsy laid out all the remaining cards of the deck, still in shock at the theft of her pet, did she deduce what the final card of the Tarot had been. 'That one!' she thought, visualizing the image on the card that was to have summarized the man's fortunes. 'Well, good riddance to it! Whoever you are, Fool—and I think I know—you are welcome to that Key—just beware of the door it opens.'

But the Gypsy was not so willing to share Audy, and she vowed she would find a way to reclaim him. 'It is a sign to me. This is no way for a Gypsy to live. I shall prepare myself to take to the road once more.' And then she had to laugh, because it occurred to her that there was not much difference between a Gypsy and a Fool.

Chapter 2

The bus pulling up to the station raised a cloud of dust. By the looks of the passengers gratefully but stiffly coming down the steps into the shade of the platform, theirs had been a hot ride. With his sandy hair, faded brown overalls, and his own coating of fine greyish dust, one passenger was virtually invisible against the background of the Caliente bus station on the outskirts of this brownish town. It was therefore quite startling to the handful of people on Platform 8 that this very person who had not even been noticed to exist suddenly exploded in a riot of cursing, snarling, and flying fur. This brief moment of amusement—provided by none other than Audy and the "Fool"—would be well embellished by day's end.

A woman humorously reported the incident to her daughter: "It all happened in a split second. There was this filthy man carrying a cat, a large skinny black cat—with beautiful blue eyes—inside the bib of his overalls, and the poor thing wanted *out*! Oh, that cat finally scratched and hissed and struggled so violently that the guy didn't just let go, he shook the thing away and shouted curses at it like it was the devil himself."

And the bus driver, who also observed the scene while he stood outside the station and smoked a long-awaited cigarette, mused to the ticket agent: "You see all kinds, dontcha? I tell you, after that fella practically threw the cat away from himself, madder'n hell I tell ya, he started blubbering! Wandering around calling, 'kitty, kitty,' and sniffling about all he'd been through with that cat. 'Master' he called it. 'Here, kitty, kitty; here, Master.' I tell you, it was more than pathetic, it was eerie. Yes indeed, I've seen all kinds but that fella gave me the creeps... Oh, the cat? Tore outta the lot faster'n you

18

can say Boo. Ran across the street and back in the weeds behind the old train station, far as I can tell. But I didn't tell you the weirdest thing—the weirdest thing is I don't remember that guy getting on the bus in the first place! *And* I coulda swore I saw him get in line to get back on the bus after he gave up on the cat, like he was going on to Pelona, but I went on the bus before it left to warn Julio to keep an eye on that guy, only *he wasn't on the bus.* Julio didn't remember taking a ticket from anyone like the guy I described. I tell you, that was weird! Hmmm, maybe I need to change routes, take a vacation or something. I tell you, that was strange! Hey, don't say anything to anyone, OK? Julio already thinks I'm nuts!"

Audy stayed close to the tracks, following them north. After his first mad dash away from the bus platform, he had slowed to a tired walk. So dazed was the cat from fear and hunger that he did not try to escape the blazing afternoon sun by resting under the clumps of tumbleweed and sage growing here and there along the tracks. The animal slunk along close to the ground as if trying to make itself a smaller target for the brutal light, which not only beat down on him but also reflected upward from the pale, sandy earth. This was a far less agreeable landscape than the Gypsy's lush vacation village.

Somewhere deep, deep within the starving cat, Malcom—the Master Seer as he was called—tried to contemplate the ever unfolding implications of his research. He had been so sure of himself, and so naive. He had thought he could simply enter the body of an animal and still be himself, Malcom, totally in control.

The cat's nose twitched and he froze. It wasn't long before his sharp ears located the potential meal in the tufts of weeds. One perfectly timed pounce and Audy was devouring a small mole. Malcom was submerged in the cat's needs and consciousness, and the cat was back in command. Appetized by the fresh snack, Audy set forth again at a quickened pace, even more alert for food. A confused and distant Malcom felt proud of Audy's prowess—'he'll survive' —and then a brutal realization brought Malcom to almost full consciousness— 'But will I? The cat's pure instinct for survival that it, we, need so much right now, could bury *me* for good.'

This shift of awareness lasted only an instant. Audy, smelling water in the dry air, had left the path of the railroad tracks and was padding casually toward a sidestreet, where a few persistent home-owners had succeeded in carpeting their front yards with sod. One lawn gleamed like an oasis through the mist of a sprinkler, and thirst took Audy straight toward the gutter running with a trickle of overflow water. He was heedless now of the dangers of the street, ignoring the dogs barking behind their fences and the children riding bicycles. The cat approached the water with the same brash determination with which it had gone to see the Gypsy, striding through her marigolds and leaping through her drawing room window.

She named him Audacious once she realized he was not leaving and ought to have a name (that is, after he had taken himself on an entire tour of the house, lapped up her proffered bowl of cream and curled up on a discarded star chart beside her reading chair). Malcom was much more present then, having just completed the transformation. He liked the name and admired the Gypsy for selecting such a suitable title. Though Malcom went to the Gypsy in the form of a cat in order to play a cruel trick on her, he soon found himself enjoying the Gypsy's kindness and affection, perhaps the only unqualified affection he had ever experienced. The cat loved to sit on the Gypsy's lap to be petted for hours on end, and to eat tidbits of cheese and fish from her fingers. Malcom's vengeance waned, and in time so did his interest in metaphysical experiments and his personality in general.

Now, a year from the day Audy the cat was christened, he was about to be run over by a car in a side street of a dusty town, one Time-spiral's turn removed from the Gypsy's drawing room. Audy was oblivious to the battered sedan lurching toward him on deflated tires. At the last second the car bumped to a stop so that the driver could call out the window to a young woman hanging clothes to dry on the line in her side yard. Audy walked around the tire that had suddenly appeared in his path, and when he made it to the far side of the street, he crouched down and raised his fur in a meaningless show of defense before lapping noisily from the gutter. Malcom was there again, conscious where Audy was not that cat-wise he had just lost a life and had—at most—only eight remaining.

The Gypsy wrongly deduced that the coarse traveler who had come to her for a reading, and left with her precious pet Audy, was the Master Seer still bent on torturing her for rejecting his love. 'Who else could have stacked the cards so, and frozen me with his voice—and chosen that card to be his?' And although the image of the Fool's giant hand petting Audy troubled her a little—that was not Malcom's hand—this detail was soon overshadowed by her over-whelming sense of aloneness. 'How much he must hate me,' she thought, 'to deprive me even of the companionship of a cat.'

She reminded herself that it was Malcom's ceaseless pranks that had driven her to the countryside of Resthaven, a remote but thriving holiday village. Here she had taken on the upkeep of an old gothic-style house which the locals claimed was haunted. The Gypsy recognized at once that this was an abandoned Witch's or Magician's house waiting rent-free for whomever might have the courage to claim it. After working her charts and crystals to determine that the previous owner was not likely to return, the Gypsy made herself at home. She began to read cards for the vacationers and to consult with the wealthy village women about the stars, herbs and dreams: the most propitious dates for engagements and marriages, remedies for sneezing and nervous disorders, the true meaning of the night's visions. The Gypsy did not dance in public or grow close to anyone. While she knew that the Master Seer's tricks were countless, after a time she began to feel that she was rid of him. 'That was my first mistake.'

Once Audy arrived, and she again felt the warmth of companionship, she even found herself having a kind thought for Malcom from time to time. She would sit at her kitchen table feeding scraps to the appreciative Audy, or sit in her drawing room with Audy in her lap, and her thoughts would turn warmly to her first months with Malcom. They had much in common, including not needing or liking a great deal of conversation, and they could sit for hours on end in quiet companionship. At least that's how she grew to picture the scene in retrospect—until now.

Now she burned inside, furious with her own weakness. 'I was right to spurn him! It was not harmonious companionship at all. It was plotting and suspicion always. How long has he been plotting to take Audy from me? How long has he been spying on me? Even while my heart softened to him, he plotted against me. I could almost have loved him. But he is heartless. How could he take Audy, the poor cat? He has probably abandoned Audy to die somewhere, now that he has achieved his aim of hurting me.' The Gypsy consulted her charts for the correct moment to launch her dual mission of rescuing Audy and retaliating against Malcom, never suspecting that these two creatures were one and the same.

She decided that her best approach to finding Audy was to go directly to the Master Seer and make him reveal where he'd sent the cat. She had no doubt that hidden inside the Fool's plain canvas sack was a magic satchel used for travel through time and space. 'Hopefully he did not choose Audy's destination at random and knows where Audy went. But even if he knows, how will I get him to tell me? I could never pretend to want him now. Not even with *his* ego could he imagine I'd willingly surrender to him after what he's done.' The Gypsy knew that if she got close enough to Malcom she could give him an herb in his food or drink which would make him speak truthfully. Malcom would be watching for such tricks and she would have to be cunning.

As she prepared her mixture, she considered how she might inflict some punishment on Malcom while she was about her other business. He deserved revenge but she did not want to waste her time with anything elaborate—she was hoping to be quickly on her way to Audy's rescue—and she was not malicious by nature. Eventually she decided she'd be satisfied with upsetting the order of the Master Seer's lands, of which he was exceedingly proud. Putting the fresh infusion of herbs aside, the Gypsy remembered how Malcom had bragged that he controlled through his great magic even the drops of rain that fell on his fields and the number of insects that populated his forests.

Smiling at the havoc she would bring, she transferred some chips of reddish rock from a dusty jar to a glass mortar and ground them to a fine powder. Then she poured the powder into a pot with some water and a handful of sumac leaves, and set the mixture on the stove to boil. Stirring the pot, the Gypsy looked around at her kitchen with satisfaction. This was the room on which she had worked the hardest. She had put up shelves for her numerous jars of leaves, oils and salts, and she had installed wide drying racks—wire mesh stretched across wooden frames—that could be lowered from the ceiling with pulleys, covered with fresh branches, and raised up again to be out of the way during the drying process. The kitchen had come equipped with many cupboards and long counters, a huge wooden kitchen table with chairs enough for a family of ten, a great cast iron stove and double porcelain sink.

The Gypsy used only a small portion of the kitchen to actually prepare and eat her meals and had moved all but one of the chairs to an unused bedroom. She would sit in the solitary chair at the foot of the long table and dine surrounded by the clutter of her magical preparations. It was during these times that she appreciated her settled life and the large house which allowed her to collect so many beautiful and useful things.

The steam wafting up from the concoction on the stove was making her dizzy. She stepped back, rubbing her eyes. "A good batch," she said out loud. She was used to talking to Audy, who loved to roam about the kitchen and watch as she worked. Keeping her head averted, she took the pot from the stove and carried it over to the sink, where she poured the murky liquid through a muslin cloth laid over the mouth of a shallow bowl. She rinsed the pot and the muslin and left the liquid in the uncovered bowl to evaporate. Later she would take the caked mass left in the bowl and grind it once more into a fine powder. Meanwhile she busied herself with other preparations.

There was much to do. The house must be put in order with each special object and book—whatever was not to go with her—set in its proper place. The plants and flowers would be set outside in a neat row to be watered by the rain and dew. The Gypsy felt her wanderlust returning as she sorted out the few true necessities from her many belongings. She would take only what she could comfortably carry, and she was vividly aware of the possibility that all she left behind—the beautiful house with all of its furnishings and gardens—she might never see again.

It was after midnight by the time the house was arranged to the Gypsy's satisfaction. All of the fresh concoctions she had prepared for her trip were lined up on the long kitchen counter in various stages of drying, congealing and cooling. The tiny vials and sachets for their storage were at the ready along with an intricately embroidered pouch. The pouch was in the shape of a hand and slightly larger than the Gypsy's own hand; stitching separated each finger into its own small compartment.

In the second-story bedroom, clothes were laid out on the bed along with a small treasure's worth of jewelry, talismans and amulets. A woven pack hanging from its strap over the doorknob was already half-filled with some clothes, two pairs of soft leather-soled slippers, a variety of silk scarves, and a tortoise shell hairbrush.

The Gypsy herself was in the third story of the house sitting hunched over on a chest in the middle of the tiny attic. She was talking to the bat, mice and spider population of the house.

"As you know, Audy has been stolen and I am going off to find him. I could be gone for so long that unwelcome strangers will try to move in here. Now, if this should happen, I am counting on you to drive these people away. You know, the old haunted house routine. It really is to your own advantages. Most folk would consider you all pests and want to exterminate you! Their pets would not be nearly so tolerant as Audy."

Here, she could not restrain her tears and had to pause for a few minutes. She had spoken aloud because this is how she could best organize and transmit her thoughts; but the Gypsy knew that language played little part in the way she communicated with the many creatures who shared her home. She spoke to them with her heart, simply by being and believing. She believed that at some level all creatures and elements of nature are made of the same stuff, and she had no doubt that if one could open oneself to this level of being, one could know the thoughts of all creatures and the workings of all things as well as one knew oneself. Likewise, one's own thoughts would be revealed to all of nature and the universe.

"So," she continued, "I'm leaving you some marbles and things to play with up here." She rolled a handful of marbles noisily across the uneven wooden floor and heard the sound of sharp nails scurrying quickly out of the way. "Sorry!" she laughed, surprised that her audience had really been so close at hand. She twisted around and put up a mobile made of cracked teacups, bent silverware and the necks of broken bottles. It was a dangerous looking array, and the Gypsy was careful to hang it so it would not be directly in the way of the small window which was always left open a few inches for ventilation and for the bats.

As she was turning back to conclude her speech, a breeze came through this window and stirred the mobile. It whistled and clanked and scratched menacingly. "I'm leaving a little cheese and bread for you, but when that's gone you're on your own. I trust you'll get by; you did before I came here." And the Gypsy reached into one of her many pockets and left a little pile of sunflower seeds on the floor next to the chest before raising the trap door and descending backwards down the short ladder to the second floor landing.

The night was wearing on but she was still on schedule. Taking a towel from the cupboard, she went downstairs and out the kitchen door into the clear night. She moved quickly and silently down a path that took her past her vegetable garden and the old pump, past a stand of blackberry bushes and through a small wood. The pond she came upon was one of many in the area. This pond, which she called the Deep Well, was especially private, for its far side was densely wooded. No public road reached the pond and few dared to trespass by foot on the Gypsy's allegedly haunted property.

Tonight the Gypsy would add yet another mysterious twist to the reputation she so carefully cultivated. She walked into the pond with her clothes on. Once fully immersed in the cool water, she disrobed. Garment by garment, she washed each article and tossed it in a ball onto a rock on shore. Once naked she swam and enjoyed the dark water and the stars. She washed herself and her hair, then swam to shore, where she took the balls of clothing, shook them out and laid them to dry on the grass.

She hoped that the gossipy townspeople and vacationers would appreciate her leaving them such a juicy detail to add to the tale of her disappearance. She could hear their talk: ". . . and she took all her clothes off and swam out into the middle of the pond where she turned into a swan and flew away." Indeed, the three swans which had been observed on the local ponds for over a month had just recently departed, and this would have been noted by the many bird-watchers in the area. She was careful to maintain her exotic image, as much to remind herself of her Gypsy blood as to keep from disappointing her clientele. The Gypsy took her work seriously.

She walked back to the house patting her hair dry with the towel and stopped at the garden to pick a couple of cucumbers, some carrots, radishes and fresh mint leaves. These she carried into the kitchen and set out on the table. She took a full loaf of brown bread and a round of cheese still encased in wax and set them with the vegetables. The half-eaten loaf and the opened cheese the Gypsy left out, covered loosely with a cloth, for whomever or whatever might need food.

Now she turned to the concoctions on the counter. She packed them in minute containers and filled some other vials and pouches with pinches of herbs and seeds from her vast collection of jars. All of this she packed into the beautiful glove-like pouch. She hung the pouch around her neck by its long, soft strap. The cloth hand, which held many powerful potions and ingredients, hung down against the Gypsy's naked belly.

She went upstairs and dressed in the clothes she had selected earlier: layers of soft silk and cotton garments, the outer skirt and quilted vest lined with many secret pockets, a narrow scarf draped loosely over her hair and around her neck. She left her feet bare, having already packed her slippers, but secured a string of small bells around each ankle. Once fully dressed and adorned with bracelets of beaten metal, strings of beads and coins around neck and waist, the Gypsy proceeded downstairs with her half-filled pack.

Taking up the Tarot deck, wrapped in the purple silk, the Gypsy was tempted to do one last reading for herself to prepare for the adventures at hand. 'No, I don't want to know. I'm going, no matter what, and I don't need the cards to scare me! Besides, the deck's a card short!' She placed the cards into the pack along with a fist-sized crystal ball, which she took from its place on the window sill and wrapped in another square of silk. Then she took a small sheathed scimitar from where it hung as an ornament on the wall and attached it to her belt, hiding the weapon among the folds of her skirt. She stood in the center of the room and turned slowly around to see if she had forgotten anything. Everything was in place. 'The tambourine! That's what I'm forgetting. What proper Gypsy would travel without her music?' And she took the tambourine from its peg on the wall and replaced its worn strap with a fresh piece of ribbon from her sewing basket, so that she could carry it slung across her shoulder.

The Gypsy had not been on the road in what seemed a very long time. She arranged and rearranged her gear, wondering how she used to carry so much. At the last minute she went back upstairs and took most of the spare clothes out of her pack. 'It's the rule of the road,' she reminded herself, 'just what one can carry on one's back.' She then put the tambourine in the pack in place of the clothes, wrapping it in the remaining garments so it wouldn't rattle.

The sky was growing light by the time the Gypsy stood with all of her belongings at the threshold of the back door. She draped a long greyish mantle over her shoulders. The heavy garment was still one more thing to carry, but she smiled as she remembered an earlier journey—her first visit to the Master Seer—on which she had not been so well prepared. 'I'll be smarter this time around,' she thought, and then said aloud, "Don't worry, House, I'll be back." But, as she drew her magic satchel from a pocket in the cloak's lining, the settled life was already beginning to feel like a dream.

Chapter 3

She had learned the secret of the magic satchel before studying with the Master Seer. This skill, like many she possessed, she had wanted to hide from him and might have, had it not been for the cloak—or lack of one.

At the beginning, he frightened her. She had been warned about becoming a follower of such men as he. "Call me Malcom," he said that first day, as if it did not surprise him in the least that a young, darkly beautiful woman, garbed exotically, had come to his door requesting to learn from him. She had said: "Master Seer, I am Esmarelda, a wanderer and a dreamer. I make my way as a Gypsy Dancer, as a Healer and as a Seer. But in this town there is no one who will enlist my services. They say, 'why bother with a woman, a lowly Gypsy, when the most awesome Master Seer himself lives among us?' I was humbled, hearing of your reputation for miles around, and I determined to seek out your tutorship. I am thinking that when the day comes that I am ready to stop my wandering, it will serve me well to have learned more of the secret arts, so I can live comfortably—respected and feared rather than scorned and harassed. Will you teach me Master Seer?"

"Call me Malcom," he said, slightly irritated by what he took as an insinuation that he was getting on in years—that is, her reference to his living comfortably, etc. "Come in, meet some of my other students." He was wishing they were not there so that he might have the company, and mystery, of this woman all to himself. But he'd been holding forth to his apprentices in his usual egotistical manner, and now he had to pay the price for his long-windedness.

The Gypsy paid for their presence as well. For some reason, she hadn't even considered that the Master Seer might have company when she came to visit; but here were four coarse young men touching her silk skirts and flowing veils. They propositioned her loudly as they eyed the coins and trinkets jingling from her belt and wrists, falling over each other in an effort to get personal attention from her. She certainly should have worn a cloak until alone with the Master Seer, but it was too late for such thoughts now. She focused on how she would get rid of the lecherous crew (she would have enough trouble just with "Malcom" alone!) and the Master Seer was also anxious to evict his now unwanted guests.

Malcom could see that slapping the louts' hands away from the lovely Gypsy and requesting civilized behavior was of no use. He was horrified at the lewdness of his so-called apprentices. 'Brutes, nincompoops, one and all; I haven't had a decent pupil in years. Not a one of these four has any significant powers. Some might do well as charlatans faking fortune tellings and seances, and some might honestly try to provide occult guidance, but truly there isn't a teacup full of psychic inspiration among them.'

However, the Master Seer liked being worshipped and feared, and these four were proving to be willing assistants—and in some cases even guinea pigs—for his ongoing "research" into the occult.

"I WILL TURN YOU ALL INTO FROGS!" The Master Seer bellowed. And though it was common knowledge that there was no one on the entire continent powerful enough to turn himself or anyone else into any kind of creature, the tone of Malcom's voice instilled sufficient fear in the apprentices for them to scurry to their seats and fall instantly silent with their hands in their laps.

"Pleased to meet you," Esmarelda said to the suddenly docile group, as if she had just walked in and been properly introduced. "I've brought a special drink all the way from Lasi. It is like a chocolate and I would gladly prepare some for you to show my pleasure at being here."

The apprentices blushed and nodded, still afraid of their Master's discipline.

"Please help yourself to cups and whatever else you need," Malcom finally said, completely disgusted that his pupils could not see what was coming. 'They are idiots,' he thought, 'and if her chocolate kills them it will be just what they deserve. She calls herself a Healer and so is probably not in the business of murder—though I'm sure she hides much from me. Well, I will let her put them to sleep. But be assured they will not rest easy. They shall pay for their stupidity with wretched dreams, dreams that will have them running in fear of this Esmarelda when they awake. Then I shall have her to myself!'

The Gypsy prepared her special beverage, careful to keep her back turned to the men so they could not see her secret ingredients or from where in her clothing she drew them. She felt like she was in the scene of a horror story, and it was all her own doing. To give herself confidence as she stirred the pot of "chocolate," the Gypsy imagined herself a wizened old woman recounting the story of this misadventure to her own young apprentice.

Meanwhile, the Master Seer strolled around the table patting each of his apprentices on the head. As he did so, he deftly plucked a hair from each of them: coarse black hairs from the heads of the twins Gregory and Thomas, a fine blond strand from Alvin's scalp, and a nondescript brown hair from Mark. The unsuspecting men felt Malcom's touch as a paternal gesture, and Malcom himself had a fatherly yearning as, particularly in the case of the dim-witted Alvin, he felt the warmth of their response to him. 'If only I could have a child of my own—a boy with my own fine blood and intellect—to whom I could teach my greatest secrets.' Malcom cast a sly glance at the Gypsy, wondering about her lineage.

The room was small; upon completing his circle around the table, the Master Seer had to squeeze past Esmarelda to get back to his seat in front of the hearth. In doing so he leaned close to her ear and spoke so only she could hear: "No chocolate for me, thank you." His low voice rumbled through her, and his breath was sweet and warm on her face. He said so little yet the humorous, secret way he spoke to her told her he knew all. Esmarelda again became conscious of the sensuousness of her attire.

It was not unusual for the Gypsy to dress in such finery, but normally the rainbow that was her costume would be concealed by a cloak. She did not like to draw attention to herself until she was ready to perform. Then she would scurry about, hunched under her mantle like a bent old woman, as she gathered an audience to the village square with enticing talk: "Have you seen the Gypsy from the East? She dances as if the Devil himself taught her. They say her gown is made of peacock feathers and precious stones and gold coins given to her by the greatest kings of Ethaleum and Cobraat. She has magic powers as well, they say, and can heal wounds and cast off demons."

Since Esmarelda was a good judge of character, she had only to pick out two or three gossipy types and hiss such words into their ears for the entire town to soon be converging on the place of her choice. Often she would enlist the aid of a youth, and not only to guard the coins thrown at her feet as she danced. For, once the excitement of the crowd had peaked, Esmarelda would twirl her cloak off of herself and onto her nearby assistant so quickly that it would seem as if the Gypsy had appeared from nowhere even as the old woman still presided. Then her costume would explode in the sunlight. She would dance to her own music, marking one rhythm with bangled feet and others with the tambourine slung from her shoulder or sometimes with the castanets or finger bells pulled from the pockets of her skirts.

From her hip hung a curved sword in a velvet sheath. This was a vital component of her dance as she displayed to the crowd her strength and agility with a prop that could, if the dancer was provoked, also be used as a weapon. The Gypsy would draw it from its sheath midway through her performance (or sooner, if necessary) and, with high trilling shrieks, dance and spin with the sword balanced on her head, her shoulder, her hip, her belly.

She would stand on one foot with the sword balanced across the upturned sole of the other and, with a quick motion of that foot, toss the sword into the air and catch it perfectly by the hilt to lunge threateningly at the astounded crowd. When Esmarelda had determined that all were convinced of her ability to protect herself, she would re-sheath the gleaming sword and proceed with the more sensuous dances, the Snake Dance and the Beledi.

Esmarelda's performances in this region had been greeted with mixed success. Many of the women and some of the more pious men would turn and flee at first sight of her, dragging away every child within reach. They'd chant prayers and cover the children's ears to keep out the music as they pushed through the remaining crowd, which pressed closer so as to grab at her. She collected very few coins and sometimes lost a few from her costume. Indeed, she often appeared better off than her audience. The sword dance became more and more central to her performances. After a while she would skip the dance entirely and remain as a cloaked medicine woman selling herbal remedies, talismans, and magic poems.

This is why she wanted to learn more about the arts of this region—the popular versions of card reading and numerology—she needed to make a better living while keeping a lower profile. The Gypsy had many skills already, but was afraid to use them here. It was hard for a woman to practice magic in these lands, one never knew when awe and respect would turn to fear and accusation. When she learned of the Master Seer, she realized that she might gain protection through association with him.

'I should not have arrived without a cloak,' she thought again as she stirred her brew. 'Whatever was wrong with me? He will suspect, or at least wonder, how I have traveled up his road in such a get-up without being molested. Will he think I have a wrap hidden somewhere outside? Will he look for it? Oh, I am such a fool! How could I underestimate him so?' Of course Esmarelda could not have traveled the roads of this country without hiding her beauty and youth under a mantle, and even if she could, there was still the matter of the vast topiary maze defending the Master Seer's grounds. The fact was, she *hadn't* come by the roads, or wandered through the maze. She had come via the complex and little known art of the Knots.

Her earliest memories were of learning the Spiral Map of Time from Huliyana, who danced Esmarelda's lessons for her. Huliyana's hip sways and dramatic twirls drew the connecting spirals of close and distant Time, while with elaborate hand gestures she spoke to Esmarelda in a very specific language. The young Gypsy learned to use percussion as a measure and to use her feet to count out the Knots around and across the Spiral. By the time Esmarelda was ten, she had already learned both the widespread dance form called Storytelling, and the Time Dance, known only to the Gypsies. Then she was free to pursue the remainder of the Gypsy dance repertoire at her own pace, while her formal instruction began to focus on herbs and minerals under the tutelage of Tibareth, the clan's medicine woman. Esmarelda understood that she was receiving the treasured secrets of the Gypsies, and her position was both a great honor and a frightening burden. She rose to the challenge and studied intensely, but her free spirit would not accept a future tied completely to the clan in the role of a wizened crone who would be called upon to heal, divine, and advise within her tightly knit, highly structured extended family. At seventeen, all she wanted to do was dance.

One night before her eighteenth birthday, Esmarelda slipped away from her father's cart and set out to complete her education independently. Eventually she found an ancient Weaver in the mountainous village of Andarra. After nursing the failing woman through a harsh winter, the Gypsy was able to convince her to share the secrets of the satchel itself. Esmarelda learned to spin fine threads from the cottony fibers of weeds, often poisonous, and to weave a satchel whose very construction represented the Spiral Map of Time. The fabric of the satchel was woven as a spiral, loosely, from the center outward, and along the way the Knots were tied to mark specific locations in time and space until the net-like circle was several feet across. The threads from the perimeter of this circle were drawn together to form a large, loose sack of cloth. Esmarelda then had much to learn about the correct method of folding and refolding the sack until it was the size and shape of any small innocuous satchel, and how to keep the special herbs in the satchel fresh and potent even during long periods of disuse.

And so, on the eve of the Gypsy's first visit to the Master Seer, she simply opened her satchel until it was large and net-like again, and then pulled it over her head and down around herself as she squatted and tied the opening at her feet. Once she was completely inside the sack, she started with the end closest to her right toe and followed the spiral weave around and around counterclockwise with her left thumb, counting the Knots. She stopped counting at the place where she believed the Master Seer to be; it was not very far from where she was keeping camp but was hidden from her by the maze. Finding the spot in the threads of her magic satchel, Esmarelda held tightly to it and allowed the scent of the herbs to lull her to sleep. When she awoke, the opening of the sack was at her head instead of at her feet, and she emerged from the spiral net like a moth emerging from its cocoon. Esmarelda stood, arranged her tousled garb, folded the satchel, tied it to her belt, and followed the smell of wood smoke directly to Malcom's door.

The Master Seer stood facing the hearth. He had the four hairs in hand and was tying them together in a knot. "She-wolves and devil-cats," he whispered and tossed the hairs into the fire.

"I smell burning hair!" Mark was alarmed, being both close to the fire and the most alert of the apprentices.

"I don't smell anything," said Esmarelda, casting a sly glance at Malcom but wondering if one of her hairs had gone into the fire and, if so, what the spell might be.

"It must be the Gypsy's chocolate," the Master Seer said, giving the fools one last chance to catch on, then when none did, "Drink up, lads!"

Esmarelda served the apprentices first. As they slurped at their drinks, she prepared two more cups, one for herself and one for the Master Seer. As she passed the mug to Malcom she said, "Please try some, I think you'll enjoy it," and nodded slightly at his questioning look to indicate that the drink was harmless. Smiling, she took the remaining seat at the foot of the table across from Malcom and sipped her own drink.

A strange stillness seemed to fill the room. The apprentices, who had been so boisterous at first, were now daydreaming. The drink was warm, spicier than chocolate but not as sweet. The men found it difficult not to down the small portions all at once and, after initial attempts at polite sips, the twins did. They sat contented and woozy at the table, heads bobbing, eyes drooping, while Esmarelda and Malcom sat patiently, nodding slightly at each other now and then, each immersed in thought and each wishing to know the other's thoughts.

The Master Seer, for his part, had taken note both of the Gypsy's lack of cloak and of the bulky woven sack hanging from her belt. 'She wants to appear as one who travels in magic circles and by magic means,' he thought, 'but I expect I shall find her cloak in the bushes. If she were truly advanced enough to use a magic sack for travel, why would she need to come to me for tutoring? Yet, it could be as she said at the door, that she is skilled but recognizes she can learn even more through me—but I sense there is more.'

As Malcom sat with the apprentices snorting and scratching around him and the elegant, lively Gypsy before him, a thought crossed his mind that was so powerful he was certain it came from outside himself. He was, in fact, certain that he was reading Esmarelda's mind and so had come upon the true reason for her visit: she wanted to be his consort! 'Of course. That explains her fine costume, her attempt to appear skilled and powerful. She wants to be appealing to me, (which she certainly is) and worthy of me (which she no doubt is not). What she said at the door must be partly true: that she heard of me far and wide is no doubt true; that she wishes to learn from me may also be true; but it is what she did not say straight out which is most true—she tires of the Gypsy's life and has sought me out as a partner to provide for her and protect her with my vast powers. Surely she was also told of my own fine appearance and my skills at seduction. Could she be testing her own cleverness and beauty by trying to seduce the seducer?' Malcom was pleased with himself—as always—for being so astute.

'He's more than just handsome,' Esmarelda thought, observing the Master Seer over the brim of her cup. 'He's pleasant-looking, gentle, not severe.' She had heard of his charms but for some reason had imagined a larger man, with craggier features and dark, dark hair, perhaps even a Gypsy himself. But the man sitting across from her had a round face, fair coloring and full, soft features. 'Like the man in the moon.' She could not tell his age, though she knew him to be in his prime; he could be thirty, forty, or fifty, for all she could see.

When he'd opened the door to her and she'd heard the voices within, Esmarelda had not even realized it was *he*, the Master Seer. But his voice quickly alerted her. He spoke to her as one who knew her and expected her arrival; he spoke to her kindly, humorously, respectfully. It would certainly have been difficult for Esmarelda to imagine Malcom as a cruel, malevolent sorcerer—as some had described him—had she not also heard the venom in his voice when he reigned in his apprentices.

'I should be grateful for these thugs,' Esmarelda realized, 'and now I am. This Master Seer commands with cruelty or charm as suits him. I must beware.' The Gypsy turned her attention to the now sleeping apprentices, hoping to gain more insights as to the character of the teacher they would soon share—for she never doubted that Malcom would accept her as a student. 'Not a very appealing group,' she thought.

As if continuing a conversation started long ago, Malcom said, "No, I haven't had much luck lately. As larcenous a bunch of misfits as you'll ever find, this crew."

"You'll find me a worthy pupil," Esmarelda answered, reminding herself of her mission. Suddenly, she was having trouble thinking of Malcom as the Master Seer, a teacher to be held at respectful distance. She wanted to simply converse with him, to lean back in her chair and share an amusing tale—he seemed that companionable. But she remembered the smell of hair in the fire and sat up straighter. 'He's putting ideas in my mind. I wonder, does he think to seduce me?'

The apprentices, sleeping with heads cradled in arms on the table or thrown back with mouths open, were getting restless; some were moaning.

"Let us walk outside and leave these foul lads to their foul dreams." Malcom stood.

"Yes, the air is pleasant outside," the Gypsy said, thinking again of her missing cloak. She was starting to feel guilty about trying to deceive Malcom regarding her skills. 'But what is wrong with me? What I said at the door was entirely—well nearly entirely—true. I'm not deceiving him. Perhaps he even knows of the magic satchel already, but I cannot be blamed for wanting to protect my secrets. He might not want to teach me if he thought it would make me more powerful than he; indeed, this may yet be the result. Oh, but why am I so jumbled? He is casting some spell on me. I should have expected this! I will not succumb to his spell.' And with this the Gypsy resolved to obtain her place as the Master Seer's pupil and to prove herself his equal—or better.

Still, there was this troubling matter of her cloak, and Esmarelda felt herself tensing as she and Malcom walked outside. The sleeping apprentices were now thrashing about in their chairs and blurting out curses, which further increased Esmarelda's uneasiness. As the Master Seer shut the door firmly behind them, Esmarelda noticed that he had taken care to collect his own cloak on his way out and now carried it over his arm, even though it was comfortably warm and sunny outdoors.

Malcom held Esmarelda's elbow lightly and steered her across the lawn toward a row of lilac shrubs in full leaf. His fingers noted that the soft fabric of the Gypsy's sleeve was adorned here and there with sharp metal beads. He felt the strength of finely tuned muscles beneath the soft flesh of her arm. As she walked beside him Malcom noticed that not a coin or bell on her costume jingled. The Gypsy moved with a smooth subtle flow, which he could only describe as sand swirling silently across a dune.

Malcom had seen such a sandy landscape only once, on a pilgrimage he'd made to a Cobraati wise man. He'd thought at the time that the man's wisdom was over-rated; and the arid brown landscape without even a touch of green had irritated him. Upon returning to his lush valley he'd vowed never to travel to those deserts again, and soon he had put the entire trip out of his mind. The holy man's advice had hardly made an impression on Malcom at the time, and his recollection of their conversations was a complete blur. Only now, with the Gypsy's gently swaying hips whispering of distant magical lands, did memories of his journey East rush back to him. For the first time the Master Seer regretted not having paid more attention to the holy man.

Indeed, though Malcom steered Esmarelda by the arm, he had a sense that it was she who was propelling him. He felt pulled into this movement of hers; it was so, so subtle. Was she walking, or did she and the Earth have some special arrangement: that the very plates of the continents would shift to this Gypsy's command and carry her where she pleased? The Master Seer stood still to see if the land would carry him along as well, but it did not, and he had to let go of Esmarelda's arm as she continued to move on ahead.

The Gypsy paused in a splash of sunshine and turned back toward Malcom in a swift movement that caused her trinkets and jewelry to sing and sparkle. Well aware of the impression she created, Esmarelda smiled with a radiance that seemed to compete with the very sun that shone on her. She knew how to widen her eyes ever so slightly so that in the right lighting sparks would appear to leap from

their black depths. "What is it?" she coaxed gently as the Master
Seer stood riveted in place.

Malcom stared at Esmarelda as if only now seeing her for the first
time. Though he'd recognized her beauty at once and was intrigued
by her exotic get-up, the smallness of his front room—filled as it had
been with his coarse companions—had cast her in a sort of veil.
Standing now a short distance away, he could take her in from head
to toe. She stood there, still but not motionless, turning slightly now
and then to follow the movement of a passing insect. She let her
smile relax, but the sparkle remained in her eyes. For the second
time that afternoon time stopped for the Master Seer and the Gypsy.

The Gypsy, while appearing so cheerful, trembled inside as she
posed for the Master Seer's scrutiny. Quite in contrast, Malcom was
maintaining a severe, mask-like expression even while a feeling of
pleasure swelled within him as he admired this jewel of a woman. He
took in every detail of her glittering form. She wore layers of
clothing: a silk skirt dyed to look like peacock feathers over
narrow-legged trousers, sheer veils of lavender and green draped
across her shoulder over a tight fitting yellow blouse and tucked into
a woven belt hung with coins. She had a nicely proportioned figure,
and the bare skin of her neck and midriff was smooth and olive
colored. Her black hair was brushed back into a long, thick braid
with a cord tied through it, ending in a shiny tassel, which made the
braid seem to come down to her knees.

The Gypsy's head was bare. Wisps of black curls escaped from
the braid, and Malcom imagined the luxurious hair blowing free in
the wind. He had an urge to examine the face framed by these curls
at close range. Were those rose-colored lips painted that lovely shape
and hue? Could the perfect curve of those eyebrows be natural? He
took the several steps needed to reach the Gypsy, while still studying
Esmarelda's every aspect as if she were a painting and not a person.

Esmarelda forced herself not to look or step away. She stood like
a statue for Malcom's observation until it was Malcom who finally
stepped back and with a swift motion snapped his cloak from over his

arm out and around Esmarelda's shoulders. At that very instant the sky darkened and thunder rumbled. Esmarelda felt a huge cold shiver shoot up her back even though the heavy cloak shielded her from the chill wind.

"I have two questions for you, Gypsy," Malcom said sharply. "Why this crazy costume? You endanger yourself traveling so in this district." Malcom reached out and fingered the silk at her neck, letting the back of his fingers touch her skin.

"And the second question?" The sky had become very dark and the air cold. Esmarelda pulled the cloak more tightly around herself.

"How did you get here?"

The cloak was now starting to give Esmarelda strength, it reminded her— The Gypsy knew what she had to do, even though it was now raining. She skipped backward several steps and swirled the cloak off of her shoulders, casting it back into the arms of Malcom. He, too, was oblivious to the cold rain.

"I dress this way because it is the way a Gypsy Dancer dresses, and I hoped to have the opportunity to dance for you." She twirled dramatically. A cold blast swept the isolated dark cloud and the rain aside, allowing the sunlight to flash off of her bangles once more. She trembled inwardly at the magic of the place. "As for your second question: as a Gypsy dances so does she travel. I'll tell you the secret of my coming here through my dance. Pay close attention. The women of my clan always said that a man could never interpret the magic language of our dance—but of course they knew not of the Master Seer!"

"The pupil teases the teacher, does she? Well, whatever method brought you here," Malcom said, pointedly directing his gaze to the magic sack hanging from Esmarelda's waist, "do not be so certain it will take you home again. I am fully in control of this space and all who venture here." Malcom made a sweeping gesture, and the black cloud receding to the north rumbled. "So, let us have the dance, I'm certain it will be entertaining if not educational."

Malcom spread his cape on the ground and sat, leaning back on his elbow. He looked up at Esmarelda with seductive expectation. The Gypsy took the magic sack and the sheathed scimitar from her waist, and the slippers from her feet, and laid them on the cloak next to Malcom. She stepped away from the Master Seer with her back turned toward him and struck a pose with her right foot tucked behind her left knee, the tambourine held in both hands high above her head. She balanced this way for minutes while Malcom fingered her belongings discreetly, watching her back for movement.

He had no doubt now that the Gypsy had used the sack—the magic satchel—to gain entry to his well-guarded estate. He was intrigued by this because he himself had had only limited success with this technique. As his hand lingered on the fibers of the Gypsy's bag, he imagined himself possessed of limitless power; he would force this Gypsy to teach him the crones' secrets. He let his hand glide from the sack to the slippers. As he gazed at Esmarelda's still immobile bare feet, Malcom's fantasy progressed to his fathering a son by this beautiful Gypsy, the son for whom he had just today begun to yearn.

Esmarelda's tambourine quivered and she returned her right foot to the ground. The quivering flowed downward through her hands, arms, shoulders, ribs, hips and legs until her entire being vibrated. She began to move with deliberate steps, still trembling, and while her coins and bells jingled Esmarelda beat a heavy rhythm on the head of the tambourine—*Dum*, chink-chink, *Dum*, chink-chink, *Dum*—taking a deliberate step and dipping a hip down low with each *Dum*, never stopping the body quiver.

The Gypsy took her steps around in a circle and back toward her audience of one. She held the tambourine before her and played it with great skill while performing the intricate steps of her dance. Malcom tried to look for the secret language in the Gypsy's performance. He was unsure of whether to pay closest attention to the rhythms of the tambourine or the patterns stamped out by her feet. Trying to attend to both, he was becoming mesmerized. 'I will make her tell me the secrets of the satchel straight out,' he thought, settling back more comfortably on his cape. 'She knows that I will be too distracted by her shapeliness to decipher the clues of her dance, if indeed there are any! I will have my hands full with this one, the little tease, the little liar. Ah well, anyone who can move like this must be forgiven a few moral shortcomings!'

Esmarelda had switched from her small energetic steps to a gliding snake-like movement. She flexed her knees so that her skirt dropped lower to cover her feet, and this made her appear to float through the damp grass. Her back again turned toward Malcom, she performed a series of hip slides, each one bringing her closer to the ground until she was kneeling, while she continued to roll her hips from side to side in a figure eight and play her tambourine high above her head; her upper torso remained balanced and motionless between the two movements.

Malcom, reminded of his thoughts while walking beside Esmarelda earlier, had a glimmer of insight. As he watched the Gypsy's swaying hips he had a sensation of movement, of the ground shifting, and he understood that although his own magic satchel was perfectly authentic (stolen directly from a Red Mountain Witch and purchased at an exorbitant price by Malcom himself several transactions later—or so his story went) there were lessons to be learned about the Knots which he had not previously considered.

Esmarelda moved the figure eight up to her shoulders, sliding her rib cage back and forth instead of her hips. She did a slow back-bend from her knees, and Malcom noticed that the tambourine now lay on the grass although he had not seen the Gypsy put it down. He still had the sense of its ringing rhythms. In the kneeling back-bend, Esmarelda danced with her hands, describing flowing waves in the air above her face. Gracefully she lowered her hands, palms down, onto the grass above her shoulders, and arching her back she raised up into a full back-bend. She let her head hang and met the Master Seer's eyes from this upside down position. The Gypsy raised and lowered (or, from his perspective, lowered and raised) her eyebrows, first in unison and then one after the other, and Malcom found himself laughing. Esmarelda's next trick was even more surprising. She kicked her feet up and stood on her hands. Her skirts fell over her head and she crossed her trousered legs like a yogi. Then she bent at the waist, lowered her still crossed legs to the ground, and rolled up into a sitting position right beside Malcom. Shaking her skirt back into place and turning toward him, the Gypsy smiled as one awakening from a sweet dream, but the Master Seer was all business.

"If you are to be my pupil, you will have to stay here on the estate; and I *will* make sure that you are unable to leave without my permission because it will not be to the benefit of your education to do so."

"What about the others, do they live here with you?"

"No, they live in town; they show little promise as a whole and I do not care to be their daddy. Besides, I trust *them.*"

Esmarelda chose to laugh at this as she put on her slippers and tied the sword and the satchel to her belt. She stood up and started back to the house still chuckling. Malcom did not try to catch up to her.

The Gypsy arrived back at the Master Seer's door and paused to wait for him, not wanting to go in alone with the apprentices still there. She was startled when the door was opened and there he was, already inside, and no sign of the others.

"Come in, come in! No sense wasting time. Let us start the first lesson; I have been waiting for you! Please, call me Malcom."

Chapter 4

"It's her, it's her, it's her, it's her! What are we going to do now?!"

A nearly hysterical Alvin was shaking Mark, who had spent the past twenty-four hours sleeping fitfully in the Master Seer's bed, his dreams full of swords.

"What? Who? Calm down, you idiot! Who's here?"

"The Witch! I mean the Gypsy! The *Gypsy!*"

"Oooooooh nooooooo," Mark groaned. "How do you know? Are you sure? Oh lord, this is not what I need, oh lord!" He staggered out of the bed and looked around at the room and through the door into the kitchen. At least the house had been recently cleaned in anticipation of the Master Seer's return. He caught a glimpse of himself reflected in the window glass and groaned louder; he still looked like the "Fool" who had gone to the Gypsy, only dirtier by about two days. "Did you actually see her, Alvin, or did you just dream this—speak up dammit!"

"I saw her, I saw her. I saw her crawling out of one of those magic bag things, like you have. I saw her, I saw her."

"Where, goddammit!? When? How long ago?"

"Just now, but way down by the stream. I mean I was going to the stream and before I got all the way I saw her through the trees. She was crawling out of the magic thing and she had a big cloak on and a big pack—full of nasty spells, I bet—and I ran as fast as I could to come tell you. Is she the reason the Master isn't back yet? Has she done something to the Master, Mark? And she's come for us now? Let's leave, Mark, hurry up; don't just stand there, hurry, let's go! What are you doing there? Don't you hear me? Don't waste time there, let's GO!"

Mark was busily cutting off great lumps of beard at Malcom's wash stand. "Shut up, idiot! We aren't going anywhere. We're going to let the Gypsy come here, and we're going to find out what she knows about the Master Seer. That is, I am going to find out what she knows. You are going to keep your mouth shut. Don't appear to be surprised by anything that I say, and agree with me on everything. Do you understand, Alvin? Stick with me and I won't let her turn you into a tree stump. Now go outside and keep an eye out; I want to know when she is near the house—but don't let her see you!"

Alvin hurried outside, not understanding at all but perfectly willing to stay out of the dreaded Gypsy's sight. He remembered vividly his dream in which she turned into a creature, half-bird and half-lion, and pulled him apart in little pieces with her claw-talons so as to savor eating him in small gory bites. It was all Alvin could do now to force himself to follow Mark's instructions and not to run for town. Even he could read the warning in the dream. And the others had had dreams, too! Why did they not drive the Gypsy away? Since the first day she had come to the Master Seer nothing had been right.

First, there was the business of these horrible dreams and the Master Seer refusing to listen to the apprentices' warnings, instead taking up *her* side and laughing at them for drinking her poison tea, and sending them back to town for good so he could devote all of his time to his new student. Then the twins started spying on the Gypsy and the Master Seer, and they became angrier and angrier. Gregory and Thomas were jealous of the Gypsy for taking their teacher away, and jealous of the Master Seer for being with the beautiful Gypsy. One day they set out to the Master's house and did not come back. A week later, two large brown rats ran into the middle of the room Alvin and Mark shared behind the candle shop; they squeaked loudly, looking right at them, before running behind the stove. Alvin had never seen Mark look so frightened. He said that the Master Seer had sent the rats to tell them that the twins would not be back, and he warned Alvin never again to go to the Master Seer's house.

All of this came rushing back to Alvin's normally untroubled mind as he returned to the spot where he had first seen the Gypsy. He found her still by the stream, sitting as if in a trance with a small crystal ball in her palm. 'Oh, she will see me in her ball and turn into that beast right here, and the dream will come true!' Alvin broke into a sweat and wanted to run but was paralyzed with fear. After a few minutes, when the Gypsy remained motionless and took no notice of his presence, Alvin adjusted his position quietly and hoped that Mark knew what he was doing.

It had been Mark himself who had brought Alvin back to this place. Some months after the business with the twins and the rats, the Master Seer came to the candle shop and told Mark he needed his help. Mark and Alvin were dumbfounded. The Master Seer had not been seen in town in many years. He'd restricted his fortune telling to only those who were brave enough to be led blind-folded by an apprentice to a tent on his estate. Surprised and nervous as he was, Mark still asked a few pointed questions: What had become of the Gypsy and why had the twins not returned?

The Master Seer was conciliatory; he said that the thankless Gypsy had run away. He now needed his best pupil back. Mark had proven himself worthy; he was not stupid like Gregory and Thomas. The twins had put themselves in a dangerous position and paid with their lives. The Master Seer, insinuating that their disappearance was the Gypsy's doing, invited Mark to help him avenge her misdeeds. Mark left Alvin in town and went with the Master Seer that very afternoon.

Mark went to the Master Seer's house each day just as he had before the arrival of the Gypsy, but he did not take Alvin. Months passed and Alvin never asked about Mark's days, he only asked for new incantations to say over the candles as he poured the wax into the molds. Alvin was content with candle-making and solitude. He didn't care that his assistant would go off with a girlfriend for long hours. But then Alvin's peace was disturbed. Mark announced that they were both to move into the Master Seer's house.

Mark would take no argument from Alvin and insisted that it was

safe; the Gypsy was gone and the Master Seer had also left. He and
Alvin were to mind the estate. Mark told Alvin that he could still
come into town and make candles a few times a week—or, if Alvin
really didn't want to help, Mark supposed he could take care of the
Master's business alone. This made Alvin feel bad because Mark had
always been his best friend and had looked after him as long as he
could remember, so Alvin started gathering his clothes while Mark
went to find their delinquent helper.

That was a year ago, and now here was the Gypsy returned and
not the Master Seer as Mark had promised. In fact, Mark had
promised to bring the Master Seer home himself and had set out
yesterday to do just that. But he had come back alone and had gone
angrily to bed without even a word to Alvin. Alvin thought of this as
he again considered escaping back to town.

The Gypsy stirred and reached for her pack, where she tucked the
crystal ball away. She turned her head to look through the brambles
toward Alvin. "You can tell the Master Seer I'm on my way now,"
she said to the underbrush and laughed softly as she heard Alvin
scurry noisily up the hill to the house.

Esmarelda stood up and, with her cloak over her arm, made her
way much more slowly along the familiar wooded paths. Her
meditation had not been satisfactory. The crystal had told her little.
The fogginess of the images warned of things not being as they
seemed. But when had that ever not been true in this place? She was
certain Malcom waited for her at the house.

Suddenly, she doubted her own heart. Why had she come? Was
it really the cat? Was Audy worth this humiliation of coming
back—or had she *wanted* to come back? Was she here to find Audy
or to see Malcom? 'Oh this place, this place! I have never thought
straight for a minute anywhere on this estate! He twists everything.'
She focused on her plan, and this calmed her. 'I should get started,
there's no telling when I'll have this chance again.'

Esmarelda carefully pulled a vial from the pouch hidden under
her layers of clothing. She walked back to the stream and tapped a

tiny pinch of the powder from the vial into the water. Returning to pick up her gear and continue to the house, Esmarelda also tapped a bit of powder onto a toadstool nearby. She put the vial in a pocket where she could reach it easily and said, "A little rain and some bright sun is what we need to begin the fun!" As the sky darkened and some fat drops of rain splashed onto her head, the Gypsy flung her cloak around herself and set out more quickly. By the time she was within sight of the house, the sun was shining again. Behind her an odd yellowish fog was beginning to rise from the woods.

Alvin ran as one pursued and, upon reaching the house, began panting his report even before Mark had flung open the door, so that all Mark heard was: "*. . . and she thinks the Master is here!*"

Mark emerged from the bedroom to find Alvin gasping for breath, leaning back against the door, eyes closed, shaking with fear.

"She does, does she? Well why don't we pretend he is here, Alvin?"

"Why don't we pretend no one is here?" Alvin pleaded. He opened his eyes, and then his mouth as if to let out a scream, but Mark rushed over and shook him by the shoulders.

"It's *me*, Alvin. It's me—Mark. You remember my learning to impersonate the Master, don't you? I've done it off and on ever since he left. Come now, Alvin, that Gypsy has got you spooked! Buck up, boy, I need you!" Mark led the sniffling Alvin to a chair. "Now sit down and collect yourself. She'll be here soon, and you just leave everything to me. Do whatever I say and don't act surprised by anything—and don't speak to the Gypsy directly, let me do all the talking. In fact, don't speak at all. Yes, that will be the best. I'll tell the Gypsy that I cast some sort of spell on you to keep you from speaking. Do you understand, Alvin? It will be safer for you that way."

The dazed Alvin nodded. The morning had been too much for him. He sat quietly and did not dare ask Mark what he was planning, or how his pretending to be their Master would in any way help to find the true Master Seer.

Mark felt sorry for Alvin, who knew nothing of the Master's experiments or the unsuccessful attempt to bring Malcom back from life as a cat. It occurred to Mark that Alvin, being so ignorant of the true events and fearful of the Gypsy, might be a liability and not a help in the encounter that was to ensue. 'Maybe I should have sent the poor lad back to the candle shop. Well, it's too late now.'

The fact was, Mark himself was afraid to be alone with the Gypsy, though he would never admit this. She was taking a long time getting up to the house, and this allowed Mark more time to think— and to worry. She knew the Master better than anyone. What if she saw through his disguise? How could he explain the Master's absence then? Mark tried to reassure himself. Of course he could pull it off; he had studied long and hard the art of impersonation from the greatest teacher of them all. None could surpass the Master Seer's ability in this area. The Master Seer could change even his physical characteristics, and not with the usual tricks of make-up and costuming. He could actually make himself taller or give himself moles and freckles or change the pitch of his voice, all through self-hypnosis and meditation.

Mark had seen the transformations with his own eyes as he assisted the Master Seer with preparations for his pranks. But these techniques alone were not enough to transform a person into a completely different creature, and Mark had also watched with awe as the Master Seer conducted his experiments in transmutations from human to animal. Had Mark not personally helped to gather the ingredients for the potions, and brought the experimental animals to the Master, he himself would never have believed such a thing as a man becoming a cat was possible.

These thoughts gave Mark some confidence. It was imperative that the Gypsy not make the connection between Malcom and the cat. Mark was counting on her to both want to find the cat and be able to catch it. This would allow him to steal the animal a second time and, with luck, get it home to the estate where the transformation back to the Master Seer could take place. And he would do things *his* way the second time around: Throw the cat into a pillow slip and make a run for it—a direct overland route to the Master Seer's land. None of this magic satchel business, he didn't care how many miles it was. 'I hate those things and—with all due respect—I don't think the Master ever really learned how to use them properly, even after the Gypsy taught him. A stupid business, this traveling through Time. A good way to get lost, and that is exactly what the Master has done.'

Mark remembered his argument with the Master Seer, one of their few. When Malcom had laid out the plan—for Mark to escape with the cat via the satchel so as to be immediately and completely out of the Gypsy's reach—Mark had objected violently. He had never used the satchel and had no wish to do so, especially without the Master Seer's guidance.

"But I will be there with you," Malcom had said.

"But as a *cat!*"

"We'll only go to the next Spiral-turn and we won't stay. We'll head straight back to this Time and the house here as soon as possible. It will be foolproof."

Mark thought of the Fool from the Tarot reading, and then of the Gypsy's impending arrival. He tried to concentrate on the current plan: As Malcom, he must pretend to try to *prevent* the Gypsy from learning the location of the cat. It had been the Master Seer's intent to make the Gypsy love the cat and then deprive her of it. Here was another aspect of the original plan that had made Mark doubt the Master's wisdom. Become a cat for a year? Who was Malcom trying to punish? Mark wondered if the Gypsy had cast some kind of spell on the Master Seer to make him insane, but with the image of the two brown rats still fresh in his memory, Mark had never dared voice this concern.

Now Mark would have to refuse to provide information about the cat's location, while in fact helping the Gypsy to discover same. He would even let the Gypsy steal the magic satchel so that he himself would not feel obliged to use it again. 'Let the *Gypsy* go rescue the

Master from that hellish world. For that matter, maybe I'll let her keep him as a house pet. If I let him remain a cat, I can continue as the Master Seer.'

Mark had never had such a thought, and he glanced guiltily at Alvin as if the disloyalty would ring out through the room. Alvin was asleep with his head on the table. Mark shook his own head to clear it. 'Let me see how I feel about this after the Gypsy has left. Perhaps she is casting a spell on me as well; or perhaps the Master is testing me.'

The knock on the door rescued Mark from these troubling ideas and caused Alvin to sit up with a glassy-eyed start. Mark patted his hand reassuringly, whispering, "Remember what I said—pretend to be mute," and went to answer the door.

Chapter 5

Audy crouched next to a fence where he was hidden by a summer's growth of vines and tall grass. Having gorged on grasshoppers beside the ditch, the cat dozed in blissful contentment, even while poised to spring to action at the slightest hint of danger.

Malcom tried to concentrate on his predicament without disturbing the cat's nap. He had discovered early on that even with the animal at rest he could not hold on to his own thoughts. The cat's state of repose would cause Malcom to also become sleepy; and when he was able to keep himself conscious, Malcom's mental activity woke up Audy, and the cat's agitation took over. After the first few months, Malcom was unable to exert much influence over the cat's behavior. The scene with Esmarelda and Mark was a good example.

Mark's arrival as the Gypsy's client had startled the Master Seer into awareness after long months of sinking into the cat's dreamy existence. The plan rushed back, and although it no longer held much meaning for him, Malcom knew that it was imperative for Mark to succeed, or the Master Seer would be buried in the consciousness of the cat for the remainder of the cat's, or his own, life. The more Malcom tried to use his powers to facilitate his rescue by Mark, the more erratically Audy acted at the exertion of the Master Seer's will. Malcom had no way of explaining this to Mark. The harder Malcom tried to communicate, the more uncooperative the cat became.

Malcom pushed the image of Audy slithering out of Mark's arms at the bus depot from his mind; the fear-memory was starting to wake up the cat. As Audy relaxed again into semi-sleep, the Master Seer's dim consciousness attended to the surroundings. Malcom wondered how such a short distance on the Time-spiral could have brought him to such a strange and distant place.

Faye dreamed of the mountains.

Just yesterday, with Zeek at the wheel of the old van, they had crossed the pass, putting the mountains on their east for the first time in their lives. It would be months before either of them would stop pointing in the direction of the mountain ridge and saying, automatically, "west." But they were the west now. The mountains stood like a visible barrier between the old life and the new life they were beginning in the sprawl of this dusty town.

In Faye's dream the peaks of the mountains were hidden by white cottony clouds. From her vantage point across the vast golden-brown plain, Faye watched as the clouds "popped" into the intense blueness of the sky and became pure white puffs of pop-corn floating off in happy metamorphosis. As the popcorn rose, the mountain peaks were revealed through windows of cloudless sky.

It was such a beautiful dream! Faye replayed it in her mind and couldn't wait to tell it to Zeek. She lay on her back in the nest of sleeping bags and blankets on the floor of a friend's apartment. She felt the sun through the window shades and knew that the sky outside was as blue as the sky in her dream. She knew also that life would not be all blue skies—she and Zeek had arrived in town like Gypsies. With little money, no job prospects, no plan, they had only luck and the kindness of friends to count on. And each other.

Faye rolled over, evicting the two cats who had wedged themselves between her left arm and Zeek's back. She curled up around Zeek, touching her lips to his bare skin. The relocated cats kneaded the blankets at her feet. 'There is still magic in the world,' Faye thought dreamily, visualizing the pop-corn clouds and inhaling deeply the fresh-baked smell of sleeping bodies. 'After all, what could be more magical than love?'

"*Only a Spiral-turn?! Only* a Spiral-turn. Just *one* Spiral-turn? I don't believe you! Did you learn nothing from me? Are you a complete idiot as well as a vicious, pompous, wasteful old devil? By the goddess, I should have stolen the satchel from you the minute I learned of it! Just as you had it stolen from its rightful owner. And for what? So you could so grossly misuse it?"

Esmarelda, circling the table where Malcom and Alvin sat, could not restrain her anger. She knew that Malcom was so numbed by her truth potion that he would remember none of her tirade and that Alvin, made mute by his own trusted Master, would be unable to repeat her vehement words, but still she berated the men. A yellow fog swirling against the windows of the house was like a physical manifestation of the Gypsy's ire.

"Give me the satchel now!" She said sharply right into the Master Seer's ear and, as Alvin stared at him in silent panic, Mark rose. With robot-like movements he retrieved a worn magic satchel from its hiding place under a loose floor board.

Of course Mark had not really drunk the Gypsy's brew; for him to fall under its spell could only lead to his revealing his true identity. The Master Seer would have been proud of how he had faked taking the potion, pretending not to have noticed Esmarelda adding it to his mug of soup. Now Mark further proved his acting prowess by pretending to be under the Gypsy's total command. As he handed the satchel to Esmarelda and returned to his seat, he wished she would go on about the Spiral-turns and the Master Seer's mistake, yet he dared not display any interest.

"Yes, it's true! You learned just enough to do it exactly wrong!" Esmarelda was red-faced as she turned the old satchel inside out to reveal bright threads newly entwined within its woven interior. The original Knots, marking a distant Witch's distant travels, were frayed grey lumps close to the bottom of the bag—the center of the Spiral. A new Knot, near the middle of the satchel, marked the Gypsy's house. Esmarelda had no doubt of this, since the Knot was tied with a twist of gold thread and a strand of her own black hair. The angle of this glittering Knot in relation to that marking the Master Seer's house (a Knot Esmarelda herself had tied) was the very same as the angle of two Knots in her own magic satchel. Of greatest concern to Esmarelda was the tiny blue string tied directly beside the Knot which marked her own house. This had been Audy's destination. She waved her discovery under the Master Seer's nose.

"Well, I don't imagine you had a very nice time in that place, did you? I see you certainly didn't waste any time getting home. And now, to get poor Audy back, I shall have to go there myself. Oh, this is the worst!" Esmarelda plopped down in a chair and forced herself to concentrate. "Let's see. If the satchel is woven so that the Spiral winds out from the center and then turns back in on itself and winds inward, that would put Audy—*one mere Spiral-turn away*—" she glanced with disgust at Malcom, "somewhere just forward of us in time and space *but in the Alternate World!*"

"What's the Alternate World?"

Esmarelda started at the sound of another's voice. It was so unexpected she was not sure who had spoken, but she leveled a very hard stare at Alvin. Alvin stared straight ahead into Mark's eyes. The Gypsy turned and saw the Master Seer staring blankly back at Alvin. "Very interesting," she muttered. Turning back to Alvin she leaned toward him across the table.

"The Alternate World, my not-very-mute friend, is a place like ours except that Magic is forbidden. The people there believe in very little and know even less. They pretend that the things they cannot explain do not exist, and so Magic is denied them. To them the Stars do nothing but mark space, Numbers are only for counting money and Cards for gambling, a Name is a label and nothing more. They treat Nature as something apart from themselves and speak not with it. Instead they adore creating machinery and complex objects of little beauty; with these things they spend their time, loving them as if the objects were living companions. Oh, I have been there, despite the warnings of my teachers, and I do not relish going back. Traveling in the Alternate World is more perilous than you can imagine. From one end of their Spiral to the other you have no idea what to expect. Monstrous machines and cities populate much of the Alternate World, and the people there are crowded together and sick of heart. They fear and hate Death, yet they die easily and are always finding new ways to kill each other.

"They dream of us and suspect we are here, keeping the knowledge, but this only torments them. They want to own the universe and control it with their machines. Those who populate the Alternate World have no insight and no out-sight. They have no true knowledge of either themselves or their universe—and this they blame on their God, who is supposed to know everything for them! They treat this God pitifully, calling him forth at every opportunity: to use as a weapon in their wars, as a salve to their wounds, as a place to hide from their own ignorance!

"But never forget, Alvin, my-friend-who-now-knows-more-than-his-Master, that the Alternate World is our Destiny, and our world is their Past. This is why they know us and our Magic in dreams, they have traveled our Spiral. And when we reach the place where the Spiral turns in on itself," Esmarelda fell back in her chair and shuddered, *"their History becomes our Future."*

The Gypsy folded the magic satchel with reverence and held it in her lap thoughtfully. She had been up all night and needed to rest now, and plan. Alvin and Malcom still sat like statues. She did not concern herself with them any longer, knowing that the next challenge lay in confronting the Alternate World. Esmarelda took her belongings into Malcom's laboratory at the back of the house and locked the door. She tapped the clock on the mantle four times to remind herself of when to wake up and then settled down in the old over-stuffed chair. She would wake and leave before the Master Seer regained control, but not before adding a pinch of her secret powder to each of his own precious potions.

Resting her head against the familiar fabric of her once favorite chair, Esmarelda's exhausted mind wandered amidst memories of her months as the Master Seer's apprentice. She had not dared enter the room which had once been hers or to sleep in the bed where so many nights had been spent longing to go to Malcom and yet resisting, convinced that her feelings of desire were somehow a trick. She would torment herself with suspicions: Had it been the lunch which she had let the Master Seer serve to her? Could he have tied an invisible string to the foot of her bed? Had he stolen her thimble? It had not seemed possible to Esmarelda that she could really love Malcom or he her. By day they were either teasing or fiendish in their distrust of one another. But they were both greedy for more magical knowledge, and so they found ways to get along. Grudgingly, they shared their secrets. They found mutual enjoyment in the study of the metaphysical arts—in the practice of magic they became friends of a sort, greatly respecting each other's talents. Alone in their beds at night, the Master Seer and the Gypsy yearned for each other with a desire each felt could only have been inspired by spells, for they had more respect for each other's magical talents than for each other's sincerity.

Here in the laboratory Esmarelda let the memories swirl around her as if they belonged to someone else. Though she slept for only a short while, she had an incredibly vivid dream: There was a mountain, and a sky so blue and bright it hurt her eyes. A single pure white cloud floated past the mountain. But then it was not a cloud—it was a feather mattress, and Esmarelda herself lay upon it in the arms of a bearded man.

Chapter 6

Away, Away
A Woe, A Woe
A woe a day
Away we go
Away, Away!

George was so intent on making out these lyrics that the Wanderers were nearly upon him before he jumped back from the road to let their horse-drawn wagons pass. They nodded to him, taking the opportunity to get a close, if quick, look.

This was the first time George and the Wanderers had openly acknowledged each other's presence, although they had been traveling the same trail since the first of the week. George had kept up with the band by day, staying within earshot but, until now, out of sight of the caravan. As best he could tell, the company consisted of five wagons, each drawn by one or two horses, and as many as twenty-five men and women as well as a number of children. The Wanderers seemed to prefer walking to riding in the wagons, and at night they slept under the stars. So did George. Then he would hear the rustle of young Wanderer boys in the woods around him, testing their bravery to spy on the strange red-haired man.

Now, as the caravan passed, George heard some of the Wanderers muttering "*Gorgio, Gorgio*," under their breath. 'How do they know my name?!' George could not fathom it. He took it as a sign.

After the last wagon had rolled by, George fell into line and followed the band to the place they would stop for the night. The high-wheeled wagons turned off the narrow path and lurched into open meadow. They formed a wide circle and stopped.

George did not follow them all of the way but stopped at the grove of trees which hid the meadow from the path. Sinking down into the grassy shade, he watched the Wanderer People make camp. The younger men were leading the horses out across the meadow and down a hill. Some women were soon following the same route with pails and urns. George tried to take in everything. Just as the old crone had said, he had taken to the road and the Wanderers had found him. Now he must try to learn as much about them as possible so that he would not accidently offend or frighten them.

The sun was setting and George watched twinkling fires leap to life in the Wanderers' camp. He lit a small fire himself and dined on some bread and wine and one pickled duck egg he had bought at a tavern the day before. He would have liked to have bought more, but he had already spent most of his funds on sea fares.

The first voyage had taken him from his own tiny island to the larger Else Island. From there he had immediately taken passage on a ship to Omanipinamo, a very long voyage. George dubbed this leg of his journey "the one hundred days at sea." It was actually longer, but he liked the sound of "The One Hundred Days at Sea" and wrote a chantey in the best tradition of his seafaring Piper ancestors. 'And lucky for me sea and song go so hand in hand,' George mused over his meager dinner. 'I'd have starved before ever making land had not my fiddle made me so many a generous dinner companion on the ship.'

It had been George's intent to try to pick up some local currency in Omanipinamo, a thriving port town, before traveling further. The sailors on the ship had told him his fiddle playing would bring him great admiration in the seaside saloons. And George did find an audience in the very first saloon at which he stopped. The inn keeper rewarded his playing with a sumptuous meal and a bath and a bed. The jovial man easily talked George into staying a fortnight. But, on George's very first morning in Omanipinamo, he found a small figure eight carved on the exterior wooden wall of the saloon's outhouse.

The rune seemed to point to the center of town. George said good bye to the disappointed innkeeper and moved on. At the town plaza, another figure eight appeared at George's feet, scratched into a brick at the base of a statue of some horsemen. Again George followed. By the end of the day George had found two more marks and had, in the course of following the direction indicated, arrived at the far eastern boundary of the town, where a single dirt road pointed like an arrow across an empty plain. Reasonably well fed and rested, but with pockets still light and little chance of filling them, George was compelled to move on.

Now he was far inland on the continent where the Dromandy Mountains reached so high into the sky that their peaks, piercing the clouds, were always veiled in moonlight. This is what George had been told on his voyage. He tried to shake off a feeling of homesickness. Why was he here? What did he want with these Wanderers?

Laughter rang through the cool night air with the strains of a mandolin. The nightly festivities were about to begin. George felt another tug of longing for his own people. He thought fondly of his last night with them at the Cory wedding. It had been their dancing that had sent him on this journey: the swirling spiral they created, his dream earlier as his head lay on the coil-etched stone pillow of the cairn, and the appearance of the old woman. Had she been a dream too? "The Spiral is their map," she had said, "they travel on the waves of Magic." Since arriving on this continent, George had felt himself swept up on such waves. 'I am more at sea than when I was at sea!' Something stirred within him. Hadn't he always felt adrift, waiting, waiting for his destiny? But a map—a Spiral Map—could one really navigate the vast sea of Time? And if one could, was this circumventing fate or only following its inevitable course? 'The Wanderers know and that is why I am here.' George turned his attention to their music. He heard ringing tambourines, reedy pipes and an orchestra of mandolins and balalaikas. George took out his violin and tuned it to the stringed instruments as best he could.

George stood and began to play softly. Once he gained confidence with the new rhythms and harmonies, he played a little louder. The music spoke to him. It made him feel at home, different as it was. 'The road is my home now,' he thought. He hardly noticed the Wanderers' music grow quiet, as if listening to him, and then loud again. They played until the fires twinkled low. When the Wanderers finally put down their instruments and crawled under their goose down quilts, George played one last tune. It was an ancient Piper lullaby, just a few short measures rescued from the past; and when he had played the last note, George carefully wiped his fiddle and bow before laying down to sleep.

In the morning, and it was late morning, George found a crock of lentil stew by his feet along with a thick slice of bread wrapped in a checkered cloth. He ate these gratefully but quickly, noticing that the Wanderers had already broken camp and were back on the road. He could hear the sounds of jingling harnesses and complaining wood in the distance. Before following, George needed to fill his water skin, and he walked to the middle of the meadow where he found a path freshly marked by feet and hoofs. It took him to a stream of clear water. Cutting north from the stream and through a thicket, George was able to pick up the cart path where it wound around the meadow. A bit of yellow fabric caught his eye as he stepped onto the path. It was caught on a prickly branch as if someone had walked too close to the bracken, but a figure eight freshly scratched in the dirt below told George that the path had been marked for him. He took the yellow scrap and tucked it into his pocket. If he walked quickly he would easily catch up with the slow-moving caravan.

As George walked along he sang his sea chantey to himself so that he wouldn't forget it, for he had not written it down:

Oh, when all of John Cory's daughters were wed
And not one of them to me

I kissed me lovin' Mum on the cheek
And then I took to the sea

From Sumweir to Else the weather was rough
And I thought of my late Great-Grand
The last of the Drumms to board a ship
And he never again saw land

Oh, he never again saw land, boys
He never again saw land
The last of the Drumms to board a ship
And he never again saw land

My music and I could not stay ashore
So teased by the ocean smells
Me coat was wet but my fiddle dry
On the rollicking voyage to Else

Here George would normally pick up his fiddle and play a wild, undulating interlude. Now he hummed this melody softly to himself as he listened for the sounds of the Wanderers ahead. When he could again make out the clatter of their carts, he took up singing once more:

Though the island Else is 300 miles long
It's but 30 from South to North
If your pockets are filled you can go
Where you will, For ev'ry town's a port

"There is a continent in tales
Where the mountains rise up to the moon
And its lands are vast as the oceans we sail"
I mused in an Else saloon

"I'll take you there" an old Captain said
"But I won't take you there for free
For a ship to reach these fabled lands
Takes One Hundred Days At Sea"

Another fiddle solo would come here, and again George hummed the part to himself as he looked around at his surroundings. He sensed that he was gaining on the Wanderer caravan. The sun was high in the sky and the terrain was growing rocky with fewer trees. George had lost count of how many cloudless days had passed in sequence. His skin was lobster red from the sun, and his hair and beard had lightened to an almost carrot color. He took a swig of water and went on with his song, raising his voice as if to drown out the dry heat with his tale of the sea:

"The voyage to Else was a rockin' crib
Next to what lies ahead
And there'll be no doubts, nor turnin' back"
The wild-eyed Captain said

"I'll take you to Omanipinamo
If you'll trust your life to me"
And so began my journey of
One Hundred Days At Sea

Twenty days passed and forty too
I felt each would be my last
Waves broke over the decks in walls
And ceaseless cold winds lashed

Then one morn' the air grew still
The ocean was warm as tea
Our sails hung limp, our spirits too
We'd been sixty days at sea

George rounded a heap of boulders. The path was climbing and so was the sun. He stopped in the narrow shade of the boulders and leaned against the cool rock, listening for the Wanderers.

"Yes, the day grows too warm for traveling."

George turned to see a robust man with a drooping black mustache approaching him. He held a wine skin in his outstretched hand.

"Here, have some wine; you must be thirsty. Singing and walking is hard work."

George took a long swig and handed back the skin, smiling broadly. "And I've still a couple of verses left."

"Well, *gorgio*, save your energy so you can sing your story to us from the beginning—we could not make out any of the words above our own noise. Perhaps, if you can tolerate such a throng, you will join our party—we do seem to be going the same way." The man raised his bushy eyebrows and grinned, "and your music is most entertaining. Was that a fiddle we heard you playing last night?"

"Yes, that's right." But George did not want to talk about music just yet. "You already know my name, how is that?"

"How is that indeed? Do I know your name? I think not!"

"You called me Gorgio, and my name is George."

"Really? How unique! *Gorgio* is just our word for 'stranger.' We had only to look at you to see you were a *gorgio*. And you thought I was calling you by name. Hah hah!"

"Well, now you do know my name, but I do not know yours." George was feeling a little ridiculous.

"Of course, forgive me. My name is Rudolfo. You may call me Rudy. My family name is delaTorre and we are Travelers, descendents of the ancient Wanderers." He slapped a friendly hand on George's shoulder. "Come, let me lead you to our camp. We have a favorite spot not far from here where we are stopping for a day or so. I'm sure we can find room for you."

George followed Rudy a short distance up the steepening path. Just when he was wondering how the Travelers could have taken their carts any further, Rudy veered off to the east. The land sloped gently downward through a pine forest, and the path disappeared. Depressions left by the wagon wheels and horses hooves in a thick bed of pine needles marked the route the Travelers had taken through the trees. The two men could now walk side by side.

"Do you have other names than George? It might be awkward for us to call you Gorgio once we get to know you!"

George laughed, finding his sense of humor again. "My family name is Drumm. I come from Sumweir Island. If you have heard of the Piper People, well, they are my ancestors."

"I see." Rudy twirled his mustache thoughtfully.

"Ah, here we are." He had led George through the pines and around to the north, where they crossed a thin trickle of water bubbling up from an underground stream. George could hear voices and smell wood smoke. The trees thinned and the ground under foot became rocky again. A great mound of rock emerged ahead, and the men followed the caravan's trail up and around to its easterly face.

George stopped to take in the magnificent scene. A great plain sloped gently down toward the northeast, and the Travelers' horses grazed happily in a nearby field. Herds of wild horses and other game were visible in the distance. But it was the huge rock itself which was most astonishing. It opened up into a cave large enough for the entire Traveler band including the carts. There was much activity in and around the cave as the Travelers moved in. A leaping fire already burned in front of the mouth of the cave. As Rudy urged George to come along and led him ever closer to the camp, George began to feel self-conscious. The Travelers, while continuing with their chores, kept looking over at him; some started to stare openly.

Entering the cave with Rudy, George saw that it was even more ideal than he had at first thought. An opening in the rock above allowed light and fresh air to pour in, permitting smaller fires to be lit within the chilly cave itself. The wagons had been parked in a semicircle at the back of the cave, and a small cooking fire lit in front of each one. The Traveler women were busy cooking; they kept the children busy fetching water and other necessities. George could smell a feast in the making and his stomach growled loudly.

"Go ahead and put your things down," Rudy said, nodding at one of the wagons. "Mama, how about a bowl of soup for this poor *gorgio*, I don't think he can wait for the big meal."

Rudy's Mama was a leathery but bright-eyed old woman. She looked up at her son with only a hint of annoyance and then ladled a generous portion of broth into an earthenware bowl, which she handed to George.

"Much obliged, Ma'am," George said, slurping at the bowl—he had not been given a spoon.

"You might as well sit to eat," she said, nodding to one of several large rocks near her fire.

George sat. He was certain that this entire exchange was being carefully observed, and he felt more conspicuous all the time. Some men had come over to Rudy; he was now walking with them over to the mouth of the cave. They stopped and spoke animatedly, occasionally laughing and periodically looking over at George. One by one they wandered off, Rudy included, and George was left in the cave with the women and children. He emptied his bowl and handed it back to Rudy's mother, who was blowing on the coals of the fire to make it burn hotter.

"I could go fetch some more fire wood," George offered.

"Good. There's an axe on the wagon. Small thick pieces like this do the best," she held up a chunk of wood before tossing it on the fire.

George found the axe and went back out to the pine forest. He was grateful for the opportunity to escape the scrutiny of his hosts.

That evening they ate a communal meal around the big fire under the stars. Then Rudy stood to officially introduce the newest addition to the Traveler band.

"It is hard not to notice our *gorgio* here," Rudy made an embarrassed George stand up. The assembled group then openly acknowledged him with calls of "Yes, who is he?" and "What is your name, *gorgio*?"

"This *gorgio*'s name is George!" Rudy answered for him. "He is called George Drumm and he is of the Piper People—but he plays the fiddle! Is this not remarkable? And that is as it should be. For we have heard his remarkable music, if only from a distance. But now, George Drumm Piper Fiddler is going to play and sing the tale of his brave adventures and how he has come to travel along this way with us." Rudy's mother thrust the fiddle case up at George. Apparently he was to be the opening act in the night's entertainment.

George put aside his embarrassment and let himself get into the teasing, playful spirit of the Travelers. He made a great show of tuning up, letting ear shattering squeaks escape in the midst of meticulous scales. The children laughed and squealed along. Satisfied that he had the rapt attention of all, George made his voice low and gruff, squinted his eyes, and held his fiddle at the ready as he began to recite in a sailor's sing-song the verses of his chantey.

George's accent, thickened with a seaman's brogue, was incomprehensible to some; but the younger Travelers were able to understand, and during the fiddle interludes they explained the story to the others, who listened and nodded carefully. George stretched out the music and waited to see that everyone had caught up to the story before going on. He was enjoying his studious audience. As he neared the end of his saga, some of the Travelers got out their own instruments and played along softly while he chanted the final dramatic verses:

Parched from sun and salt
Resigned to a watery fate
Seventy days and eighty gone
There was naught to do but wait

Then just when hope would perish
The wind once more did blow

And after One Hundred Day At Sea
We made Omanipinamo

Yes, Omanipinamo, boys, Omanipinamo!
Again our sails were pulling us
towards Omanipinamo!

George swung into one last rollicking instrumental and his Traveler accompanists joined in with vigor. Some young women got up to dance, starting and stopping often and giggling all the while, unsure of how to move to the Piper sailor's jig. As if by unanimous consent, George gave up the lead to the Traveler musicians and the jig became a raga. Now it seemed that all of the young women had jumped up and were dancing with a grace and passion George had never before experienced. He was afraid to watch them too openly. He turned aside and put down his fiddle and bow so that he could shake out his hands and arms and mop his face with a bandana. The men and boys now came over to him and slapped him on the back and shook his hand as they told him their names.

Some married women were brought over and introduced by their husbands. They were beautiful and some were flushed from dancing; the husbands held them around the shoulders or waist and winked proudly at George. At one point, while George was surrounded by several middle-aged couples, Rudy came over and made a big show of asking George if he had a wife. It was obvious that his answer was of great importance and would dictate his position among the Travelers. George looked at Rudy who looked back intently, as if wishing he could tell George how to answer.

George hung his head and bit his lip. When he looked up there was a tear in his eye. "I've a wife on Sumweir Island. She—she lies buried atop the Corbel Shernyie, struck down at the peak of her womanhood. But you see, since I am here and she is there, I can imagine her alive, my wife still, my wife forever—someday I shall cross the sea to be with her once more." George wept real tears. The story was so sad, he could almost imagine it was true.

"What took the dear girl?" a woman asked gently.

George looked off into the distance and spoke as if in a dream, "I won't speak of it. I must remember her in her health. None will ever be more beautiful. Her hair was the color of sweet apple wine and her eyes as green as a spring leaf. And her skin, her skin was white as a pearl." He brought his eyes back to the Traveler men and their dark-skinned, black-haired wives. "Oh, excuse me, I shouldn't be saying these things."

The Travelers were quick to reassure George and to console him. Rudy threw an arm around him and said, "There, there, George Drummer Fiddler Piper Traveler, forget we ever brought this up. You're one of us now. We'll share your sorrows if you'll share our joys!" And with that George was prodded into taking up his fiddle once more.

George's tragic story spread quickly during the next few days. Over the course of that time George met all of the Travelers; it was not long before he was an accepted member of the company. He was careful to keep his place among the married and elder men and women, and not to socialize with the young fellows actively looking for brides. At each evening's festivities, George would play his fiddle and observe the dancing freely; but he would put a somewhat distant expression on his face as he watched the girls spin and undulate, pretending they bore little appeal to him next to the memory of his fair wife.

In truth, George had never found the female form more enticing: every black braid, every brown arm, every dusty, bell-clad ankle, spoke to him of romance.

Chapter 7

The extra run had been especially gruelling. Julio was glad to swing into the station, and he sighed in unison with the pneumatic doors of the bus as they opened to release his passengers. He felt odd and wished he'd never agreed to cover for Bob, even though he owed him one and would get time-and-a-half for the extra hours. Now Julio thought only of home and the fresh enchiladas his girlfriend would have for him. As he stood ready to help the women and old people down the three steep steps, he saw only Teresa and he could almost smell the pungent green chile sauce which would be simmering on the stove. He smiled to himself and took a deep breath, but the odor of strong spirits jolted him to attention. An inebriated old gent was pushing a nearly empty whisky bottle into Julio's hand.

"Take it. Take it!" he urged hoarsely. "I am going mad. Just like the preacher man said. I got the hallucinations; I got the cold sweats. Take it. Take it—there's a mission up the street. Maybe it ain't too late."

Julio took the bottle and pushed the man away. Passengers were lining up to disembark. They went past Julio quietly, nodding but avoiding his eyes, not laughing as people often would at such a scene. 'Everyone's had a rough day,' he thought, trying again to visualize his living room with Teresa and the kids scurrying around, talking loud and laughing, waiting for him. He nodded automatically as each person stepped off the bus, watching their feet and offering a hand without seeing their faces.

Too late, he took notice of an unusual pair of shoes quickly revealed as old fashioned skirts were lifted to avoid the metal steps of the bus. The shoes were more like slippers and were embroidered in metallic threads. 'Oriental,' Julio thought. But the skirt was more like that of his Spanish grandma—layered flounces all the way to the ankle. By the time he looked up, Julio could see only the back of a tiny cloaked figure as it disappeared into the crowded station. He assumed it was an old woman—who else would dress so on such a warm day? Although he didn't remember such a woman getting on the bus at Silverton, he didn't bother to speculate. Old grandmothers—grandfathers too—were known to sometimes sneak onto the busses. When caught, they would be adamant about their rights to travel free: "How else will I get to see my children? It isn't right to keep families apart!"

Julio raised his shoulders to his ears and rolled his head back, hearing the joints snap and pop. The old lady had been the last off the bus. Julio hopped back on to clean up the aisles. As he picked up some candy wrappers and soda pop cans from under the seats at the back of the bus, he smelled something fresh and spicy, not the usual odor of stale cigarettes. He shook his head and rolled his tired shoulders again. "Teresa, I'm on my way!"

Esmarelda hurried through the bus terminal, easily finding the room marked WOMEN. She'd discovered these public conveniences on her previous visits to the Alternate World. Though horribly unnatural settings, they at least afforded some safety and privacy.

Esmarelda sat down carefully without lifting her skirts. She just needed to think.

'How disgusting—arriving on a moving vehicle. Malcom is an utter idiot and I suppose I am, too, for using his magic satchel. Of course the satchel would act mischievously, having been stolen and misused as it was. But it was my best chance to find Audy.' The Gypsy had a disturbing thought: What if the whole thing had been a trap? Perhaps the blue thread had nothing at all to do with Audy but had been intended for her from the beginning—to land her in this odd place. 'It was too simple! I should have suspected he was tricking me when he made it so easy for me to doctor his soup. His looking so tired and a little sick, having the soup ready in the first place—it was all a nasty joke. Oh, have I learned nothing?!'

The Gypsy plunged her hand into her pack and pulled out the crystal ball. She toyed with it nervously, rolling it from hand to hand, distracted by the dreadful feeling that she had played into Malcom's most dangerous trap yet.

Something glittered out of the smooth crystal. Esmarelda caught her breath and steadied the ball on the palm of her left hand. She took several deep breaths with her eyes closed and then focused all of her attention and energy on the crystal. It was sparkling brightly now, even though the unpleasant lighting of the restroom had not changed. As Esmarelda stared, the sparkle became pinpoints of light bouncing off of water. It was just a tiny trickle of water, but around it plants and insects flourished. And then the glittering water became Audy's blinking blue eyes. A toilet flushed, making Esmarelda jump, and the scene dissolved.

'So, he is in this Spiral-turn after all. And it looks like he's found a reasonably safe place, too.' Esmarelda was so encouraged that she quickly put her unpleasant thoughts of the Master Seer aside and turned her attention back to the rescue of Audy. 'I wonder where that oasis is. My only hope is to try to contact Audy with my thoughts and to let his energy lead me to him.' As more toilets flushed, the Gypsy decided this would be more effectively attempted outdoors in the fresh air. She wrapped herself up in her cloak and, hugging the bulky pack close to her chest, she emerged from the stall.

Esmarelda let her mind go completely blank as she quickly made her way out of the station. The less she thought, the less attention would be paid to her. This was a trick commonly known among the Gypsies of Esmarelda's clan and many other clans as well. It is the reason Gypsies are rumored to be able to make themselves invisible though they cannot, not in the physical sense. But with this special talent for quieting the ego, becoming completely neutral, and holding the aura in close, Gypsies like Esmarelda could go so unnoticed as to be as good as invisible even while moving about freely and acting as circumstances dictated.

It was this very neutrality and calm that took Esmarelda instinctively around the corner and across the street to an abandoned railroad depot. She rustled through the sun-dried stalks of wild plants which she did not recognize, making her way around to the back of the old building and out of sight of the busy bus platforms. Although the plants were unknown to her the sun, so high and hot, and the cloudless sky felt reassuringly familiar. This was from her dream. Standing beside a criss-cross of rusty tracks, the Gypsy found herself surprisingly alone. Ahead of her—beyond the overgrown lot, the barbed wire fence and an elevated roadway—blue-grey mountaintops hovered in the distance. The dream again.

Esmarelda was feeling more confident by the minute. There was something magical here. At least her own magic seemed to be working. She now had no doubt that it was only a matter of time before she found Audy. She took a pendant from around her neck. It was an eight-pointed star fashioned of silver, the size of a large coin. The talisman hung heavily from its long silk cord. which the Gypsy held high with her right hand while steadying the star with her left. There was no hint of wind as Esmarelda took her hand away from the star and stood motionless. And there was still no hint of wind when moments later the pendant began to swing, first to the Gypsy's left and then to her right. Back and forth it swung, gaining momentum and swinging higher, and always highest to the left. Esmarelda caught the star in her left hand and returned the talisman to her neck. She turned purposefully a quarter-turn to the left and began to follow the thread of track stretching before her. She was heading north, following the same path Audy had taken.

When the path along the tracks became too rough for her, Esmarelda turned west and then north again along a road marked First Street. Large, noisy vehicles continually jolted her out of her invisibility meditation. This seemed of little consequence, since the few pedestrians the Gypsy did pass appeared to be Gypsies of a sort themselves. They wore many layers of clothing, and they carried bulging sacks or pushed their piles of belongings in wire carts. The vagabonds, those that noticed her, paid no attention at all to Esmarelda; and to the men driving the huge machines and working in the greasy warehouses and garages, Esmarelda was simply another street person.

The Gypsy walked almost three miles and noticed that First Street became more residential as she went. The large industrial lots gave way to houses with yards, and these yards seemed to be full of animals. Cats leapt up onto fences and walls behind which dogs barked as the Gypsy passed. Some yards even had pens full of pigeons, chickens or geese. Esmarelda tried to make a mental connection with these animals, asking silently if any had seen Audy, but the intensity of these thoughts was drawing attention to her in this more orderly neighborhood. Some children were already watching her curiously; again she let her thoughts grow silent.

When the street ended in a cul de sac, the Gypsy slipped behind an old shed in a dusty yard and consulted her pendant once more. Again it swung to the left first. Esmarelda retraced her steps and took the first side street west. The streets were getting busier—Esmarelda could feel her nervousness and uncertainty returning. It seemed to her that the sun in this place would never set; she was hot under her cloak and the pack felt heavier with each step. But she kept walking west—not knowing what else to do—and wondered how she would ever find Audy in such a sprawling town.

Anxiety gave way to numbness, and Esmarelda no longer cared that people were noticing her or worried that someone might speak to her. When she reached a busy commercial street, the Gypsy stood resolutely on the corner and looked up and down. She ignored the cars swooshing past her and concentrated on making sense of the chaos of glass, neon and billboard lettering that represented the storefronts along the street.

A window on the other side of the road caught her eye. She saw prisms and beautiful pieces of stained glass sparkling among baskets of hanging plants. When she noticed a picture of a unicorn painted on the glass door of the shop and the words above it, "The Lost Unicorn," Esmarelda said a silent prayer of thanks to the goddess. Bravely she crossed through the traffic. The Gypsy found her safe arrival at the door of The Lost Unicorn as miraculous as the existence of the shop itself.

Entering the cool dark of the building from the bright sunlight, Esmarelda could not see anything at first. But she smelled the familiar smells of incense and drying herbs, and closed her eyes to better concentrate on the aromas.

"Can I help you?" a woman's voice said. The Gypsy opened her eyes and saw the room for the first time. There were shelves cluttered with candles and jars, and glass display cases brimming with gems and jewelry. Leather sacks adorned with beads and feathers hung from pegs on the walls, old fashioned straw brooms and driftwood walking sticks were leaning in the corners. Esmarelda turned around and around, not believing her eyes.

"Can I help you?" the woman asked again, and this time Esmarelda turned toward her and saw the tallest, blondest woman she had ever seen standing behind a counter at the back of the store. She had a very kind and knowing face, which was framed by a brilliant green scarf and giant moon-shaped earrings. Her sleek blond hair flowed down over her shoulders and back. She wore a long paisley-printed caftan, and a moon-and-stars pendant around her neck. Her fingers were full of rings, which flashed as she dusted an assortment of small sculptures lined up on the counter.

Esmarelda approached and saw that some of these were beautiful silver figurines of unicorns with crystals inset for the horns, and others were unusual rock and crystal formations or smooth balls of serpentine, amethyst or quartz balanced on lovely sculpted bases. Esmarelda stood in front of this array and looked up into the woman's eyes, holding them in a steady stare. She lowered her pack to the floor between her feet and let her cloak fall away from her shoulders so that her own magnificent costume was visible.

"I'm looking for my cat. I have seen him in my ball and think he is nearby." Esmarelda looked down at the one pure crystal ball on the counter. There was the image of the trickle of water surrounded by plants, exactly as she had seen it in her own crystal. She looked up excitedly, could this woman also see the image?

"If I were a lost cat in this neighborhood," the store's proprietress said, bending over and leaning her elbows on the counter so as to be at eye level with the Gypsy, "I would find my way to the irrigation ditch. There's water there and lots of bugs to catch, not too many people, and plenty of places to hide." Though apparently oblivious to the miniature landscape which the Gypsy now saw repeated in every reflective surface of the store, the woman had described it exactly. "Yes, the ditch would be the place to look. That's where my cats run off to when they manage to get out. If I could be sure they wouldn't run into the street I'd let them out all the time—but it isn't worth it, I'd hate to lose them. I know how you must feel."

She touched the Gypsy's arm as if to comfort her; in truth, she wanted to make certain it was a real person who stood at her counter. Robyn's clientele tended toward the eccentric, and she was used to meeting all manner of mysterious characters, but there was something even more unusual than usual about this visitor. The woman had brought a strange light into the room when she mentioned the cat, and a smell of water.

"How do I get to this irrigation ditch?"

"It's just one more block to the west. Here, come on out the back way and you'll be practically there."

Esmarelda followed the woman through a cluttered office and storage room, noticing again how very tall and graceful she was. "What is your name?" Esmarelda asked, as the woman unbolted the heavy back door and opened it. Sunshine poured over them, and the two women looked at each other for the first time in full light.

"Robyn." She pointed out toward the junk-strewn lot behind the store. "Just go out to that big tree—there's a place to squeeze through the fence over to the left there—and follow the irrigaton ditch. It's shadier and quieter to the north; there's a little path you can walk on.

Is this your first trip to Caliente? Are you sure you don't need anything before you go? A glass of water or something? It's been unusually hot today for this time of year."

"You have done a great deal for me already, Robyn. I cannot tell you how fortunate I feel to have found you. I would like to come back and spend some time looking at all of the wonderful things in your shop, but I doubt I'll have the opportunity. I must go look for Audy now before he gets even further away."

Esmarelda rummaged through her pack and withdrew a shiny object, which she pressed into Robyn's hand. "There's something for your display," the Gypsy said, flinging her cloak across to again cover her elegant costume. "I must be off. When you think of me, Robyn, wish me luck—send me magic!"

Robyn didn't know what to say. She watched in amazement as the beautiful fairy-woman disappeared into the folds of her grey cloak and moved off through the yard to become one with the lengthening shadows. Opening her hand, she found an intricately worked bracelet. Nine flat pieces of silver, cut into tiny pentagons, hung from a silver chain. A letter was engraved on each bangle. Robyn turned the bracelet to its clasp and followed the letters around clockwise. "E-S-M-A-R-E-L—ESMARELDA! Esmarelda—wow! Whoever you are, Esmarelda, I do wish you luck finding your cat, and magic, too, though you seem to have plenty of that. Oh, and I hope you'll come back and tell me your story!"

The buzzer sounded in the back office. Robyn hurried back into the shop. Two customers browsed nonchalantly among the treasures and shook their heads when she asked, "Can I help you?"

Robyn sat down on the stool behind the counter and put the bracelet first around her wrist and then, finding it too large, around her ankle. It fit perfectly. She went back to dusting the stock, trying to remember every detail she could about Esmarelda's visit. Every once in a while she had to shake her right foot and feel the bangles against her skin just to assure herself that the incident had been real. 'A fairy queen came to see me, looking for her lost cat!' Robyn smiled to herself and decided not to mention Esmarelda's visit even to her most metaphysical friends, though keeping such a story secret would require great discipline. 'If anyone asks, I'll just tell them the bracelet is an inheritance from a long lost aunt. I think Esmarelda would prefer it that way.'

Robyn stared into the crystal she was dusting, looking for Esmarelda's cat, and saw instead a perfect spiral winding outward from the center.

When Esmarelda arrived at the irrigation ditch she knew immediately that she had found Audy's hiding place. As she walked slowly along the dirt path, she held Malcom's magic satchel at the ready. Her plan was to put Audy in the sack and send him back to her house while she returned in her own satchel. It would be a little tricky sending the cat back alone, but in this strange place, after all he'd been through, the Gypsy did not believe Audy would be cooperative enough to be held. She did not want to try to hold onto him while she got into her sack and traveled the Spiral; if he struggled, they might both end up someplace even worse than this! Esmarelda rubbed catnip into the Knot in the old satchel that represented her house. Audy would chew on the Knot and the satchel would take him home—she hoped.

Something rustled in the high grass beside the path. Esmarelda silently lowered her pack to the ground and opened the neck of the satchel wider. She squatted and tried to keep her voice steady as she called softly: "Audy, here boy, it's me! Here Audy! Come on, boy, I'm here to take you home!"

This time there was no conflict between Malcom and Audy. They had both sensed the Gypsy's presence and then smelled her spicy scent while she was well down the path. Now, with united intentions, Audy/Malcom emerged from the tangled growth of plants and trotted toward Esmarelda, who could hardly suppress her excitement. She forced herself to be calm and did not let herself jump up and try to grab the animal.

"Good boy, Audy, good boy!" she cooed as she reached out her hand. Audy came up to her, and she stroked his fur with her right hand while she maneuvered the satchel with her left. As she brought the satchel toward the cat, she pressed down on his back firmly so he wouldn't run away. She felt him tense when she started to pull the bag over his head. "It's all right, Audy, I'm sending you home and I'll be right behind you. There's catnip in here, you'll like it. Trust me, Audy, you know I'd never hurt you . . ."

Both the cat and the Gypsy were nervous and, as Esmarelda's hands trembled, Audy slithered. His claws stuck to the loose weave of the bag; Esmarelda could not get him in far enough to smell the catnip and find the special Knot. She did not know that part of the problem was that Malcom could not repress his own urgent desire to be rescued, and the energy of his will was further frightening the animal.

Suddenly a trio of boys on bicycles came speeding down the path on the far side of the ditch, calling out loudly to each other. The commotion broke the Gypsy's concentration and Audy, terrified, broke from her grasp and scampered down the path, dragging the magic satchel behind him.

"NO! NO! NO! AUDY, COME BACK! COME BACK!" Esmarelda shrieked, running after him—until she remembered where she was. The boys across the ditch had stopped and were staring at her and laughing. "Hey, it's not Halloween yet, lady!" one called out. "Yeah, and you forgot your broom!" another teased.

Esmarelda turned and stared at them with such fury that they hastily mounted their bicycles. "You're lucky I don't have my broom!" Esmarelda shouted back, "or I'd come cut out your noisy little tongues! You wouldn't be interfering with my work then, would you?" The boys' eyes bulged and their faces were white as they peddled away as fast as the rutted path would allow. But the Gypsy took no pleasure in the scene. She trudged despairingly back up the path. Reclaiming her pack, she considered returning to The Lost Unicorn but thought better of it.

"I'm going home," she said out loud, as if Audy might hear her and return so that he could go home also. But there was no sign of him or the old satchel, and the sun was finally setting, making it difficult to see. The Gypsy moved off the path and leaned exhaustedly against a tree. The old gnarled bark comforted her. She leaned her ear against it and heard the tree laughing. "You too?" she said, feeling hurt and crying a little bit into the tree trunk. The tree seemed to reach out and hug her, and she stood there until it was completely dark.

The Gypsy put her few spare garments on over the clothes she was already wearing. She had not expected it to get so cold, after such a warm sunny day. But with the cloak wrapped around her, Esmarelda was warm enough, and she curled up beside her tree for the night. She was not about to give up on Audy so easily. She would take him with her in her own satchel if it was possible, if she ever got another chance.

The night passed quickly for Esmarelda. Worn out as she was from her adventures, she slept soundly. When she awoke she thought for a moment that she was comfortable in her own bed. Reality washed over her as she raised her head to feel the cold morning air on her face. But still she felt remarkably cozy. Then the Gypsy noticed Audy curled up close beside her, purring contentedly.

"Audy, oh Audy, you sweet thing, you poor kitty. We'll get you home now. No more tricks, I promise, but do cooperate this time, I only have one satchel now." Esmarelda was stroking the cat with one hand and trying to get at her bag with the other. She had been so cold the night before that she had put her extra skirt and tunic on right over the belt that held the bag to her waist. Now she realized she would have to stand up and rearrange her garments to get at the satchel, and she would have to act quickly. She could hear the neighborhood waking up. Someone might come up the path and frighten Audy away again.

Esmarelda fed the cat a morsel of cheese. The animal ate hungrily. She stood and put a whole pile of cheese on the ground to keep Audy busy as she quickly slipped off one skirt, stuffing it into the pack, and grabbed the satchel from under the tunic she still wore for warmth. Now she grabbed the cheese and, cooing to the cat, picked him up and balanced him under her left arm so he could eat out of her hand. She hoisted the pack over her right shoulder. With one shake she opened the neatly folded satchel.

A scent of musk and cardamom filled the air and instantly the cat began to struggle. "Oh, please, Audy, please be good, it's all right, I promise, Audy. Oh, please don't do this to me!" Esmarelda squeezed more tightly with her left arm so Audy would not get away, but he was about to pop out of her grasp. She reached over with her right hand, which still held the satchel at the ready, and the cat became uncontrollable. He hissed and spit, a sharp claw pierced the back of the Gypsy's hand and then another. Still she held on and tried to calm him with her voice. The enraged animal twisted around with all of its force and leapt into the tree behind them, leaving three bloody gashes on Esmarelda's forearm.

Tears of anger and pain streaming down her face, the Gypsy peered up into the tree where Audy perched in the highest branches. Shivering, she pulled her cloak around her, heedless of her bleeding arm. A dog barked, and many dogs joined in. She heard footsteps on the path and saw a man running toward her with a dog at his heels. Quickly gathering the satchel into a ball under her cloak and pulling the hood up over her head, Esmarelda slipped around to the other side of the tree, pressing herself close to it. As the man ran by, the dog took a detour over to the tree, ate the crumbs of cheese from the ground, sniffed, urinated, and trotted back to his master. Neither had noticed the Gypsy.

Chapter 8

"I have a present for you."

"Why should you give me a present?"

"Because I'm fond of you."

"If you were really fond of me you'd let me get my own room in town where I could have some privacy. I would still come for my lessons every day. It would be more—more civilized. Who knows, perhaps I would find it more romantic, too. Romance needs anticipation."

"Oh, *I'm* full of anticipation, Esmarelda. Every day that I wake up and know you are in this very house with me, I *thrill* with anticipation.

"And you know 'town' is not a private place to be at all. Trust me on this one. 'Town' is every nosy woman and man snooping after you. And once they discover you come to see me, well, that would not be beneficial to either of us to say the least. No, absolutely not. You will not move to town. I will not have you as my pupil if you move to town."

"Well, I could camp in the woods. I've spent most of my life sleeping under the stars. I don't need that room in the back; I *am* a Gypsy."

"Do my personal habits offend you? Am I so overbearing? Have I been less than a perfect gentleman? Is my teaching inadequate? You seem to take some interest in the Tarot and the mixing of potions. And I have many more tidbits to share with you. You will be the hit of any gathering and a force to be reckoned with if you continue with me.

"But if you would really rather sleep in the woods than under the same roof as your respected professor here—well, I just don't think my feelings can bear it. Not to mention my nerves. Gypsies generally travel in bands, remember? Your people know there's safety in numbers. It's a wonder you've managed alone for so long— Now don't give me that look! I'm paying tribute to your independence; you don't have to prove anything to *me*."

"So, what's the present?"

"Never mind. You don't deserve it. Why should I give you a present? You would rather sleep in the woods than in my house. You would rather eat your meals with the squirrels than with me."

"I have a something for you."

"A present? For me?"

"Perhaps more of a gratuity, for being such a good teacher."

"So, you're happy with your lessons?"

"I tried the cloudburst potion this morning. Yes, that was me! It worked wonderfully. That will really come in handy sometime when I have an ugly audience. If they turn on me, I can turn the water on them!"

"Ah, then you feel you're getting your money's worth here?"

"What money's worth? You haven't charged me a thing. It makes me a little nervous, if you want to know. Are you running a tab? If so, I'm sure I'll never afford it."

"A tab? Why, you sweep up and wash my dishes. It's the usual apprentice's arrangement. There's nothing to be nervous about, darling. True, I have suggested that we might enjoy something more than the usual arrangement; but as you are unwilling and I am not a brute, I must be content with a little cooking and cleaning—and a small gratuity from time to time, if you insist..."

"Malcom, I wish you would stop bringing up your unwelcome propositions. Your insinuations make me very uncomfortable."

"Forget the whole thing, Esmarelda. I am your teacher and you are my pupil. We will leave it at that. Now what is it you have for me? An apple?"

"I keep offering to dance for you but you won't let me."

"Offering to torture me, you mean. Now, Esmarelda, I cannot guarantee my continued chivalrous behavior if I must watch you writhe and quiver. You're not really going to offer me another dance are you?"

"I'm trying to help you learn the Knots as I promised I would. But there's no point if you won't attend to the dance—it's the key to the Spiral Map."

"So, you promised to teach me something you knew I would never have the patience or fortitude to learn. This way you keep both your word and your secrets. So, this is how the Gypsies keep their bargains, is it? *I* say, if you *want* me to learn something, you will tell it to me straight out."

"You're being impossible."

"Me? It was you who said you had a gift for me and then you offer only a dance. You know I don't want a dance!"

"*Not* a dance. Not a dance; but it has to do with the dance and the Knots. You never let me finish!"

"So finish, finish! Tell me what the present is already, I'm sure I'll love it."

"No. Not now. I can't be nice to you—I wonder why I try."

"I know you're going to leave me, Esmarelda."

"Then you won't try to stop me?"

"You've always been free to come and go."

"You mean to go and not come back."

"Don't forget, I can get all the apprentices I want. I gave up four for you."

"Well, you shouldn't have. I mean you didn't have to. I could have held my own with them. Malcom, it was never my intention to hurt you—or to use you."

"Of course not! Don't feel badly. Pretty girls are allowed to be insensitive. Now, we *could* talk about how you ended up a lone Gypsy in this inhospitable district in the first place—I never needed to ask because, as Master Seer, I saw through you at once. A spoiled, unappreciative little ingenue. She takes the secrets of her clan and skips out. No thought of family obligations. No concern for the responsibilities of being a vessel for generations of Gypsy magic. Off she goes looking for a shortcut to wisdom, bartering ancient truths for cheap tricks. How could I have expected to be treated any better?"

"Enough! You sound just like my Gypsy teachers. They called me ungrateful too. Should I really be grateful for having had my whole life decided for me before I was born?"

"Ah, Esmarelda. In so many ways your life *is* decided before you are born. But not by the likes of me, or your Gypsy family. That is why we must let you go—we must all let you go—much as we hate to lose you."

They fell silent. The sky darkened and big drops of rain splashed on the tin roof.

"Really, Malcom, how sentimental can you get?"

"Disgustingly so. I have a gift for you. Please accept it. I sense this is my last chance."

Esmarelda waited coolly. But when the Master Seer pulled a bangled chain from his vest pocket, and the clouds broke to send a shaft of sunlight dancing through the window and off of the silver, her eyes lit up.

"I knew you would like it. Now take a closer look. It's very finely crafted, don't you think? I had it done while on my trip to Ochersfeldt some months ago, remember?

"And you've been trying to give it to me all this time. Now I'm sorry that I put you off. It's perfect, Malcom, thank you."

"Then put it on. Let's hear how it sounds."

Esmarelda snapped the chain around her ankle and the nine bangles, each engraved with a letter of her name, jingled against each other when she shook her foot. The urge to dance suddenly overwhelmed her. It was as if the dancing that had been forbidden in Malcom's presence would now burst out of her, heedless of either

Malcom's—or her own—will.

'Steady, steady. Don't succumb. He wants me to dance now, but I won't. He thinks it will make me stay. The smiths at Ocherfeldt made him a little chain to hold me here, did they?'

"It's so lovely. Thank you again, Malcom." Esmarelda acted as if nothing out of the ordinary was happening, but her feet burned with the need to dance while her hands itched, longing to tear the chain from her ankle. 'If I can just stay calm I'll be able to get away. It's up to me—he said he would let me leave.'

"Now I have something for you."

"At long last. You know, I do feel for a dance after all this time."

"Here, I mended this old magic satchel for you. I want you to see that I do keep my promises. Given how uncooperative you've been about studying the Spiral Map, fixing up the satchel is the best I can do for you in regard to the secrets of the Knots. Be careful with this, Malcom. I know you'll figure out how to use it when you're ready—but you're not really qualified. And of course it's stolen, which is not good at all. You shouldn't be using it. Don't blame me for the trouble you get into with this thing."

"Really, go ahead. Show me the dance now. I'm ready."

"No, it's too late."

"Then I'm going to blame you for absolutely everything. I've just decided that. Thanks for the bag."

Malcom stood and lurched angrily into his bedroom, slamming the door. The sky darkened once more, without rain, in a premature dusk.

Esmarelda quickly gathered her belongings and left the house. The bracelet on her ankle jingled like an alarm, but she could not stop to take it off. She ran out of the house and down to the maze, where she skipped and danced and bounced against the shrubbery as the darkness became complete. She could not stop moving. She gasped for breath as her legs carried her faster and faster and spun her around in circles as if she were a puppet on a string.

"Away! Away!" She cried. Pitching her body forward, she fell to the ground and was able to tear the chain from her ankle. But she could not cast the bracelet away altogether. Clutching it in her fist and her pack in her arms, she crawled into her own magic satchel.

"Away! Away!" she sobbed, fingering the Knots clumsily. "Anywhere, anywhere! Away! Away!"

Chapter 9

"Oh my!" Tears came to Esmarelda's eyes once more as Robyn dabbed at the gashes on her arm.

"I'm sorry. Really, it should only hurt for a minute. Let me get you some tea." Robyn bustled over to the stove while Esmarelda sat at the cluttered kitchen table holding a soft pad to her stinging wounds. She closed her eyes and leaned back, grateful for the warmth of the house and Robyn's kindness. She could hear Robyn run water into a teapot and then quietly step out of the room. A moment later Esmarelda could hear Robyn's voice talking softly in the hall, although she did not sense that anyone else was in the house. She could just make out Robyn's words:

"...Something came up. No, I'll be here—it's just that I can't leave the house. An old friend showed up this morning and I want to spend the day with her... Yeah, we have a lot of catching up to do and I'm not sure how long she'll be in town... Yeah... Anyway, can you do the store? I really appreciate it. You're a doll to do this on such short notice... Well, I'd like for you to meet her too, but, uh, well, she's having some, uh, problems, you know... yeah. This might not be the best time... That's why I want to stick around—you know, and find out what's going on with her... I knew you'd understand. I owe you one, Faye, you're great... Thanks, talk to you later."

Robyn returned to the kitchen just as the kettle started to boil. "How're you doing?"

"It feels much better now. Is someone here?"

"Here? Oh no, I was just making a phone call—getting someone to mind the store for me so I don't have to rush off. I can fix up a bed for you so you can sleep. You look wiped out. You didn't sleep on the ditch did you?" Robyn brought a steaming mug to the table and looked disapprovingly at Esmarelda.

"I was in no danger." The two women were silent for a moment. A fluffy grey cat came into the room and looked from one woman to the other. The Gypsy said, "I do feel I owe you an explanation, Robyn. I mean I *want* to explain—it's just that I don't think you will believe me. I might even frighten you and I don't want to do that."

"Well, now you've got me so curious you will have to tell me everything no matter how frightening. You can't say things like that and then just leave me hanging!"

Esmarelda laughed. "Very well, but tell me something first: what is a phone call? Is it like sending your thoughts to somebody? I didn't think anyone in the—I mean anyone here—had that power."

Robyn took a deep breath and let it out slowly. "'Phone' is short for 'telephone;' a telephone is a device which people use to talk to each other when they are not in the same place. You can talk to someone around the corner or across town or in another country, if there is a telephone at each end. Mind reading is not usually involved. Esmarelda, there are telephones *all over the world*. Now, would you mind telling me where *you* come from?"

"Of course. I mean, I shall try. Do you have a piece of paper? I think I should draw you a map."

Esmarelda drew the Spiral for Robyn with a skilled hand. It wound out and then in again so that the ends connected in the center and created one continuous line. "This is my world," Esmarelda said, tracing the coil outward with her finger, "and this is your world, where we are now," she continued, following the coil back to the center. "We call your world the Alternate World, because the path of your Spiral alternates with the path of ours. You can look at each world's path separately by opening the spiral up into an 's' shape, but keep in mind that the center points of the two spirals are the same." The Gypsy drew a second spiral on the page.

Robyn was silent for a minute staring at the drawings. "Well, what do you call your world?" was all she could think of to ask.

"We don't call it anything really. It is just our earth, our reality. All in all, there are not many of us who truly understand the Spiral Map or give your world any concern whatsoever; just as you have—just as you *had*—so little knowledge of us."

"Then you must be someone special in your world as well as in this one, to know about the Spiral, to come here. How did you do it? How did your cat get here?" Robyn realized she had better try to get some details while she had the chance. She had always felt there was another side to things. Now she formulated her questions not with suspicion or disbelief, but as one hungry for confirmation of events already known.

"Let me try to tell this in my own way," Esmarelda said, taking a sip of tea. Robyn sat back and the cat jumped into her lap. The two looked at Esmarelda expectantly.

"I know the Spiral Map and am able to travel it because I am a Gypsy. Just as here, there are many different cultures, peoples, and places in my world. But the Wanderers, the Travelers, the Journeywomen, the Ethalees, and the Gypsies are known to travel to all places and to, in fact, make the caravan their home. Of these groups, however, it is only the Gypsies who travel through Time. Of course Witches travel through Time as well, and some other dimensions I'm not qualified to discuss, but keep in mind that they do *not* travel excessively from place to place."

"So it's only Gypsies and Witches from your world that I'm likely to run into here?" Robyn interrupted with a grin. She was feeling giddy. Esmarelda gave her a stern look. A second cat padded into the room. It collapsed dramatically on the floor, flicking its tail.

"You know, we have Gypsies in our world too," Robyn continued before Esmarelda could go on. "Only I don't think *they* can travel through time..." (It was Esmarelda's turn to grin.) "... and if they can, maybe they should. You know, we expect people to settle down and be predictable in this world, and we don't trust folks who don't conform—I mean we in general, of course, and not me specifically. I hate to say it, Esmarelda, but our Gypsies are known mostly as thieves and vagabonds—or at best just storybook characters."

"Well, that would be us. The storybook people. Your 'fairy tales' demonstrate that you are not so unaware of our world as you think. We really are two sides of the same coin. If you look over your shoulder, you will see us."

"That's very poetic, but how do you and your cat actually travel from one side of the coin to the other?"

The Gypsy brought out her magic satchel. She unfolded it and put her hand inside so that Robyn could see how loosely it was woven. "Consider that the coin is a net, and we know how to fall through the open spaces."

The scents rising up from the satchel filled Robyn with memories of dreams. She felt herself in the vortex of the swirling Spiral. 'Where *is* here?'

However it might work, Robyn was convinced that the strange sack was true physical proof of what the Gypsy said. She felt awed but not frightened. Her own investigations into magic and the occult (into which categories she also lumped science and religion) had taught her that there was more to life and the universe than we could ever know—and yet very much less to our minds and human knowledge than we would like to admit.

She liked the image of falling through the spaces; she was always looking for the holes in reality and scratching through the superficial to see what lay beneath. When she was a little girl she would sit upside down on the couch with her legs propped up on the backrest and her head hanging off of the seat cushions. In this position the ceiling became the floor, and stairs and doorways took on a surreal aspect. A mirror added whole new dimensions. What would it be like to live in such a landscape?

Mirrors and glass, prisms and gems, all things to do with light and color fascinated Robyn. In high school and college she explored such subjects as astronomy, photography, gemology and geography; but she could not settle into any of them. 'Too many facts. Too many experts. I don't want to know what they know—I want to know what they *don't* know.' Robyn dropped out of school. She worked as a waitress, a model, a secretary, and a sales clerk, moving from her quaint college town to the city.

She learned to read palms in a snobby Russian Tea Room which happened to employ an authentic Gypsy fortune teller. One day Madame Violetta, as she was called, handed a beautiful deck of cards to Robyn and asked if she would like to buy them; Madame was a little short on cash it seemed. Robyn recognized the deck as a Tarot deck. Without hesitation she said that she would buy it, if Madame would teach her how to tell fortunes with the cards. Apparently, this was out of the question, but after some haggling Robyn did purchase the cards and was given a scrap of paper with the name and phone number of an associate of Madame Violetta's scrawled across it. That was on a Sunday. On Tuesday, Madame Violetta had left town and Robyn decided to quit her job as well; the Tea Room had nothing to offer without Madame. She looked up Oscar Too, not knowing what to expect, and found a rather mousy middle-aged man. He could not teach her the Tarot but was willing to employ her in his Crafts Of The World shop. She took the job.

Some months later a Navajo rug weaver came in with some of his work. He was a huge, barrel-chested man with long shiny black braids and a handsome craggy face. He wore giant turquoise rings on almost every finger, an extravagantly beaded necklace in place of a tie, and a grey pin-striped suit. He was enchanted with Robyn's tall grace and blond tresses. Smiling broadly, he took her hands in his and practically drooled as he told her how beautiful she was. While not normally one to put up with such behavior, Robyn could not resist the man's charisma. His name was Black Star. She let him take her to lunch, at which he spoke nothing but flattery and she said nothing at all while his black eyes drilled through her. They went back to the shop and Black Star finished his business with Oscar.

"You must come to the land of the sun," he said to Robyn before he left. "The big sky will tell you what you need to know. What are you doing wasting away here with Mr. Too?" He handed her his card, which gave his address as a post office box in Caliente, and went out chuckling.

Things like this kept happening to Robyn: unusual people showing up in unusual places and giving her things, teaching her things, telling her things. She had never given much thought to it—until now.

Now, as she sipped tea with the Gypsy, Robyn realized that there was possibly no one else in the Alternate World who was as prepared as she was to listen to, believe, and help, this Time traveler from another world. She listened carefully to Esmarelda's story of how a stranger had come to her house to have his cards read and had then stolen Audy. And how Esmarelda, knowing that the Master Seer was behind the theft, had gone to confront him and had discovered that Audy had been brought here, to Caliente, in the Alternate World. It *was* like a fairy tale. Robyn had many questions about how the Gypsy's world differed from the world she knew.

"Our worlds are different because we think of them differently," Esmarelda tried to be generous about the Alternate World. Now that she had met Robyn she felt that her judgement of the Alternate World may have been too harsh. "We do not strive so much for change, or 'progress' as you call it. We are not so interested in mechanical things, in harnessing energy in that way, or in explaining why and how things happen in those terms. It seems to me that in this world, where you are unable to travel through Time, the Present is never enough. You are either waiting for the Future or longing for the Past. Yet in our world, where some of us *are* able to travel through Time, we find the Present the most satisfying place to be. In fact the Past, the Present, and the Future are all very much the same in my world. I can travel forward and back on my world's Spiral path and not feel out of place in any Time. In my world we understand that which is constant and that which is not. But here in your world, that which is constant is made uncertain by your trying always to explain it; and that which is not constant—yourselves, your minds, and your explanations—is given the weight of Truth. There is suffering in my world—poverty and cruelty and lost love—but nothing to compare to the suffering of this world. The pain of this world is the pain of confusion, mass confusion!"

"But why are we so confused?"

"Because you are riding a Spiral but you think you are driving a straight line! You say, 'I'm going around in circles,' as if that was bad—but that's what you're meant to do!" The Gypsy started to laugh and then couldn't stop.

At first Robyn thought that the Gypsy was making fun of her, but when Esmarelda's laughter turned into coughing Robyn realized how over-tired the woman was. She convinced Esmarelda that she needed to rest and took her to the small downstairs guest room to lie down.

While Esmarelda slept, Robyn went to check on Faye, walking through the backyard and an adjoining lot to the back door of the Lost Unicorn. She paused at the stoop where she had said good bye to Esmarelda the day before and then found her again so early in the morning, spotting her from the bedroom window. Robyn looked back at the house. Would the Gypsy still be there?

Robyn spent only a few minutes with Faye and then returned to the house. She decided to take advantage of her unexpected day off and went to work in the kitchen on her favorite recipes. As she stirred ingredients into a pot and watched the swirling liquid, Robyn thought about the Gypsy's Spiral Map.

It made a lot of sense, the concept of time as a spiral. Why hadn't she thought of it before? But this notion of two worlds would take some getting used to. 'Everyone takes for granted that we live in a less than perfect world—but who would have thought that a better world exists just a Spiral-turn away?' Robyn stopped stirring and picked up Esmarelda's drawing of the Spiral Map of Time. Such a simple little drawing, but she felt her life changing.

"That smells delicious!" Esmarelda came into the kitchen and stood a moment, inhaling deeply, before sitting down at the table.

Robyn noticed how silently the Gypsy moved. "I've been thinking about this situation with Audy: You have so many powers—you seem to be able to do almost anything—why don't you just *ask Audy* what's going on?

"You mean make a phone call to him?" Esmarelda joked.

"I know! You could turn yourself into a cat. That would make it easier to communicate with him, wouldn't it? Can you do that?"

"Why, no, I *can't* do that. What an alarming idea!"

"Sorry," Robyn said defensively. How could she have known this would be such an unwelcome suggestion?

Esmarelda felt sorry too, Robyn had only been trying to help.

"You do have a point about my not communicating with Audy. He's always been a mystery. I never knew where he came from."

"Perhaps if Audy could speak to you, he could tell you how the Master Seer is mixed up with all this." Earlier, Robyn had wished that the Gypsy would tell more about her relationship with the Master Seer, but Esmarelda had only said that he had been her teacher and that it was his magic satchel that had brought Audy—and then her—to Caliente.

Esmarelda did want to share more with Robyn. Her hostess had listened with fascination to what surely must have seemed the most unbelievable stories. But it was hard for the Gypsy to speak of more personal matters, it had been so long since she had tried.

"I guess you live here alone," she ventured, looking around.

"Mostly. I have a boyfriend. He stays here with me sometimes. It's nice when he does, but that's because he's not around all the time—if you know what I mean."

"You mean you wouldn't want him to be here all the time?"

"Right. Ramon wouldn't want to be around me all the time, either."

"I see."

"Do you have a, uh, husband in your world?" Looking at the Gypsy, Robyn could not imagine her with a husband—unless of course it was someone like a Master Seer.

"No. I have not been much interested in men, lately." Esmarelda seemed uncomfortable.

"I bet they're interested in you!"

Esmarelda smiled. "That's my problem, I guess. You see, the Master Seer, Malcom, was especially interested in me. And he still keeps finding ways to pester me. That's why he stole Audy and brought him here."

"You didn't love him?"

"I was attracted to him, certainly. A brilliant and handsome man. And we spent so much time together when I was his apprentice that we were almost like a married couple. But we were not lovers, and that made him angry. Over time things got worse and worse. His attitude just confirmed what I had suspected from the beginning—that he really only cared about himself. He did nothing to reassure me, to show me that my feelings mattered. He just pushed and pushed. After a time we could no longer be friends and I began to feel unsafe in his house. I had to leave."

"You lived with him?"

"Yes. You can imagine how it got difficult."

"Hmm, I'm beginning to get the picture. And he just let you leave?"

"It wasn't that easy but, yes, he let me leave. Of course I was not really rid of him."

"What happened then? Where did you go?"

"It was awful. I got into my magic satchel and asked to go Anywhere and ended up near Ochersfeldt, which didn't really surprise me."

When Esmarelda told Robyn about the bracelet, they both looked down at Robyn's right ankle. She shook her leg and the silver pendants clinked against each other softly.

"It seems to have no effect on me. I haven't felt anything sinister about it—and I can usually tell those things."

"Oh, I would not have given it to you if I thought it were really dangerous. It's something between Malcom and me. That's why I couldn't just throw it away I guess; but now I'm sure giving it to you was the right thing. It has no power in this world except that of its beauty—I think that's why I was able to finally surrender it. I had not even touched it since that morning I woke up in Ochersfeldt and tossed it in the bottom of my pack—I was afraid to."

"Tell me about Ochersfeldt."

"There's not much to tell. The town is known for its artisans, particularly the metal workers, glass blowers and crystal cutters. In fact, there are many shops not unlike the Lost Unicorn there, and it's a popular place for Witches, Seers, and Magicians to visit. They trade among themselves and commission new tools of the trade from the craftspeople."

"It sounds like my kind of place!" Robyn was bustling around the kitchen. It looked to Esmarelda like she was making some sort of vegetable pie.

"Oh, you would fit right in there, Robyn. The local people are blond like you, and they would honor you for your great height. But the Gypsies generally stay away. We are different in more than just appearance—it's hard to explain. An Ethalee—a 'Gypsy from the south,' as we call them—once told me that the music and dance the Gypsies carry in their hearts outshines the gold of the Ochersfeldt smiths and makes us unwelcome there.

"I for one did not stay to find out. I purchased a mule and set out for the lake region of Sky, a place I had always wanted to visit."

"What was that like?"

"It's a vast and beautiful country. The people are honest and friendly wherever one goes, and all variety of races live there in harmony. It seemed to be just what I needed. I could travel freely dancing and telling fortunes; I even thought I would meet my true love there."

Robyn stopped chopping vegetables and looked over her shoulder expectantly. She had heard the disappointment in Esmarelda's voice.

"I met a man named Lyle. He was a hunter. We met when I took my cart down to the bank of a lake where he was hunting for swans. He was hiding in the reeds down in the shallow water, and when Bruno—that's what I named the mule—and I clanked down to the water's edge all the swans flew up and away before he could get an arrow in his bow. He was furious and came splashing over to me bellowing about his swans."

"I'm glad he didn't get any!"

"I was too. But I apologized and offered to read his fortune to make it up to him. When he calmed down he was rather nice and quite handsome. His fortune suggested that he would meet a woman from a distant place who would change his life. It also indicated that he would find a new kinship with the animal world and change his profession."

"And you were that woman."

"But he was not that man."

"What?"

"He was not who he appeared to be: I was so intrigued with him that I stayed in the area, and we saw each other often. I thought I was falling in love with him. Then he disappeared for several days. Just when I was becoming convinced that he had been killed by a bear or a wolf while out hunting, he showed up. But he was no longer Lyle the hunter—he was Malcom."

Robyn put aside her chopping and sat down, absorbed in the Gypsy's story.

"You see, one of the Master Seer's special talents is impersonation. He can change almost everything about himself."

"Do you know how he does it?"

"It is as if his body is totally fluid—malleable like clay. This is
not unheard of in our world but a talent like Malcom's is rare. I can
only say he has the right combination of inherent physical traits, great
mental discipline, and years of practice."

"But was Lyle a real person or not?"

"At first I thought Malcom had come and done away with Lyle
and then learned to imitate him. I wanted to believe this, even though
it would have been horrible, but it just wasn't true. Lyle was the
Master Seer's invention all along. His point was that if I didn't love
him as Malcom he could turn himself into someone I would love."

"That's creepy."

"It gets worse."

"How?"

"He continued to trick me in this way. No matter where I went,
no matter how many miles I put between myself and Malcom, every
six or eight months I would find out that someone I was getting close
to was *him*. I never saw it coming. I played right into the trap each
time. In the Fashah district he was a merchant with an eye for my
Cobraati beadwork. He followed me from town to town joking and
bartering until we actually began traveling together. I enjoyed his
company. But it was Malcom all along. Off I went again in my magic
satchel, trying to get as far away as possible. What can I say? It
happened a couple more times before I finally felt so defeated I just
cloistered myself up in Resthaven. I figured if I stayed put and didn't
let myself make any friends, then I couldn't keep getting hurt."

"Well, that explains what a Gypsy is doing with a big old house."

"Not very traditional, is it? I think *you* would like my house very
much. I should like to have you there someday." Esmarelda meant
what she said. Talking with Robyn was easy. She had forgotten what
it was like to have a friend.

"But right now I want to make certain that I can find my way back to you. I hope you don't mind my making this my outpost in the Alternate World."

"Oh, you must!"

"Well then, do you have a small thread or something I might tie into my satchel to mark this place?"

Robyn jumped up and rummaged through a drawer next to the sink. "How's this?" she asked, handing Esmarelda a tiny glass bead. "I'll get you a needle and thread."

"Perfect."

The Gypsy excused herself to work on the satchel. It would take some concentration to get the bead in just the right spot.

Faye was exhausted when she got home from working at the Lost Unicorn. She'd been on her feet all day. Except for the few minutes Robyn had stopped in—wouldn't it figure—the store had been quite busy.

"All the regulars showed up today," she reported to Zeek over dinner. "And some not-so-regulars, too. You should spend a day with me over there sometime. I mean, you wouldn't believe it—and today was the weirdest yet. Three people, *three people*, came in at different times and told me they had gotten these, like, vibes to come over. They were bummed that Robyn wasn't there; but then when she finally showed up the store was empty—I mean dead! It was weird. And she was really distracted. I'd like to know who this friend of hers is that showed up today; I have a feeling all of this is related."

"Maybe there was no friend. Maybe Robyn was just up to some magic spells and stuff and didn't want to be interrupted."

"Well, I guess that's a possibility." Zeek had been half joking but Faye pretended not to notice. "Anyway, the vibes were rubbing off on me, so I bought some incense and candles. Don't worry, nothing too heavy. The incense is called 'Travels End.' I thought that would be fitting, since we seem to have settled down here."

"That sounds good. Let me see those candles." Zeek got up to find some candle holders.

They burned the candles and incense all evening. Faye went to bed early and then woke up in the middle of the night to the sound of a cat wailing. Soon every dog within blocks was barking. Faye imagined a chain reaction—perhaps every dog in the entire city was barking. She drifted back to sleep imagining the dogs barking out messages to each other. What were they saying?

Chapter 10

George was careful not to acquire too many possessions, although he certainly was tempted by the Travelers' exotic wares. The trading of hand-crafted treasures from every corner of the globe was the principle livelihood of the delaTorre clan. They traveled far but always within a specific region. Over the course of a year they would circle from Omanipinamo far inland and make their way south through widely scattered farming communities to the Bay of Khios, where they would turn to the north again and follow the coast back to Omanipinamo.

To the sheep herders and corn growers Rudy's company brought soaps, spices, metalwork and glass collected from the ports along the coast. And to the bayside and seaside towns the delaTorres brought cheeses, wool and wine. They themselves lived the richest and poorest of lives, feasting in times of ease and plenty, going hungry when a horse grew lame or repairs to a wagon cost all of their goods. Much trading was done with other Traveler clans, some of whom shepherded their own stock and always kept inland, and others who traveled further along the coast—either to north or south—than the delaTorre company.

George noticed how Traveler territory overlapped in a beneficial arrangement. He also recognized that if he wanted to continue to cover new ground he could not stay with the delaTorres indefinitely. Rudy understood, and agreed to find a place for George with another caravan.

"We will have a confluence of several clans when we reach the Bay. There are many possibilities. Where do you want to go?"

"Send him to the Gypsies," Rudy's mother chirped.

"Beyond the Dromandy Mountains?"

"Very good! So you know of the Gypsies already. Don't worry George, you'll find no Wanderer People actually in the mountains themselves. The Dromandies are reserved for Witches, Weavers, and Moon watchers—those who can stand the cold and dark!"

"Whatever you say. But why the Gypsies?"

"Because of your fiddling, no doubt. Right, Mama? The Gypsies sing, dance and play as their work. They travel light—not like us—living in large companies on the outskirts of the cities of South Hedzaj Province where they come and go freely. Some Gypsies have been able to amass great fortunes entertaining the nobility and politicians with music and dance, palm reading, and feats of magic."

"Hah! They spend as quickly as they earn! They stay in taverns when in town and carry their wealth back to the caravan in the form of fine jewelry and clothing."

"Well, then, see that? What a life you will have with the Gypsies, George Drumm. And the journey to their territory should be long and arduous enough to satisfy even your wanderlust."

"How long and arduous?"

"From the Bay you will go on with the Ettruria clan." Rudy's mother seemed to have already given some thought to this. "They can take you to the Launfel Valley. There you will find Shane or possibly Royston, Elia's son. Look for someone who can take you to the Ney Adz District. It will take you many months to reach the Journeywomen, but sooner or later you will find them. They trade with both the Gypsies and the Ethalees."

"But will they trade with a *gorgio*?"

"I think with this *gorgio*. Look at this." She took a sheet of paper from her pocket and showed it to Rudy. George recognized his own drawings on the page. Soon after joining up with the company, he had drawn some of the glyphs from the cairns of Sumweir Island to show Mrs. delaTorre. She had shown much interest in the page. On it George had drawn the "s"-shaped spiral, the vertical figure eight, a plain circle and, across the top of the page, a square wave pattern which he labeled "Piper People." At the time, Mrs. delaTorre had offered no comment.

Now, as George and Rudy looked over her shoulder, she added more symbols to the page. Above the "s"-shaped spiral she wrote 'Gypsy' and below George's simple circle she drew another spiral, one that coiled out and then back to the starting point to make a single continuous line. Under "Piper People" she added a graceful curvilinear wave pattern and wrote "Wanderer" beneath. Under this she drew a horizontal figure eight, the word "Traveler," and another figure eight. Finally, at the very bottom of the page, Mrs. delaTorre drew two symbols side by side: a concave triangle pointing downward, which she labeled "Journeywoman" and a crown-like, leaf-like shape which she labeled "Ethalee."

"Now, when you meet a Journeywoman, show her this at once." Mrs. delaTorre handed the sheet back to George. "And tell her that Letta delaMar delaTorre suggested you visit the Gypsies. If she sees that this is the correct course for you, the Journeywoman will introduce you to the nearest Gypsies; if she does not agree with me, she will send you back to us.

"Of course you need not come directly back in that event," both delaTorres were grinning at George, "you might want to see a bit more of the continent and visit the Ethalees before returning. We would be so happy to have some of their fine baskets and dyed cottons. The saffron yellow and lapis blue are especially rare—oh, we could fetch a fine price with those on the coast. And the Ethalees' interest in music is great; they will likely be very generous with you, George."

Now George was grinning too, and shaking his head in mock disbelief. 'So, it is a shopping expedition to the Ethalees they really want me to take.' George had heard the tales of the black-skinned Ethalees and their many talents, even aboard ship. Their craftwork was greatly prized and eagerly displayed by its lucky owners, Traveler and *gorgio* alike. But he had heard little of the Journey-women.

"How will the Journeywoman know if I am meant to go to the Gypsies or not? Who are these Journeywomen? Are there any Journey*men*?"

George looked at Rudy who looked at his mother. She sat for a moment and gathered her thoughts before answering.

"A Journeywoman might travel with her man, or her children, or perhaps with another woman," she raised her eyebrows meaningfully. "She might have been raised a Traveler, or an Ethalee or a Gypsy. She might be of city stock or from the farms or the daughter of a Weaver from the mountains. What makes a Journeywoman a Journeywoman is her ability to divine. There is no match for a Journeywoman when it comes to the reading of dice, cards, dominos, runes, throwing sticks . . . "

"They say a Journeywoman can tell your fortune with a handful of pebbles scraped from the ground," Rudy interjected.

"Each Journeywoman is so different from the next that they rarely travel in the traditional caravan, but only come together for short times at their special places to rest and advise each other. We see far too few of them on this side of the continent, but who can blame them? The population is so scattered and full of distrust that a Journeywoman would find it hard to feed herself in this territory."

George, Rudy, and Mrs. delaTorre spoke for a long time about the ways of all the different Wanderer peoples. George folded and unfolded the sheet of paper which was to be his entrance pass to this world of the Wanderers. Mrs. delaTorre had added her notations so as to indicate that his own Piper People were descendants of a Wanderer tribe. Just as George was overcome with a feeling of real belonging, he also felt a wave of sadness. It was the moving on that made one a Wanderer, and George's time to move on was near. He thought of how he had left his mother and felt guilty. Then something struck him. He mused out loud:

"Letta delaMar delaTorre. Letta. And Mum's name is Greta. More than a bit similar I think. Letta delaMar delaTorre. *DelaMar* is *of the sea* of course; and *delaTorre* is *of the bull*, which by astrological extension could also be *of the earth*. And Mum is Greta *Marie Moor* Drumm. Yes, that's it. Letta-Greta of-the-Sea of-the-Earth. These are my mothers—the Sea and the Earth."

George was overcome with emotion and found it hard to go on. He stared at the ground and heard Rudy ask quietly, "What about your father?"

"He died in the mines—the coal mines—fire. I was just a boy. And Mr. delaTorre?" George had wanted to ask about Rudy's father for some time.

"Oh, Papa's still with us. We just don't know where, right Mama?"

Mrs. delaTorre rolled her eyes and spat ceremoniously into the fire.

"Papa is the Traveler's Traveler, you see. He cannot stay with one caravan, he cannot trade just soap and candlesticks. His mind and heart range free as a bird, and, if at all possible, his legs follow. Perhaps you will even run into him in your travels. Last I heard, he was following the coast far to the north. He heard they make a flavored ice desert from snow and maple sap up there and he wanted to taste it!"

"Just so he doesn't try to bring it back with him! Ah, my husband is a fanciful fellow, George—not unlike you. Do not be sad about being apart from your mother and father. You are a Wanderer. How true it is that your mothers are the Sea and the Earth. And you have two fathers as well: Fire and Air. The Sun is your brother, the Moon your sister, and the Stars are your distant cousins. Yes, we Wanderer peoples are lucky; we are always together, even when apart—everywhere we go, we are surrounded by family."

Chapter 11

This time the Gypsy arrived unannounced and entered without knocking. Her day and night with Robyn had given her new confidence and reassured her of her powers. And when Audy had sprung away from her, hissing and scratching, she had felt her heart harden, so that now her mission was not so much to rescue the cat—who apparently did not want to be rescued—but to uncover the secrets surrounding this strange course of events.

'Perhaps the Master Seer has never stopped considering himself my teacher, and this is his idea of a lesson. Or perhaps this is his way of forcing me back to the road so he can plague me even more. Without the bracelet tying me to him, I really don't care. Why didn't I get rid of that thing years ago?

'I can't believe that I am actually looking forward to seeing Malcom, but I am! I can't wait to laugh at the mess I left him. After what I have done to his laboratory, his magic will be weakened. This time *I* will have the upper hand and I will make him tell me everything.'

"Oh, it's you." Esmarelda was disappointed to find Mark and not Malcom stoking the fire. She was also dripping wet. It had been raining on the Master Seer's estate since her visit two days before. Her zeal for mystery somewhat dampened by the wet walk up the hill, the Gypsy plopped down in the chair closest to the fire and let her soaked cape drop to the floor.

"Wood's too damp," she said, squinting up through the smoke at Mark. He looked old to her, though she knew him to be a young man. "So your dear Master left you to clean up the mess, how kind of him . . ."

109

"Yes, that's it all right," Mark answered. The Gypsy's arrival had taken him completely by surprise, and he was glad for her to provide the excuse for the Master's absence herself.

His voice sounded hoarse too. Of course she hadn't seen him in years; he wasn't here the other day—but Alvin was. Esmarelda reminded herself to be alert despite how wet and cold she was; all was not ever as it seemed here.

"Where's Alvin?"

"You saw to that now, didn't you?"

"What do you mean?"

"He didn't care for your pranks. In fact, I thought he might die of apoplexy after just half a day of pouring rain, yellow fog, everything in the lab percolating, orange fog, frogs hopping in circles around the house, green fog, toadstools growing three meters high right outside the door here, purple fog . . ."

"You're doing a good job then," Esmarelda broke in, proud of herself for creating such havoc. "The place already seems reasonably under control."

A loud burbling noise erupted from the laboratory. Mark just heaved a sigh and, ignoring the Gypsy's compliment, finished, " So I took him back to the candle shop. And when I came back the Master Seer was gone."

'He's definitely hiding something,' Esmarelda thought. "Where were you, Mark, when I was last here?" Something was nagging at her—something Robyn had said about Audy—what was it?

"On business for the Master."

He was sounding and looking more like Mark all the time, but this only made Esmarelda more suspicious. She stood up to get a better look at him.

It was no good. The Master Seer was unexcelled at the art of disguise. Esmarelda had spent so little time with Mark that she could not judge if this was really him either by appearance or behavior. Besides, her eyes were watering from the smoke, and her wet garments were beginning to make her feel exceedingly irritable.

'Why can't I just walk a normal road where the climate and environment do not change so drastically? Now, that would be pleasant. A fortnight's hike across the Gila district is what I really need . . .' Esmarelda turned her attention back to Mark who seemed content to stare at her breasts, for every contour was made apparent by the clinging of wet silk.

"You're *Malcom* aren't you and not Mark? And—yes, of course—I believe *Mark is Audy*."

"Excellent, Esmarelda!" Mark said in Malcom's voice. How could he resist?

Esmarelda felt thrilled and frightened as she always had when made to realize the full extent of the Master Seer's powers. He *had* learned to do it—to turn man into cat.

"And I suppose Alvin is really still here, and warned you of my approach as he did the last time."

"No, the part about Alvin is true, he really couldn't take it. I knew of your arrival, darling, because I am the Master Seer." Mark was starting to have fun, but he was concerned that he himself might become confused about who's role he was playing. "Do let me change back into my own form."

"Yes, please do. I want to talk to you seriously, Malcom."

Mark retreated to the bedroom and, with a few strokes of the razor, a dab of hair lotion, and a moment of self-hypnosis, became Malcom. He had played the part of the Master Seer so often lately that the transformation was becoming automatic. And today the wet Gypsy had aroused him so that he felt he understood the Master as never before. When he returned to Esmarelda at the fire, he was totally Malcom.

"Don't you want to get out of those wet clothes, Esmarelda? I'm sure I have some lovely veil or something that would keep you nearly as warm—and provide an even better view for me."

Esmarelda was digging deep into her pack in the hope of finding something dry. She looked up when Malcom spoke, "You are a horribly cruel man, Master Seer, to turn your best apprentice into a cat and abandon him in the Alternate World. Knowing that it is Mark as a cat and not Audy makes his being there worse. How can you leave him there? *You* should be rescuing him and not me!"

Esmarelda's concern surprised and touched Mark. He became still more attracted to her.

"Well, my dear, given how you barged in, drugged me, stole my satchel, and sabotaged my laboratory, how do you expect I could have gotten Mark back? I was counting on you to return with him, but if you will kindly return my satchel I shall take care of it myself. Of course, I won't be able to return him to human form until I get my Restorers corrected." There was another loud pop from the laboratory. "You really did make a mess of things, darling."

Esmarelda felt a momentary twinge of guilt. "The satchel is gone, Malcom. I'm sorry it was lost, but it was never meant to belong to you. I suppose I shall have to fetch Mark with my own satchel, but only on condition that you tell me everything about how you did it—changing him into a cat—and how you intend to undo it. I might even help you with the laboratory, but only as a humanitarian gesture, you understand." Cleverly, the Gypsy did not mention that she had already located the cat, and had failed twice to get him into a satchel.

"Tell me how the satchel was lost and what happened in the Alternate World. How do I know I can trust you to really bring Mark back?"

"So, today you know about the Alternate World? I knew something odd was going on the last time I was here. And you speak of trust! I'm your only hope; you'll have to trust me if you want Mark and your precious laboratory restored—truly, I wonder which is more important to you."

"*You* mean the most to me." Mark said the words Malcom could never utter. "Let me make love to you and I will share every secret."

"Perhaps you are right, Malcom. Perhaps our time has come." Esmarelda could not believe her own boldness. Of course she had no intention of being the Master Seer's lover now; his unconscionable experiments disgusted her. The thrill of his power could never overcome that. Yet she felt the warmth of his emotion and realized it could be used to her advantage.

"I think I may have left a robe or something in my old room. I'll go and try to get dry—and I'll consider your offer." Esmarelda turned to Malcom with her sweetest smile and then retreated to the tiny bedroom at the back of the house.

She had hoped never to enter this room again. Just as she had expected, not a thing had been changed since her departure, but all was coated with a layer of dust and cobwebs. The very walls seemed to murmur reproaches, and the Gypsy was reminded of how she used to hear the walls whispering love poems and pleas of longing. This had been one of Malcom's most insidious spells: the sound would become audible only as Esmarelda drifted off to sleep. Once it had lulled her to sleep, the chanting would swell in volume until it woke her up again. But each time she jerked to wakefulness—silence.

Esmarelda found several caftans in the closet and chose the one with long, tight-fitting sleeves. She had been counting on it being there; it would hide the still-fresh claw wounds on her arm. The walls tisked and growled. Esmarelda, fearing that they would give her away, closed herself in the closet. In the dark, cramped space the Gypsy removed her wet clothes. From the hand-shaped pouch still hanging around her neck, she extracted several ingredients and prepared a small capsule. When this was ready she reluctantly removed the pouch—Malcom would notice its contours under the lightweight gown. Esmarelda slipped the dry caftan over her head and then tucked the capsule into her sleeve.

Leaving her pack in the closet and closing the door behind her, Esmarelda stepped resolutely back into the room. The tone of the walls was menacing as she went to rejoin Malcom.

The Master Seer was already at work in the laboratory. "Now, help me fix all of this and I'll tell you about Mark and Audy. *Then* we will share our *deepest* secrets with each other."

Mark turned to Esmarelda with Malcom's most lascivious look. "Nice dress."

"Nice of you to keep it for me. Shall we go ahead and get to work?" Esmarelda stepped close to the Master Seer and touched his arm, "Once we take care of business, we can play."

Esmarelda felt Malcom catch his breath and let it out again in a slow sigh. It was a sigh that made her heart ache. It was a sigh of pleasure, relief, surrender; it was honest and basic. Esmarelda realized she had never even given Malcom reason or opportunity to express this vulnerability. She had been so aloof, and had hated *him* for *his* attitude of superior control.

Now the two stood awkwardly close. The air around them filled with static. The laboratory candles flickered madly.

'By the goddess—who knows what he's capable of!' Esmarelda broke away, remembering Audy. She steadied herself, forbidding the horror to sound in her voice.

"So, Master Seer, I am ready for today's lesson: how to turn a man into a cat."

"And so you shall have it. I think you will be both enlightened and entertained—not to mention humbled. For it was your own Gypsy magic that inspired me, and there's no reason you shouldn't have thought of it yourself."

'She wants me, I can tell. All I have to do is keep my end of the bargain and she will keep hers. This is perfect! The Master Seer's prank in reverse: instead of his pretending to be someone else, someone else is pretending to be him! He will thank me for this . . .'

'How can he imagine this pleases me? If he has used Gypsy magic in some perverse way many creatures could suffer, and I will be to blame. Mark must not be lost because of this.'

"Really? Gypsy magic? And I thought you never paid attention."

"It's amazing how things come together in dreams." Mark remembered the Master Seer's words exactly; he repeated them now to Esmarelda as if she were he and he were Malcom.

"I had so much trouble understanding the satchel and the Spiral and the Knots. Yet in my dreams I had a marvelous insight: Crawl into a satchel, travel through Time. Crawl into a satchel, travel through Space. Crawl into a satchel, travel through *Being*."

'Ochersfeldt.' Esmarelda knew it but did not speak it. She didn't want to remind Malcom of the bracelet now or distract him from his explanation. "Go on."

"The satchel is made from feathers and fur as well as the magical thread spun in Ochersfeldt of gold and silk." Malcom did not mention his other business in that renowned city, much to Esmarelda's relief. "The herbs are administered to both subjects, and the animal is put into the satchel. The human subject is locked in the same room and . . ."

"What herbs?"

"Black cohosh, licorice, mugwort—the usual. Unfortunately they, like everything else in the laboratory, have gone bad since your last visit. I say unfortunately because these same ingredients are the Restorers as well as the Transmuters. You have to undo your spell or we don't have a chance with Mark and the cat. I can't even bring fresh herbs in here without their going foul."

"I see. I didn't know I had done such a good job." The Gypsy was indeed surprised by this last revelation and wondered how she would undo such a spell in the location of the spell itself. Would her own herbs and powders work here? 'The capsule! That might not work either; then I'd be foiled by my own magic.'

Motivated as much by concern for her own welfare as Mark's or Audy's, Esmarelda immediately launched into the task of removing her spell. She devised a system of taking the leaves and powders into the kitchen and mixing them with pinches of her own stock of substances, which remained safe in the unenchanted closet of the back room. Back and forth she went, collecting minuscule portions of herbs from her pouch and bringing them to the Master Seer, who sifted, stirred and boiled one concoction after another at the Gypsy's direction. Periodically the two ventured into the laboratory to cast some spells and see how things were doing. It was a slow process, but eventually the murdoch could be brought into the laboratory without growing long fibrous roots or turning color, and the spell was pronounced undone. But the Gypsy did not dare rest or let down her guard.

"Well, I did it. Now back to my lesson. Show me the satchel."

"It is right here."

Esmarelda had not realized that the woolly black cloth on which they worked was the bag itself. Far from being the net-like vegetable fiber of a traditional magic satchel, this bag had the texture of dense, hairy felt. It appeared large enough to accomodate a quite sizable animal. The Gypsy tried not to think about this.

"So, the cat is put inside the bag after ingesting your herbal brew. The man has also taken the brew. The two—the cat in the sack and the man—are locked in a room together. Is that all?"

"Well, the human has undergone hypnosis by a Facilitator, myself of course; and this Facilitator is present—but outside of the room—to help channel the energies. Again this is Gypsy inspired: *a drum rhythm, at the tempo of the animal's heartbeat, at the pitch of the human's voice*, is the pivotal ingredient. If all is done correctly, by the time the hourglass has run out, the satchel shall be a flat empty rag," Mark ran his hand over the double layer of felt, "the man shall have dissappeared, and the two subjects shall be combined into one animal form—the cat—now running freely in the room."

The Gypsy sat quietly, absorbing all the Master Seer had told her. She wasn't sure what horrified her more, the idea of the poor cat being taken over by the human or the thought of Mark trapped inside the cat. When she felt composed enough not to give away her true feelings, she asked: "And what becomes of the human body? Where *is* Mark's body?"

Mark was ready. "I think I've told you quite enough for now. It's been a long session. Isn't it time for you to keep your side of the bargain? After all, I have to save one secret to keep you honest."

He hovered beside Esmarelda and tentatively fingered her curls. The Gypsy was also willing to end the game; her curiosity regarding this last point was dimmed by her distaste. 'If he tells me any more, I may not be able to go through with the plan—he will have repulsed me too much to even pretend to want him.'

"Let's go to my room," Esmarelda said, leaning against Malcom, an arm around his waist. "That's where I always imagined we'd be."

As they entered the room, Esmarelda pretended to cough. Putting her hands to her mouth, she slipped the capsule inside her cheek. The sound of snarling and gnashing teeth erupted from the walls.

"Why didn't we reverse *that* spell while we were at it?" she laughed and then reached her arms around Malcom's neck and turned her face upward to be kissed.

Mark trembled. He had never felt so good; he didn't even notice the walls. Now he fully understood the Master's infatuation with the Gypsy. 'This is for you, Master,' he thought, as he pulled Esmarelda's soft body close and put his parted lips on hers. The warm sweet wetness that met his mouth filled Mark with almost uncontrollable desire, and he swept Esmarelda up and carried her to the small bed in one step. Laying down with her, he rolled onto his back with Esmarelda on top, groping clumsily at their clothes. Esmarelda kept kissing him and did not let herself struggle away.

Suddenly, Mark's body grew limp and his arms fell away from the Gypsy. She rolled off of him and stood up, spitting out the empty shell of the capsule. This she left on the nightstand for Malcom to discover when he awoke. "Really, I thought the Devil would be smarter, Malcom, and not so swayed by his heart! Which reminds me, about my Tarot card..." The man snored loudly. The walls were eerily silent. Esmarelda felt so sleepy. "It's another trap! The last thing I want to do is fall asleep *here*." The Gypsy determined to go at once; the Tarot card would have to wait.

Sylvestor was a big docile tabby cat but he was not meek. He liked to explore far and wide. While his brother Felix ruled over the Del Sol apartment complex, Sylvestor took to the alleys and ditchbanks in an ever widening circle.

Both cats were unusually friendly with strangers, humans and animals alike. Faye attributed this to their being raised on the road during the migration to Caliente. At rest stops, campgrounds, motels, and the homes of friends around the country, the cats had learned when to make themselves unobtrusive and when to be completely irresistible.

Now, in Caliente, when Sylvestor found himself hungry and far from home, he would simply visit one of his human friends who would rustle up a tasty meal for the orange-striped cat. Each of these benefactors enjoyed Sylvestor's visits and rewarded his return with lavish treats. The cat developed a regular route. He even had a stop right behind the Del Sol so he did not have to compete with Felix at the dinner bowl on his occasional visits home. Faye and Zeek, noticing how well fed Sylvestor was each time he reappeared, had an idea of what was going on, but they missed him nonetheless.

On the night of the Gypsy's visit to Robyn, Sylvestor stopped for a long time to investigate the smells around the back door of the Lost Unicorn. Out of the darkness came a low growl. A lanky black cat emerged, bristling.

Sylvestor, failing to respond with typical feline territoriality, moved toward the strange cat, nose twitching. Sensing no threat, Audy became subdued and let himself be sniffed. And when Sylvestor turned and trotted off, Audy followed.

As if by prearrangement, Sylvestor led the black cat to the house behind the Del Sol and cried at the back door. When the door was opened he sprang away, leaving the bedraggled Audy on the stoop.

"Why, I'll be—you're not Red. But you sure sound like him. Jerry! You won't believe this—a black cat came to the door and impersonated Red's meow! I suppose I should give him some milk for that trick..."

The neighbors' voices faded behind him as Sylvestor made his way home. Faye and Zeek greeted him joyfully but Felix stalked off—he was getting used to being an only cat!

Esmarelda arrived back at her house at midnight and found everything as she had left it. There were already some new spider webs, but the food she had left out was only slightly nibbled. She had been gone four days but it seemed so much longer. She had traveled to the Master Seer's house, to the Alternate World, and back to Malcom's. Now this little plot of land and orderly home felt tame to the Gypsy, glad as she was to find them safe.

Esmarelda decided not to get too comfortable. She would set out before the next nightfall to resume her mission to rescue Audy, a mission made more urgent by the knowledge that a man was trapped inside the cat. 'One part of my bargain with Malcom I could not keep; but I *will* go back for the cat. If I had stayed out of this, Mark might already be restored to human form. But since I botched things up so badly by losing the satchel, I guess it is my responsibility to make things right.'

Now the Gypsy knew why the cat's behavior had been so erratic. She decided not to go straight back to the Alternate World, but to learn more about human-animal transmutations first. 'The Alternate World is no place to start experimenting. I must know precisely what to do before I go back. It seems that at the very least I need a way to first calm and then transport the cat. I could administer a sleeping potion, but in combination with the ingredients the Master Seer used to make the transformation in the first place, anything could happen. Tibareth would know what to do if anyone would . . .' Esmarelda was tired and could no longer concentrate on her dilemma. She went upstairs and dropped into bed.

Esmarelda slept heavily for many hours. When she awoke it was mid-day. The images of Huliyana and Tibareth were fresh in her mind. Though poorly remembered, the dream convinced her that these former teachers would have the answers she sought. She took her cloak and pack and went to the pond to bathe before setting out once more.

Esmarelda sat on the soft grass to dry in the sun before putting on the clothes that lay untouched from the other night. In their place, she would leave her unwashed garments. She gave little thought to the Resthaveners' gossip now, for she had too many other things on her mind. What would be in store for her on this next leg of her journey?

The Gypsy had never traveled to the Past in her magic satchel, and she tried to remember everything the Andarra Weaver had told her about going back. Ehrte's rule was never to go back to a Time-place one had already been. Never retrace your steps. Disregard this, and one could actually find oneself being two people in the same place! The ancient Ehrte had recounted with horror the experience of her sister Venness:

Venness, as an old woman learned in the arts of the Spiral Map, had returned to their girlhood home, thinking to become carefree, healthy and young again! Instead, she found she was still *herself*, the old woman, but here she was again as *herself*, the ten-year-old girl. Venness was observer of her own life—and a very real observer. Venness the girl and the young Ehrte woke up one morning to find a dreadfully familiar old crone in their tiny bedroom. She spoke to them as though she knew them, and was particularly interested in young Venness, who grew more and more frightened. The old one finally took pity and said that she was there by mistake and that if the girls would leave the room and not say anything, she would go without hurting them. They left gratefully.

From that time on Venness, who was older than Ehrte, took a great interest in magic and convinced her parents to apprentice her to the village Magic Weaver. Ehrte joined her two years later, and together the sisters mastered the secrets. Venness instinctively solved the mystery of the crone, yet when she had aged into this very same old woman she was still compelled to repeat her mistake and return to the bedroom of her girlhood—or risk upsetting the course of Time itself.

Ehrte told this story at every opportunity, anxious to teach

Esmarelda the great responsibility of Time travel. Esmarelda always found herself becoming dizzy as she considered the implications of the Time-loop Venness had created for herself, and up until now she had chosen to avoid the whole issue. Even traveling to the Alternate World didn't seem as risky as working the Spiral backward.

'But why not, after all?' Esmarelda thought. 'This whole business has become a series of tests for me. Now it seems I am to travel back. At least having lost Malcom's magic satchel for him I need not worry that *he* will show up in some disguise to further confuse matters. Let's see, I can return to the clan at a time and place *after* the point at which I ran away. That way I won't bump into myself anywhere! Huliyana and Tibareth will be angry with me, and will probably have a new apprentice or two; but, if I know them, their curiosity will overcome the bad feelings. I shall trade my own tales for advice about this cat business.'

The Gypsy was anxious about how she would be received by the family she had left so remorselessly, even as her excitement increased at the thought of seeing her people again and resuming her studies with Tibareth and Huliyana. Before she could be carried away by speculation, Esmarelda dressed, assembled her gear, and once more unfolded her magic satchel. "I want to be with my clan at the time I was actually far away, studying with Ehrte, about four years after I left their caravan." This said, Esmarelda crawled into the satchel and carefully fingered the Knots, following the landmarks back to the very first Knot she had tied, Ehrte's Knot. As she rolled an adjoining piece of thread between her fingers, she concentrated on her memories of the sights and smells and sounds of her journeying clan—specifically, the faces of Huliyana and Tibareth. She hummed an old Gypsy lullaby, one she had forgotten until that very moment.

Chapter 12

Each night that was fine enough for sleeping under the stars found the Gypsy bedrolls and quilts arranged in a spiral around the coals of the camp's central fire. Huliyana, Tibareth, and the clan Elders slept near the center of the spiral where they would be the warmest and most protected. It was therefore impossible for any of the wise ones to arise and walk in the night without the entire company knowing about it. And when either Huliyana or Tibareth went for a nocturnal walk it was generally understood that magic was afoot, and in their hearts and dreams every clan member participated in the event. So it was that while only a small number of Gypsies were fully initiated into all of the many magical secrets known to the wise ones, every Gypsy played a part in the expression of these secrets. All contributed to the powers of the wise ones with empathic, flowing energies.

George, the lowly stranger, slept on the very fringe of the spiral and was for the most part ignored, except when his music was requested. George's fiddling did not win him immediate acceptance with the Gypsies as it had with the Travelers. Even though he had been traveling with this particular caravan for some months, he was still treated with the utmost indifference. This suited George fine, as it left him free to observe the various members of the company and pursue his investigations into the mysteries of the Spiral.

He was particularly interested in the wise women, Huliyana and Tibareth, and their young apprentice, Stepha. He had become adept at finding the women's secret places and spying on them, in part through learning Stepha's lessons himself. He had quickly mastered the techniques of emptying his mind so as to become "invisible" and using a swinging talisman to point him in the right direction when he wanted to find the women. Often, Huliyana would be instructing Stepha in some magic dance that George could never quite understand, and Tibareth would be roaming about collecting plants and roots. Sometimes George worried that Tibareth would stumble upon his hiding places, but she never did.

Lying awake at night, staring into the vast star-filled sky, George would remind himself that what he was doing was meant to be. It was as if the crone on Sumweir Island had shown him a path and, setting foot upon it, George had found it a flowing river and himself a leaf riding the current. The river had carried him to the Travelers and to Rudy, who arranged for the stranger to be passed from caravan to caravan. Then George had traveled far into the vast continent, where the Travelers' territories gave way to those of the Journeywomen and the Gypsies. It was Huliyana herself who had granted him permission to stay.

"This is the *gorgio* who has been looking for us," she told the company's leader, Oskar, who was snarling at George and glaring angrily at the elderly Journeywoman seeking to introduce him into the Gypsy caravan. Oskar withdrew, and Huliyana apologized to the Journeywoman, who went off with a nod. Huliyana then turned to George and said:

"You would not be here if you did not have true Wanderer blood, and since you do, I trust you—but do not try my patience. The knowledge you seek is usually reserved for women. This is not because women are selfish, but because men have other interests. They willingly leave the mysteries to the women, and are satisfied well enough that *we* have command of the secrets—they themselves do not feel the need to *know*."

"I grant you that I know nothing; but I want to learn and I'm not disinterested," George dared to interrupt.

"You know more than most. You know more than you know you know. Know how to ask a question and know what question to ask, and perhaps then I can help you. Until then, do not speak to me."

Well, what was George to do but take up spying? Each day he tried to follow Huliyana or Tibareth or both. Each night he remembered Huliyana's instructions and considered if he had learned what question to ask or how to ask it. All of the questions he came up with grew out of the secret sessions he had heard or witnessed; how could he ask about these things without giving himself away? And so, since that first day, George had not spoken to Huliyana, nor she to him. But he was learning.

As George took in Stepha's lessons, he also took in the magical spirit of the Gypsies, and he soon became one with them. Ostracized by all but the musicians and a few teenage boys, often intensely lonely, at night shivering on the very fringe of the Gypsies' camp, George began to have Gypsy dreams. He would wake up knowing that the day had come to move on or to make camp, that they would meet up with another caravan or descend on the cities for a fortnight of wild gambling and music making. Perhaps it was the dreams he should ask Huliyana about—perhaps it was the dreams that would tell him what to ask. Each night, George tried to dream a question.

"Who?"

George woke up with the one word lingering from his dreams. 'Who? Who what? What kind of a question is that? I can't just go up to Huliyana and ask *Who?*'

George opened his eyes and noticed that it was not dawn yet. But he had heard something, someone getting up. He rolled over onto his stomach just in time to see Tibareth wrapping herself up in a shawl and scurrying off into the darkness. No sooner had she disappeared into the night than Huliyana jumped up and followed behind. Some of the sleeping Gypsies sighed heavily, others tossed about under their quilts. Stepha, sleeping beside her family, sat up with eyes closed and asked, "Who?" and then lay back down. She, and all of the others, still slept. George sat up, put on his shoes, stowed his bedroll, and set off after the two wise women.

"Who do you think it is?"

"I don't know; but it must be someone known to us or we would not have dreamt it so."

"It will be light soon. Then we can get a better look at the sack and see if we recognize it. I hate to be surprised."

"It will only be half a surprise either way."

"Yes, it was a very strong dream."

The sun was rising quickly, and George moved carefully toward the women's voices until he saw where they were sitting. He made a wide loop around them and found a low perch in a tree where he could hear and observe them without being seen. They were sitting with their backs against a rock on an overgrown cart path. It was not the path that the Gypsies had taken to their present camp, but George had been on it before while following Huliyana and Stepha. Now there seemed to be something right in the path almost at Huliyana and Tibareth's feet. George assumed it was the sack they had just spoken of, but from his vantage point it looked more like a great lump of clay or an oddly shaped rock.

"I don't recognize it, do you?"

"No. I've seen fibers like that around Andarra, but I've had no dealings with the Weavers there in years."

The women grew silent. George was close to drifting off to sleep when the object moved and, much to his amazement, a person began to emerge from the brown folds of the sack. It was a Gypsy woman in full regalia, and George almost fell out of the tree straining to get a glimpse of her face. Even from a distance he could see that she was a great beauty.

"Esma, Esma!"

"It is, it's Esma," the teachers whispered, "Esma, Esma."

The Gypsy had crawled all of the way out of her sack and stood up, lowering a pack from her shoulders. She shook and then folded the sack before addressing Huliyana and Tibareth, who continued to sit and stare.

"I am called Esmarelda now," she said. She had not expected her teachers to be right there, waiting for her; but why not? They were all three powerful women, connected by blood, spirit, and dreams.

'So, they know each other,' George thought, 'but it is a less than warm reunion, I'd say.'

"What—are you passing yourself off as Queen of the Gypsies now?" Tibareth asked nastily. "Such pride is not becoming to one so young, especially one who has deserted her training. How have you come to use the magic satchel? Whose knowledge have you stolen?"

"I do not think she is so young, Tibareth," Huliyana said, approaching Esmarelda and fingering her face and hands gently.

Esmarelda longed to throw her arms around Huliyana and beg forgiveness. The touch of the woman who had been teacher, friend and sister to her brought back a flood of memories. How could she have left her people as she did? For her it had been almost fourteen years since she ran away; the intense need she had felt then to be on her own was softened now by nostalgia. To the clan, it had been less than four years since her departure, and the hurt was still fresh with them. But this was not the time for regrets, tears now would only hurt her cause. She must demonstrate her knowledge and talents, her worthiness to be welcomed back. She could never again be the favored pupil; her only hope was to prove herself an equal.

"Huliyana is right, Tibareth. I come to you from the Future. And I come to you for help. I lengthened my name to Esmarelda because it draws more interest and respect in the districts where I have been traveling. I have never claimed to be a queen of the Gypsies, but some have called me that. Of late I think that Queen of the Fools would be more appropriate, for I have gotten myself into a horrible tangle. Call me whatever you like, but let us be friends and learn from each other. Please tell me it is not too late for me to make things right."

Tibareth softened at Esma's humility. She stood and went over to Esma and Huliyana, and the three women embraced. Esma could sense the excitement in her teachers. Nothing delighted a Gypsy more than tales of Time travel, trouble, and magic. Esma hoped that her story would not disappoint Huliyana and Tibareth. She broke away from them and said, "Now, let us go someplace private where I can dance for you. I will dance my entire story for you, I cannot think of a better way to tell it."

Huliyana and Tibareth nodded to each other with satisfaction. They were already accepting Esma back into the clan, and they were willing to take some credit for her magical skills.

As the women set off down the path, George scrambled down from his tree, almost forgetting to maintain his invisibility meditation. This was it! The secrets of the Spiral Map and Time travel were about to be revealed, and by such a magnificent woman! George followed the women at what he hoped was a safe distance. Sometimes he caught an aroma of spices in the air, and he imagined it was Esma's perfume, for he had never smelled that scent around Huliyana or Tibareth. 'Calm down, lad,' he chided himself, 'they will hear your heart pounding and come cut it out for spying on them.'

But the women remained unaware of George's presence, and soon all were getting into position for Esma's dance. Huliyana and Tibareth settled down in the shade of a tree and George scaled another tree a short distance away. The Gypsy stood barefoot in a grassy clearing and faced her teachers. "I am Esma," she said in the formal way she had learned to present ceremonial dances as a girl, "I am a Gypsy Dancer, a Time Dancer, a Magic Dancer. Open your hearts to me that I may dance for you."

"Dance for us, Esma," Huliyana and Tibareth said in unison, "dance into our hearts."

"Dance for us, Esma," George repeated under his breath, "dance into our hearts."

Esma looked up sharply to where George hid. He did not consider whether she could really see him or not, but turned his thoughts quickly to the songs of birds.

"What is it? Is someone there?" Huliyana asked.

"Oh, I am hearing things, I think; perhaps it was a sparrow."

With that, Esma turned back to her teachers and proceeded to dance. She employed a combination of two dance forms: the Storytelling dance and the Time Dancing. The Storytelling was a mixture of pantomime and sign language, and every dancer in every part of the world learned the universal expressions, gestures, and hand articulations in one form or another. Styles and details varied from place to place, as well as the music and other dance elements used as accompaniment; but within a particular ethnic group, the dance could be used to convey the most subtle of concepts and the most intricate detail. For important occasions and delicate situations, the Storytelling dance was generally preferred to verbal explanations.

George recognized many of the Storytelling gestures. He had often enjoyed the dance performances of his island, both contemporary and re-creations of the old Piper dances, and many of them incorporated quite similar techniques. After several minutes he seemed to understand most of the movements and was able to follow the Gypsy's story fairly well, although he was sure he was missing much detail.

Then came the Time Dancing, and George did not pick up on this at first, with the Storytelling to distract him. He thought the segments of dance interspersed between the Gypsy's story were pure dance, a break from the action, and he let himself be carried off by the hypnotic, sensual motions of Esma's hips and torso. Then he noticed that Huliyana and Tibareth were taking a very great interest in this part of the dance, and were even humming and chanting along. The three women paid close attention to each other, and George began to get the feeling that they were talking back and forth using chanting, clapping, and the stamping of Esma's bangled feet.

It appeared to George that Huliyana and Tibareth were repeating back to Esma what they heard/felt/saw in her dance, and she responded with minor corrections until they were all in unison; then Esma would move on to something new. When Esma again returned to the Storytelling mode, George noticed that this other aspect of the dance remained, and he recognized that the stamping of the feet and swaying of the hips had as much meaning as the gestures of the hands and eyes. How was he possibly to attend to everything? He refused to feel discouraged; already he had missed some of the story just by worrying. When he freed his mind, the sense of the dance came to him. '*Open your hearts that I may dance for you*, she said. Now I understand better.' George opened his heart, and even the Time Dancing began to make some sense.

Esma danced until the sun was high. She left nothing out. She danced leaving the caravan and setting off on her own. She danced that first winter with Ehrte, the weaving of her magic satchel, the trips she took in it, and all of Ehrte's lessons. She danced the meeting with the Master Seer, and she even danced the dance she danced for the Master Seer. Huliyana and Tibareth took much interest in this and the events which followed, but it was at this point that George started to get lost. Esma was using a rather colloquial sign language to describe Malcom and his apprentices and was doing so with a generous portion of humor. Huliyana and Tibareth giggled uncontrollably when Esma made a great joke of having arrived without a cloak and the trouble it caused her.

Esma danced her relationship with Malcom, and George got the drift of that pretty well. He wondered how, in fact, one was to go about courting such a lady as Esma. Could a fiddler succeed where the Master Seer, with all of his charms and powers, had failed?

Esma danced leaving the Master Seer and the events leading to her settling down in Resthaven: Malcom's traps and tricks and her increasing paranoia. Huliyana and Tibareth tisked and spat. They were an excellent audience.

Esma danced her life in Resthaven and, again, the tale turned comical as she mimicked the local residents and her clientele. Then Esma danced Audy's arrival and made this very dramatic, alerting Huliyana and Tibareth that this would prove to be significant. Next came the reasonably happy year with Audy, the arrival of the strange client, and the theft of the cat.

By the time Esma had danced through her first visit to Malcom and was dancing her arrival in the Alternate World, George was truly lost. He could tell that the adventure was becoming more and more serious; Huliyana and Tibareth leaned forward to beat the ground with the palms of their hands. Tibareth hummed a nasal, mournful drone. George surrendered himself to thinking about the Gypsy: how beautiful she was, how graceful and skilled in the dance, how magical, and how she was neither a very young woman, nor an old woman, but appeared to be just about his own age.

'What am I thinking? She's come from another *Time!* Now how does one overcome that?' George brooded while he watched Esma sparkle like a jewel in the sunlight. He imagined himself swinging out of the tree on a vine as he had seen the monkeys do and snatching her up in his arms. 'The very sight of me will either repulse her or make her laugh. Of course, making her laugh wouldn't be so bad. Some girls like a good laugh. Oh, there I go again, forgetting about the Time thing. That really could complicate matters.'

Esma was now dancing her second visit to Malcom and was finally revealing the tragedy of the man turned cat. Both Huliyana and Tibareth wailed, and George felt like he was witnessing a wake. But it was over soon and Esma was dancing the Time Dance again, dancing her return to the Past, her return to Huliyana and Tibareth.

George thought he was going to fall out of the tree. He clung to his limb and looked around and around. Everything seemed to be as it was, but he was certain he had felt the ground quake. He looked down. Esma was standing with feet together and with her hands pressed together above her head as if in prayer. She was trembling from toe to fingertip. *She* had done that. *She* had made the earth move, or seem to move! Esma stopped trembling. She danced a Spiral then—George could see it perfectly from his perch above—her tiny steps circled out and out and then in and in. And when she had come back to her starting place, she pantomimed waking up, slithering out of her satchel, and presenting herself to Huliyana and Tibareth. Her dance was over, and at that very instant George understood what he had seen. He had seen the Time Dance—and the dance, the spiral, and the satchel were the secrets of traveling through Time. 'Perhaps if I learn how it all works, I *can* woo the Time Dancer.'

That night Esma was asked to dance again. The company had welcomed the three women back with diffident respect. Preparations for a feast were under way. George fetched load after load of fire wood and many pails of water. Then he was asked to sit with the family of Amet, a young musician, and he enjoyed his meal with his fiddle at his side. Now and then, he caught a glimpse of Esma. She sat with Oskar's family.

Oskar's youngest brother and his wife appeared to be Esma's parents. The parents, brothers, sisters, aunts, uncles, and cousins all treated Esma with great restraint, almost severity; but their pleasure and excitement at her return could not be disguised. Esma herself maintained an unreadable expression. When the time came for music and dancing, all waited for Esma to be first.

George and Amet joined the other musicians. The instruments were tuned with more precision than usual. Finally, the group launched into a lively folk melody which George recognized at once. He played along with ease. Esma played her tambourine as she performed the favorite Gypsy dance, a dance full of energy and joy. When she had finished, she embraced first her family members and then many others who came up to her; and at last everyone talked and laughed in true reunion.

The musicians played on and the young girls got up to dance. They looked toward Esma for approval; when she smiled and winked at them they blushed and grew clumsy. Then the men and women danced as couples, and then the women and women in a circle, and the men and men in short lines, and finally everyone together in a great line spiraling around and around the fire. When the fire grew low the dancers stopped dancing, the musicians stopped playing, and everyone settled down for the night.

The evening had passed without Esma acknowledging George's

presence or taking any notice of him whatsoever, even though he
stood a full six inches taller than the tallest Gypsy man in the
company, and his red hair and beard had glowed like an orange flag
in the firelight.

Chapter 13

The next day George followed Huliyana, Tibareth and Esma to their
secret place. At first the women spoke about Stepha, who had been
furious at being left behind, and George paid little attention. But soon
it was he they were discussing:

"Oskar must be getting soft, allowing a *gorgio* to join the
caravan," Esma said.

"The *gorgio* sought us all the way from Omanipinamo, all the
way from Sumweir Isle. The Travelers passed him from company to
company, and finally to a Journeywoman who passed him to us. We
could not turn him away—do you know his name is actually George?
George Drumm, the fiddler! His fiddle is an addition, don't you
think? Why else he might have been sent to us I do not know—but it
was his great interest in the *Spiral* that he thinks brought him here."

'That I *think* brought me?' But that was the last the women had to
say about George, and he was left to wonder what it meant. He
followed them as they continued on in silence to the same spot where
Esma had danced the day before. George resumed his perch in the
tree and watched as Tibareth rubbed the soles of Esma's feet with
salve. Huliyana danced a little bit. The three talked softly, and
George could not make out what they said. He imagined it was he
rubbing Esma's feet. Esma looked up at the tree, but George was too
lost in fantasy to notice until he heard her ask: "What does this
George do each day?"

"He follows us and spies on us," Tibareth answered. "That seems
to be his job."

"He has set out to learn something," Huliyana added.

'Discipline, discipline!' George commanded himself. He would not let himself feel angry or embarrassed that they'd known of his activities all along. He thought of Stepha and how Huliyana and Tibareth tested her constantly. George had imagined he was gaining without such repeated humiliation, but here it was. They'd been testing him, too. This was just another manipulation to see how he'd behave. He sat silently and attentively. Everything the women said from now on, that he could hear, was meant for him to hear. And what they had spoken of before so softly, he was definitely not meant to hear. It had been too easy. Now George was sure he had missed something vital.

'They're lowering their voices again, not letting me listen. The free ride is over now. I think it's time to go legit. I could ask that question. I could ask about what Huliyana said. Why was I sent here—implying that my own will had little to do with it. She knows I overheard her, she *meant* for me to overhear her, so it wouldn't matter now if I asked . . . but I don't really buy it. I wasn't sent here, I came here. Though maybe I was led here! Yes that's more like it. I was led here by the Spirals and the Figure Eights . . .' George's thoughts rambled as he gave up trying to make out the words of the women below.

Whimsy, however, was not the mood of the three Gypsies. Huliyana and Tibareth were lecturing Esma prior to suggesting how she was to proceed, or sharing their insights as to human-animal transmutations. They went on and on about fascinating but irrelevant bits of magic, taking the opportunity to show Esma how much she had missed by running away. They wanted to show their wayward pupil that, for all of her seeking, great springs of knowledge had been left behind with her clanswomen.

Esma had expected this attitude, and she endured the chiding gracefully. Sooner or later they would have to get to the point. After all, Huliyana and Tibareth would have to provide some meaningful advice before they could collect the reward for which they had bargained so insistently: the secrets of the Tarot. Esma had resisted agreeing to this exchange. She made light of the cards, saying that the system was highly overrated, a game of fools. But this only made her teachers more eager, suspecting that Esma was trying to keep a great mystery to herself. It was to show her lack of regard for the Tarot that Esma finally not only agreed to teach Huliyana and Tibareth all she knew, but also to leave her beautiful hand-painted deck with them, although she had no other.

This still did not completely satisfy the wise women, and they extracted one last promise from Esma. She would seek to reclaim the stolen card and return the card to Huliyana and Tibareth, so that they might have a complete deck. This would not only signify the resolution of Esma's trials, but would properly re-establish Esma with her people; for she was not to travel back in Time with the card, but was to meet up with her clan in the Present—her Present—when it would be possible for her to stay with them if she chose.

As it was, Esma could not stay with the clan for very long. She was lucky that they were camped for an extended period for the benefit of two clanswomen who were pregnant and close to delivery. Once the babies came, the company would soon be on its way again, and it would be out of the question for Esma to travel with them. The caravan would be heading toward Andarra, where even now Esma's younger self was settling in for her first winter with Ehrte.

Esma did not want to be in the proximity of Andarra, nor did she want to "trick Time" any more than was necessary. To trick Time was to spend a certain period of time on one part of the Spiral, but to return to the original Time location without allowing an equal amount of time to elapse. In Esma's case, she could not do otherwise. She might spend days with her clan in the Past but would have to return to a time immediately after she had left Resthaven if she was to have the best chance at rescuing Audy and Mark. Esma knew that putting oneself out of sync in this way could take its toll on a Time traveler. She had hoped to stay no more than a day—but, as Huliyana and Tibareth rambled on, Esma felt she would be lucky to escape within the week.

Esma thought about her teachers' sudden interest in the Tarot.

She was sure they must have had many opportunities to learn the cards in their travels. When Esma was a young girl and had asked about such methods, they had laughed and told her not to bother with them. Why, now, had the positions been reversed? As Tibareth chided her for her ego and stupidity, and Huliyana pointed out the many mistakes she had made in her dealings with the Master Seer, Esma began to understand that it was the return of the lost Tarot card that was of greatest significance.

By making the Tarot deck complete again, Esma was to bring closure to the magic she had worked with Malcom. That the deck would not be restored until Esma was reunited with her people in Time was a lesson in the rippling effect of magic: Once a course is set in motion, events and energies touch off one another. How is one to control the great waves of circumstance as they build and build? 'Only by standing and breaking the wave, standing and facing the wave.' Esma felt anxious now. 'They are telling me I have to face Malcom again, truly face him—with honesty—and them too, everyone. They are showing me that I have given up the deck but not the Devil. Even if I can save Mark and the cat, I will have no peace and no true power until I have resolved matters with the Master Seer—and rid myself of him.' A dark feeling came over Esma. She wondered why in all this time she had been unable to extricate her life from Malcom's, and if she would ever succeed. 'Perhaps I actually do love him...' the thought depressed Esma terribly.

"Well, it's no surprise that you're in such a spot," Tibareth was saying. "This is what comes of studying with the wrong person. And this Malcom of yours is a fraud! I'm not saying he has no talent; why, he must be a genius of impersonation just to have pulled off the 'Master Seer' act in the first place."

"Now, Tibareth..."

"Listen to me, Esma! No true Seer would have tried those human to animal stunts. A Seer sees; he would have seen the disaster ahead. No, Malcom is no Seer. And as for Master, well! He is master of nothing and no one—not himself, you, his apprentices, or the wretched creatures he uses in his experiments. By failing to master his own conceit he has entrapped you all."

"I can't understand why he tried that with the animals," Esma said, not wanting to defend Malcom so much as to draw Tibareth out more on the subject.

"Pure stupid pride. He found he could take on many different appearances and personalities, and then became confused about what he was doing. Impersonating a person is not becoming a person. I can impersonate you, but I do not do so by taking something away from you or depriving you of your liberty. I become *like* you but I do not become you."

"You see, we are already more alike than we are not alike just because we are humans," Huliyana added. "The great differences we see between one person and the next are quite inconsequential in the scope of things."

"Yes, we have all of the tools necessary to impersonate another human already within us. But it is not possible to *impersonate* an animal. We simply do not have enough insight into the animal consciousness to mimic it. An unprincipled magician like Malcom can find ways to make his being enter an animal's body, but no good will ever come of it. This is not mere mimicry—it is two souls existing within one body. Both creatures are in grave danger. Your helping Malcom by teaching him to use his stolen magic satchel has made you a party to this nonsense, and you must help to undo it. At least you recognize that."

Esma felt miserable. "Truly, I had no idea about the cat until just the other day," she sniffed.

"Oh, Esma," it was Huliyana's turn to berate her, "you knew from the beginning that there was something you did not trust about Malcom. Why would you not have him? Why did you leave him? Why did you suspect him the moment Audy was taken?"

"Well, what am I to do now? I await your unerring wisdom! And if he's nothing but a charlatan, why are you so eager to learn the Tarot—those are *his* secrets, after all?" Esma felt like she was seventeen again. Here she was ready to flee just as she had before, and if she was not careful she would be asked to leave. The danger of returning to the Past became vividly clear to her. An endless, wretched Time-loop loomed before her, and Esma bit her lip and hoped it was not too late. 'You must help me,' she begged silently.

Huliyana ignored the outburst and went on. "First you must retrieve the old satchel. It has no place in the Alternate World. You will leave behind another vehicle. This will be a magic vessel of clay. Tibareth and I will help you build it. Meet us at sunset by the river where the willows grow. The clay must be dug when it and the sky are most red."

"How will the vessel work?"

"We will build it out of coils of clay, which will represent the turns of the Spiral, but only a small piece of it. The rim of the bowl will be your dusty town in the Alternate World, the bottom of the bowl will be Malcom's house. If the cat enters the bowl, it will return to Malcom. Then it will be in his hands to restore the man and the cat to each one's individual self."

"Do you think Malcom can do that?"

Neither Huliyana nor Tibareth would look Esma in the eye.

Tibareth finally spoke, looking beyond Esma, into the woods. "The man and the cat have been one for a year, you say. That is a long time. We wonder about the man's physical form. Where is it? How has Malcom cared for it? We wonder about the cat's spiritual form. Did it stay with the animal? Has it been cared for? You see now why they are both in danger. Seek to return the cat to Malcom's laboratory. Seek to reclaim the Tarot card. Seek to settle your own accounts with Malcom and to resolve that which you have begun in the Alternate World. You can do no more."

Esma had nothing else to ask. She would wait until sunset to learn more about the magic vessel. There was no doubt in her mind now that Audy was lost to her.

Huliyana and Tibareth stood. "We must go back to camp now," Tibareth said. "Kalili will deliver today. Go to the river at sunset; we

will be there to meet you." And the two women left Esma to her
sorrowful thoughts. They weighed so heavily on her that she lay back
and closed her eyes.

George watched Tibareth and Huliyana walk off in the direction
of the camp. Esma remained behind, reclining in the grass. He eased
himself stiffly out of the tree and went over to her. He had no idea
what he would say.

"Hello, George," Esma said, hearing him approach but not
opening her eyes. "I enjoyed your playing last night."

George sat down nearby. "And I enjoyed your dancing."

Esma sat up and took a good look at the stranger. He had a nice
face, what she could see behind the bushy beard and mustache.
Knowing that she would be leaving the company very soon, she felt
she could afford to be tolerant. In some ways she was a *gorgio*
herself—having arrived as she had—and she had some sympathy for
the red-haired stranger who was permitted to live with the clan, and
yet kept at a distance.

"Why did you leave your family? Why did you leave Huliyana
and Tibareth?" George asked, seeing that the Gypsy was waiting for
him to continue the conversation.

"Why am I so anxious to leave them again? I have been here little
more than a day, and if I did not need their help so badly, I would
run off exactly as I did before."

"And you don't know why?"

"Why did *you* leave your Sumweir Isle, George Drumm?"

The two looked at each other, recognizing that the answers, if
they could be put into words, would be similar.

"Could *I* help you?"

Esma laughed. "You'd probably be more help to Huliyana and
Tibareth delivering Kalili's baby than you could be to me!"

"I'm sorry I asked." George looked hurt.

"Really, though, you are helping. At least you are not telling me
what a stupid fool I am; and you could take my mind off my troubles
if you'd stop asking about them." Esma did not want to offend

George. She had not felt so at ease with a man in a long time. 'It's nice not to be suspecting him of being Malcom, or to have to think much about him at all—in a day or two I'll be back in my own Time and that will be that.'

"What shall we talk about, then? May I tell you how beautiful you are?"

"Well, there is probably no harm in that." Esma blushed. She found George's roguish smile appealing, and there was a softness in his grey-green eyes when he looked at her that told her his words were more than mere flattery.

"Let's walk a little bit—that is, if your feet aren't hurting you too much. I've been spending far too much time perching in trees lately." George stood up with exaggerated stiffness and offered a hand to Esma.

Esma let him pull her up. Now, standing right beside him, she noticed how tall a man George was. The top of her head barely came to his shoulder, and her hand seemed so small in his. Though he had given her an opportunity to reprimand him for spying, she had no desire to do so. In fact, she had little interest in conversation at all but preferred to walk along quietly, lost in her own thoughts. Sensing this, George did not speak again for some time, nor did he let go of Esma's hand.

"When I was first brought to this caravan, and Huliyana convinced Oskar to let me tag along, she told me I had to learn how to ask a question and what to ask before she would teach me—before she would even speak to me," George finally blurted out, squeezing Esma's hand hard in his earnestness. Even if she didn't need his help, he needed hers.

"That sounds like Huliyana all right," Esma answered, withdrawing the hand he was starting to crush. "Still, I can't tell you what to ask her. What is it you want to know? Ask her anything at all—she probably just wants to see how brave you are."

George now rested his hand on Esma's shoulder. He did not want to stop touching her. She did not seem to mind. "Brave, eh? Was crossing two seas and an ocean of unknown land not brave enough?"

"No question you are well on your way to becoming a Traveler. But if you are looking for the secrets of the Spiral—if you would learn what the Gypsy wise women know—you must be brave enough to travel through Time. And believe me, that takes courage indeed."

George felt Esma shiver and was reminded that she had done just that. For all of his travels he knew nothing of what *she* had been through or what still awaited her. His usual confidence left him and, shoving his hands in his pockets, he walked on ahead.

"But George...George!" Esma ran to catch up to him and tugged at his shirt gently. He stopped and looked down into her dancing eyes. "Do you know what takes the most courage of all? It is the *sharing* of these secrets. That Huliyana and Tibareth are so selfish with their knowledge shows they are not very courageous themselves. I cannot tell you how it angered me the way they used to tease me with promises of the great mysteries I would learn 'when the time comes.' Yet there was always one more lesson, or one more test, or one more favor to perform, and the time never seemed to come. You see how they treat Stepha! And I see clearly now that these very games, which drove me away, I have fallen prey to myself. Suspicion and secrecy, lack of courage and lack of conviction are what have brought me back here to my foolish Past. And if I am not careful, the whole cycle will begin again. *I* think you are worthy of the mysteries, George, and brave enough. Go to Huliyana and ask her any question; see if she has courage enough to share her knowledge with you. If she does not—find another teacher!"

"Perhaps I already have," George suggested. There was no one he would rather learn from.

"I can help you get started. I will draw the Spiral Map for you and tell you how to read it, but there won't be time for much more. You will have to continue your lessons with someone else once I've gone back."

"But I have nothing to offer you in exchange." Despite Esma's talk of sharing, George had learned enough of Wanderer ways to know that for every favor given, one was expected in return.

"That is not necessarily true," Esma said, putting her arms around George's waist and pressing against him. Her heart hammered against her chest and her stomach felt weak. This was no spell. There was something special about George; he seemed familiar, although she had never met another man like him. 'Perhaps I am only adding to my troubles, but I don't care. I want to be with him for whatever time is allowed.' She tilted her head back to look up into his eyes.

George seemed to be reading her thoughts. He cradled her cheek in his hand and stroked her hair. Then he kissed her with great tenderness. As his lips touched hers, all of his worries and fears left him. Esma also felt that she was in a timeless, painless place while George held her. They sank to the ground and their caresses became more passionate. George squeezed the tiny Gypsy as she playfully slipped her hands under his shirt. "I love you, Esma," George caught her hands and pressed them to his lips. The birds were beginning to sing their evening songs, it would soon be time for them to go.

Esma frowned and could not look at him. How could she profess her love for a man she had just met and would only know for a few days? "I must go to the river now and meet Huliyana and Tibareth. Please do not follow us anymore, George. I will find you tomorrow as soon as I am free and give you your own lesson in the Spiral." She kissed him once more and gave his beard a soft tug before reluctantly standing and heading off alone.

There was no dancing at the camp that night out of deference for the newest clansman and his tired parents. Everyone assumed that Huliyana, Tibareth and Esma were spending their evening with Kalili and the boy, but only Stepha attended to the new mother. Once again the women had left her behind, but this time Stepha took pride in her responsibilities and her teachers' trust in her. She had almost had to deliver the baby herself, Huliyana and Tibareth had stayed so long away from camp. Stepha was glad then that she had not been invited along. If she had, Kalili would have had no midwife to prepare her for the birth.

The company was quiet and contented. Occasionally a solo instrument or voice would sing out a sweet ballad. George took a turn and played the melody of a song his mother had sung to him when he was young. The Gypsies rocked and nodded. Old men turned to each other and said that the *gorgio* had a deep soul. Even Oskar, standing alone in the dark smoking a cheroot, had to admit that he heard the cry of a distant ancestor in the strains of George's fiddle. Returning from the river, three Gypsy women stopped and listened in silence. Esma stood longer than the other two, letting them walk on ahead. Her heart ached with exquisite longing.

Chapter 14

"I have a question," George said, stopping Huliyana as she returned to camp. He had in his pocket the Spiral Map which Esma had drawn for him.

Huliyana stopped, "It's about time."

"Yes, it is about Time!"

Huliyana waited without acknowledging the pun. George struggled to phrase his question. It was an important one.

"Huliyana, is it possible that two people from vastly different places, even from different *Times*, might be *fated* to be together, and that all of the circumstances and events in their lives will inevitably lead to their meeting and falling in love, and that through the power of their love they will be able to overcome all obstacles and barriers to their everlasting union?"

Huliyana looked George up and down and giggled. She scratched her head and stroked a downy beard and examined George some more. She turned around and around until she was doing a little dance. Finally she stopped and took George's hands in hers and said:

"I don't see why not."

"You don't?"

"Not if you put it that way."

"Will you help me?"

"Help you what?"

"Follow Esma."

"Hmph. Esma is not going anywhere until she gives us the Tarot. We exhausted ourselves over her today. I'm not as young as you. I need some rest now. Leave me alone."

George wondered what the women had been doing. Esma had

also been tired and irritable after their session. She explained the Spiral Map, as promised, but seemed impatient with George's many questions about the Alternate World and the magic satchel. After a while she refused to continue and would not even linger to exchange kisses, although she did agree to see George again that night.

Now George was left alone to consider how he was to go about obtaining a magic satchel, locating Esma, and learning how to use it, all in the space of a day. For tomorrow Esma was to surrender the Tarot and all of its secrets to her teachers, after which she would not only be free, but compelled, to leave.

'A day can be time enough if it is the right day.' George tried to approach the problem as a Wanderer would. 'A woe a woe/Away Away/A woe a day/Away we go.' He wasn't sure if the rhyme applied, but he took comfort in his memories of Rudy and his first meeting with the delaTorre clan. 'I became a Traveler and crossed a continent. Now I will become a Gypsy and travel through Time. If only Huliyana will help me!'

There was a song contest around the camp fire that night. The presence of Esma and the birth of Kalili's child had combined to inspire the performances of the clan's favorite songs of children, parents and ancestors. Everyone was having a fine time, until Esma's father got up and sang a mournful song about a daughter running away. Esma hung her head, and when the song was finished everyone sat in awkward silence. George jumped up and announced "The One Hundred Days at Sea," which he had not yet performed for Oskar's company. His exaggerated brogue and lively fiddling soon lightened the mood of the evening once more. Esma smiled gratefully at George from her place on the other side of the fire. She coaxed Stepha and two of her friends into acting out George's story with the Storytelling dance, and everyone became engrossed in the tale. During the fiddle interludes, the girls attempted the Time Dancing, egged on by Esma's tambourine. George delighted in this accompaniment, but some of the Elders disapproved and cast sharp looks at Esma, who pretended not to see.

Even the eldest Elder forgot about propriety, however, when he and all assembled distinctly felt the swell of the ocean erupting from the solid ground beneath. The circle of light cast by the fire on the hard packed dirt became the deck of a ship, which rocked and swayed, and the girls danced as if transported, careful to keep their balance atop the swells of an ocean they had never seen. George played on, his face wet with tears which, when he tasted them, became the salt spray of the ocean. Esma's tambourine mixed with the surprised whoops of the adults and the children's squeals to create the sounds of the sea: waves breaking, gulls shrieking. George was grateful to all of these Gypsies, every one of whom was filled with magic. They were giving him the gift of the sea. He imagined himself astride the craggy cliffs of Sumweir Island surveying the glittering dance of the water far beneath, and took up the verse of his chantey once more.

'At last we open our hearts to him,' Tibareth mused. She swirled the dark contents of her mug and tapped the ceramic with a silver ring. 'Now I suppose we must give him what he wants.'

Huliyana swayed dreamily, looking from Esma to George. They stood on opposite sides of the fire, but Huliyana could see that they watched each other and felt the music together. She thought she could see a ribbon of golden light connecting them even as George had implied. 'If Esma had stayed with us, she and George would have met, but Esma would have been much younger than he and under our tutelage. We would never have permitted the match and they would have faced great hardship. Now, as it stands, we can assume that the two *will* meet again *if* George stays with us, because Esma is a smart girl and more powerful than she realizes—she will certainly put things right and return to us with the Tarot card. Of course, we will not see this come to pass for at least ten years. George will be older and his memories of Esma faded, while she will be more youthful and her love fresh and sure. Here again the obstacles will be great, the greatest one being to keep the impetuous George with us for that long once the lovely Esma has gone.'

These thoughts troubled Huliyana. She wanted Esma to be happy, and George too. She moved over to where Tibareth was squatting by the fire and squatted beside her, accepting a sip from Tibareth's mug.

Huliyana talked into Tibareth's ear and Tibareth listened intently. As she did so she watched George and attended to the progress of his song. When it was finished George was engulfed in a crowd of Gypsy men who slapped him on the back and passed him flasks of wine. A group of admiring women circled the men, and Tibareth looked to see if Esma was among them, but she was not. A trio of women were preparing to sing. Tibareth watched as George slipped off into the darkness, nodding at Huliyana's whispered discourse.

"Oh, my Gypsy Dancer, Magic Dancer! How can a Gypsy beauty as magical as you have any troubles at all?!" George had picked Esma right up off the ground in a big bear hug and was taking deep breaths of her cinnamon-scented hair.

"Your song was marvelous; and weren't the girls excellent? That will give the Elders something to think about!" Esma laughed with delight and held on to George as he swung her around and around to the tempo of the Gypsy songs filtering through the darkness. "But tell me about those daughters of John Cory's."

"Ach! I was supposed to skip that verse! What's the matter with me?" George set Esma down gently on the cloak she had spread out on the grass and plopped down beside her. "You see, it contradicts my tale of the poor dear wife I buried on Sumweir Isle."

"Don't worry, no one believed that anyway."

"You mean you've heard that story already?"

Esma wished she could see George's face, but it was hidden in shadow. "Already? I heard it the first night I was here! Just because the Gypsies ignore you doesn't mean they don't talk about you. Why you've entertained them with more than just your fiddle."

"That's me, righto, a born entertainer."

"And on Sumweir Isle you entertained John Cory's daughters?"

"Oh, leave off about that now! The closest I ever got to the Cory girls was to play at their weddings. It was right after the wedding of the youngest that I left the island; so I begin my chantey with 'When all of John Cory's daughters were wed.' That's all there is to that, I swear. But now *you* tell *me* about this Master Seer character who's after you."

"I wanted a teacher, not a lover. As a result, I have made a formidable enemy. Must I tell you more?"

"Tell me you don't care for him one bit and that you won't let him hurt you. Tell me that I can come with you and get rid of him for you once and for all."

"Now stop. I have taught you enough to know that it is impossible for you to travel through Time with me. We would need a very large satchel indeed to carry two of us through Time together—even if we held each other very tight." Esma tried to distract George by showing him how tightly they would have to hold each other. "Malcom means nothing to me now except that, if it weren't for him, I would never have come back here and found you. We can thank him for that, anyway. We have so little time together, must we spend it all on talk?"

"Well, not all of it . . ." George returned Esma's hugs and kisses but kept interrupting himself to ask more questions about the magic satchel, the Alternate World, and the Master Seer. Though he longed with all of his being to consummate his love for Esma, he knew that if he wanted to hold on to this love he could not afford to waste time. He needed a plan.

Esma answered George's questions about Time travel but refused to say any more about Malcom. She was happy to feel George's warm arms around her, and would have gladly drifted off into blissful sleep, but he kept pestering her for more and more details.

"I know what you're up to, George," she finally said, sitting up, "but you are not going to be able to follow me through Time, and I can't bear the thought of your trying. Besides, it can take years to learn everything one needs to know about making a magic satchel and then to actually make one. And don't think you can steal a satchel, because if you do there's no telling where you might end up. It's very bad luck to steal a magic satchel. Even if someone amazingly *gave* you a satchel, how on earth would you find me? For all that I've told you, you don't know the first thing about how to travel the Spiral. It takes much study in the Time Dance to understand..."

"So it *is* the dancing that's the secret. Of course. Esma, if I can't learn the dance, perhaps I can learn the *song*," George spoke excitedly, thinking of how he and the dancers together had created the magic of the sea on dry land.

"Well, that is very interesting. I had not thought of it, but why not? George the Time Fiddler, that's funny."

"Is it possible? Can you teach me?"

"You make me nervous, George. I'm afraid I won't find you here when I come back, and that's what I'm counting on. After all, if you just stay with Oskar's company we'll certainly meet again—for I have promised to return to my people in the proper Time. It won't matter that you'll be a few years older, Tibareth's herbs will keep you young."

"Esma, ten years is more than a few. Don't ask me to wait that long or even longer. Could you? Would you say the same things if our situations were reversed?"

"I only want us to have a chance of being together again. Please promise you won't do something foolish and loose yourself in the Time Spiral. You could become lost to me *forever!*" A tone of panic crept into Esma's voice and she started to weep. George kissed her wet lips and face.

"I promise that the next time we meet we won't have to part. And I promise that time will come. When and how I don't know, but the time will come that we are together again and forever. You want that, don't you Esma?"

"Yes, I only wish that time was now."

"Well, I don't see why we should have to wait all that long. You made your satchel in just a year or two, didn't you?"

"But think, George, once you have made your satchel, how will you find me? I don't know where I'll be in two years time. You could destroy yourself searching."

"Esma, my love, can you explain to me how we happen to be together *now*, across all of *this* unlikely space and time?"

Esma sat quietly for a minute. "I think I might," she said softly.

George waited anxiously, willing her to speak, 'Tell me, Esma, tell me—and I *will* find a way.'

"I love you, George." Esma finally said, putting her palm over his heart.

"Then trust me, Esma; trust love. Teach me the Time Dance. That we have found each other at all convinces me that anything is possible. I have crossed half the globe to find you, and if I can make a way I will cross the Time Spiral to be with you. I'll not promise not to try. How will I find you? My heart will find your heart," and he put his hand over hers.

Esma sighed. 'Is he meant to be my reward or my punishment?' she thought, remembering what still lay before her.

"Tomorrow will be my last day here. I will dance tomorrow night and then leave when everyone has gone to sleep. Play your fiddle for me while I dance and pay close attention, perhaps you will be able to relate the Time Dancing to your music. That will be your challenge. I have my own tests to meet." She pressed her face into George's bearded cheek and held him close.

George was taking a bath in the river. He had gotten up quite early in order to find a remote spot and avoid embarrassing anyone else coming to the river to bathe or fetch water. The Gypsies were very careful about privacy and personal hygiene. Not only did they learn at an early age how not to be seen, but also how not to see. It therefore surprised George when Huliyana and Tibareth came to the river so early themselves, and instead of tactfully going upstream headed directly for his small cove.

'I guess they want to see me.' George waded out of the water and shook himself off before throwing a coarse blanket over his shoulders and turning to greet them.

"We're prepared to help you," Huliyana said. "We have a satchel for you." She patted her belt proudly.

"Your own satchel, Huliyana? Are you sure? I mean, why? Will it work? What do I do?"

George was practically babbling. It had been a long night and an early morning. He wondered if he was hallucinating, but when Huliyana withdrew her satchel from the folds of her skirt and placed it in George's hands, he was convinced that all was real.

"We've taken a look at Esma's satchel," Tibareth said, drilling George with her gaze. "We've copied her Knots into Huliyana's satchel. You are to go to Esma's house in Resthaven and wait for her. That is all. She will not go directly there herself but *you* must. Go there and wait. You are not to go gallavanting here and there. Resthaven is the *only* place you are to go until Esma is ready to return to us. Then you will come back with Esma and return the satchel to Huliyana."

"Oh, absolutely! No problem at all. That's all I would want to do: Go to Esma's house, wait for Esma to join me, accompany her to you, return the satchel. Great plan. Thank you so much! Now show me how to get to Resthaven."

"Just one more thing..."

George did not like the tone in Tibareth's voice. Huliyana looked uncomfortable.

"You must leave us something to seal the agreement."

'Uh oh, here comes the Gypsy's deal.'

"And what might that be?"

"Your fiddle."

George was stunned. He held the satchel in his hand. It was his only link to Esma. But how could he agree to such a bargain? He looked for help from Huliyana, but she turned away. Only Tibareth would meet his eyes with her steely stare.

"Your fiddle, George Drumm—just as collateral of course. Once Esma completes her tasks you will both be quickly on your way to us. You won't be without the fiddle, or Esma, for long."

"But my *fiddle* will be without *me* for ten full years; and I'm to trust its care to you two? There'll be nothing left of it!"

Tibareth looked pointedly at the magic satchel in George's hands. "You're a large fellow, George, and that satchel is made to fit Huliyana—yet she trusts you."

George felt himself growing hot with anger and shrugged off his blanket, not caring about his nakedness. The two women looked up at him expectantly, and a little fearfully. He glared back, too furious to speak, and shoved the satchel back at Huliyana. She took it, surprised.

"Are you sure, George? I thought you loved Esma. It's just a fiddle—surely you can find another in Resthaven."

George spoke in a quiet, controlled voice. "When I left Sumweir Island, me own Mum told me never to be without my fiddle—*this* fiddle. The voices of the wee spirits are here in this fiddle, don't you know?" He wished *she* was there to help; *she* would put these two meddling crones in their place.

Huliyana and Tibareth turned then and walked off quickly. George could hear them talking in low angry tones.

"Very well, ladies," he muttered, "if you won't help me, I'll help me-self."

Esma dozed fitfully as her teachers handled the cards and quizzed each other on the meanings of the images. It had taken her most of the day to go through all seventy-eight cards and their six most popular spreads. Added to all of George's questions the night before, the session had made her hoarse. It felt good to lay back in the grass for a nap, but strange half-dreams troubled her.

"Oh, no! That would be terrible!" Esma sat straight up. Tibareth and Huliyana looked up from the cards.

"You must not let George near Andarra! *I'm* there—*now*. And *he* wants to learn how to make and use a magic satchel. Andarra is the obvious place for him to do that, but he is not supposed to meet me there. He doesn't, I mean, he *didn't*. We can't let it happen now. You two must keep him away from Andarra for at least three years—that's how long I stayed with Ehrte. Oh, promise you won't let him bump into my younger self somewhere!"

"But we are all heading right in that direction. We could send George away, but if he leaves us we will have no way to stop him from doing whatever he wants." Huliyana was speaking to Esma but looking meaningfully at Tibareth.

"If he doesn't go to Ehrte, he doesn't go to Ehrte. You know that he does not, for it is done already. Whatever has been, shall always be so," Tibareth intoned philosophically. But she returned Huliyana's gaze and sent an unspoken message to her: 'All right, all right! We will give him what he wants.'

Chapter 15

Mark wondered if he would know when the Master Seer died, or when the cat died, or if Malcom would die when the cat died, or vice versa. Since the Gypsy had come and restored order to the estate, the dream images of death had become more persistent. Mark was becoming convinced that these were not mere hallucinations caused by the Gypsy's spells, but true portents. But how should he wait for the inevitable?

He put the Tarot card on the mantle. The fanged, horned countenance of the Devil grimaced out at the room.

"The Fifteenth Key—this could be a clue. Let me see—you have been gone just over twelve months," Mark spoke to the card as if it was Malcom himself. "Perhaps I should not expect you back until the close of fifteen months."

The Devil stayed on the mantle. Mark took to conversing with it regularly. It was as if the Master Seer was really there again. Mark realized that he had missed his mentor, and that his days had grown even lonelier without Alvin.

"You know, I like you better when you show your true face," he said to the card one day. "The Gypsy may be confused as to which of us is the cat, but she is right about you being the Devil. No wonder you always relished teaching this Key and gave it your most memorable lectures: 'The Devil is the Lord of the Underworld. Here he was sent as punishment for his inventive manipulations in our—shall we say, *surface*—world. But the Devil is not punished, is not humbled—he revels in the world of darkness, which hides his secrets. Interpret the Devil as cleverness, covert actions, ambition. Should your subjects grow cold with fear at the sight of the Devil in their cards, and look about them suspiciously for the wolf in sheep's clothing, instruct them that the Devil is not to be feared, but emulated. The Devil is our model for the soul which plunges, plunges, plunges—yet is never conquered. Creativity is the hallmark of the Devil, who is now man and now beast—who is Death itself yet who never dies . . . '

"So you think you are immortal?" A chill ran up Mark's spine.

"My dreams tell me this is not so, Master. How would your other pupil, Esmarelda, have told this card?"

Mark mentally reviewed the reading Esmarelda had given that day he went to fetch Audy, and noted that her interpretations had been only slightly altered from those Malcom taught. 'I'd have thought a Gypsy could do better by the Fool. Naturally, our old Devil Malcom gives the Innocent no respect—but I do not see him as being so harassed and foolish. Does the Dog always snap at the Fool's heels—does he really try to bite the Fool? In *my* deck, the Dog barks playfully—and the Fool relishes his adventures all the more with his friend Death at his side. The Innocent is enlightened as he travels through the deck, aware of the transience of all existence.

'Esmarelda listened to the Master too much. She would have benefited more from my perspective on the Fool—maybe she wouldn't have had to hide herself away in that house. She is some kind of Gypsy!'

Mark had no ill feelings toward Esmarelda. They had deceived each other reciprocally. Not only had Mark pretended to be the Master Seer, but he had also lied about knowing the details of the transmutation process. In truth, he had not the slightest idea of what became of the human body once the subject was transmuted to animal form. Even if the Gypsy had gone through with her part of the bargain, Mark would not have been able to complete his. As it was, he had gotten the laboratory restored, which is what he most needed, and he tried to put aside his other thoughts of the Gypsy. Still, he sometimes daydreamed about how Esmarelda would someday return and . . .

Mark knew these were pointless fantasies. It would be better for him if he never saw the Gypsy again. It would be better for him to go far away and start out fresh, his own man. He resolved to leave for good in a few month's time, whether or not Malcom had returned. He would just wait a little bit longer. While he waited, he would put the estate in tip-top shape. When the time came, Mark wanted no unfinished business delaying his departure.

And as his dreams grew more vivid, Mark also resolved never to impersonate the Master Seer again under any circumstances. "I'll not let Death catch *me* in *your* trap, old friend."

George woke up in a cold sweat. At first he thought he'd been bound, and that the dreams of the horned wolf—the fanged bull—had been true. He felt his fiddle case pressing into his ribs and realized his eyes were squeezed shut. Now fully awake, he opened his eyes to glimpse blue sky through the netted windows of Huliyana's magic satchel.

"Oh, *this* blasted thing! Well, here we go again. I wonder where I've gotten to this time." He gently wrestled his way out of the too small sack. "I can tell already that I have not made it to Resthaven yet. Such dreams! There's no rest to be had here."

George folded the satchel in thirds, rolled it up, and stuffed it in the large inside pocket of his coat. He looked suspiciously at the clear stream burbling beside him. He didn't like anything about the place, although he couldn't say why. There was nothing overtly sinister about his surroundings—but those dreams! The dreams were a warning and he should heed them.

'I could always go back to Sky. It's nowhere near Resthaven, but it is a jolly place. To think I had a chance to play for the Prince of Canary—and here I am ready to fiddle for the Devil instead. *Unlucky to steal a satchel*, she said, but I didn't think Sky was so bad. Perhaps I'll receive my come-uppance here; or perhaps my punishment will be the waiting and dreaming of it. George, me lad, you've done a wicked thing—stealing that satchel from Huliyana.

I've no idea even how to fold the thing properly, and here I'm thinking I can get it to take me to Resthaven!'

Turning around and around, wondering what to do, George finally allowed that his surroundings seemed innocent enough. The nightmare images were fading. A hummingbird hovered at his right shoulder for a moment. Then the bird flew away to the west, so George went in that direction as well.

The house he discovered was not Esma's house, could not be. It was low and rambling with deep eaves that cast dark shadows across the windows. George thought better of going to the door. He cut quickly across a lawn and down a path leading away from the house. He hoped to get off of the obviously private property and to a road marker that would tell him where he was. But the path led to a great topiary maze. George cared neither to enter the maze nor to try the magic satchel again so soon. He determined to return to the house and present himself to its occupant.

'Why not find out where the magic satchel has landed me? I might as well learn what I can while I'm here.' George tried to bolster his courage with curiosity. 'Thanks to Esma letting me see her satchel before she left, I know I have been working with the right group of Knots—the Knots Tibareth copied into Huliyana's bag. Though I don't know which Knot represents Resthaven, I do know that all of these Knots have something to do with Esma's life. Even if I do not find my love right away, it seems I may learn something more about her in the trying.'

George returned to the house and resolutely knocked on the door. No one answered. He pushed and the door swung open. The first thing that caught his eye was the image of the Devil on the mantle. He recognized the card at once as belonging to Esma's Tarot deck. George walked through the front room and found the laboratory. Now he had no doubt that he had found the Master Seer's house. He continued to look around. In Esma's room the caftans in the closet smelled faintly of cloves, and the green one seemed to have been worn recently. One sleeve was stained with drops of blood.

'Those scratches on Esma's arm...' George's own skin prickled. He thought he heard murmuring. 'Whatever you're up to, Esma, I won't let on that I've seen you. But forgive me if I stay to meet the famous Master Seer.'

George returned to the front room, which doubled as a kitchen, and sat down to wait. He tried to put together the pieces of the Gypsy's puzzle. He had seen her Storytelling dance but had missed vital details. What was so special about the cat? He had never asked this, so preoccupied was he with trying to understand the Spiral Map and the Time Dance. Only at the very last minute, as she stood holding the heavy ceramic pot, with the satchel ready to drop down around her, did Esma give George any specific information as to what she was about to do.

"I'm going to the Lost Unicorn to see if I can catch Audy in this magic vessel. This is what I came back for: for Huliyana and Tibareth to teach me how to do this. Wish me luck."

"Good luck." George could see there was no point in asking for more explanation. She was poised to go. "Wish *me* luck."

"Good luck, George. Now don't you go getting lost."

George wondered then if she knew. He kissed her quickly—guiltily—and stepped back.

"I'm going to watch if you don't mind."

"You can try, but you'll probably fall asleep. Now..." Esma took a deep breath. "Farewell, George Drumm. Let us meet again in good health."

"Yes, in good health, Gypsy, and in good speed."

Esma crouched and let the net fall about her. It was dark, and George could see only a squirming, compact shape. As he watched, he was engulfed in even deeper darkness, until the world became so black he could see nothing at all. He struggled to stay awake and keep his eyes open. There were no stars. There was no moon (yet earlier he had seen the moon rise, three quarters full). He was afraid to move. He heard and made no sound. Perhaps he finally dozed.

Dawn came. The Gypsy was gone.

∞

"Well, who have we here?"

George stood and faced the man coming through the door.

"Artie. Artie delaMar. I'm looking for the Master Seer." George sensed he had not found him yet.

"The Master Seer's not here."

"When do you expect him back?"

"Perhaps in three months. Perhaps never. What is it to you?"

"I heard he was in trouble—Can I trust you?" Now that he had given himself a new name, George had easily invented a story to go along with it. He was enjoying turning the tables on his suspicious host.

"I am the Master Seer's first apprentice. Who are *you* and what do you know of the Master Seer's troubles?"

"Don't you have a name, Master Seer's First Apprentice? I have already told you mine."

"Mark." He stood waiting, menacingly, for the stranger to answer *his* questions. This visitor was too cocky.

"I heard that Malcom had some trouble to do with a woman," George said. He winked at Mark. "Not the usual kind of trouble either—I'm referring to actual enchantment, by a Gypsy."

"Sit down, Artie. Let me get you something to drink." Mark was completely changed. "Sorry for being so rude, but you never know around here. We have had some trouble, as you know—but how? How do you know Malcom? How do you know about the Gypsy?"

George accepted only water; he had to stay on his toes. "The Master Seer is one of my own teacher's greatest idols. Yet Malcom would probably not recognize either the name or face of Wilbur Strumberg, the Master Player. Wilbur was just one of many who flocked to the Master Seer whenever he visited Ochersfeldt," George watched Mark closely to make certain this detail would be accepted. From what he knew of Ochersfeldt, it seemed plausible enough. Mark pulled at a grog and attended to George's every word, giving nothing away by his expression. George pressed on with his story.

"What Wilbur was able to learn from Malcom on those few times when their paths chanced to cross, he applied to his own science of Music. After a time, Wilbur discovered that of all the artisans of Ochersfeldt, there was not a one who could build an instrument to match his newly perfected talent. And so the Master Player underwent much discomfort journeying by sea to my own Sumweir Island, where we have the greatest of all fiddle makers, drum builders, and flute carvers. My humble fiddle here, which I've had since I was a lad, is finer than any made on this entire continent, and in some ways superior even to the one made for the Master Player—for it was made not for a coin, but for a cousin!" George proudly displayed his worn, but finely crafted fiddle.

"Yes, 'twas made for me by me own Mum's cousin, who learned the trade from his father and so on before them. So you see, fiddles and fiddling's in my family, and when the Master Player arrived at Sumweir Isle and everyone learned who he was and heard him play—well, I was apprenticed to him at once.

"Listen to this, won't you? I see you are not overly impressed with my friend here. Yes he is old and faded, but listen to him sing." George took up the fiddle and played an eerie mixture of his ancestral sea ballads and the ragas he had learned from the Travelers. The plaintive strains of his fiddle belied the feverish pace of George's thoughts as he rushed to invent the remainder of this Artie delaMar's explanation for being in the Master Seer's house.

Mark grew more convinced of Artie's story as he listened, and was soon so convinced that he became concerned the magic fiddler would cast a spell on him.

"Enough playing now. It is a fine instrument, Artie. The finest I have ever heard. And the playing—well, if you are the pupil, your Wilbur must be a Master indeed. I only hope I can stand as such a worthy example of my own Master. And it is he who concerns me now. Once again: What details do you know of Malcom's current circumstances, and how do you know them?"

"I was just getting to that. Please bear with me—where was I? Oh yes. Wilbur. Wilbur brought me back to Ochersfeldt with him, but inevitably I went my own way. I traveled to Nedjaz in search of the Gypsies who sing and play in the cities of that region. I found ready employment in the town of Moro where I played each night with whatever group of Gypsies was staying at the Path Light Inn. This is also where I resided. I was quickly accepted by the Gypsies, and they used me as their messenger, leaving word with me for the next party who would be coming through town. They trusted me and they knew I would be there at the Inn—I became the non-wandering Gypsy. After a while, I knew as many Gypsies by name as the Gypsies themselves.

"But there was one name I never learned. There was a woman whose name was never mentioned. It was like a curse. She had left her clan and gone off on her own. All of the Gypsies were very angry with her. Apparently, she was to have been their star dancer, and had been trained by the Gypsy wise women in their special arts. Still, the woman's family tried to keep track of her, and the other clans helped when they could. If word was passed through me of 'The Gypsy,' it was news of *her*. Honestly, I had so much to remember—for the messages were never written—that I thought little of this nameless person. But when I started to hear the name of the Master Seer mentioned, I began to pay attention.

"At first the messages said: 'The Gypsy has gone to the Master Seer,' and, 'The Gypsy remains with the Master Seer.' But after a while I was told: 'The Master Seer can't live without The Gypsy,' and, 'The tables have been turned for the Master Seer and The Gypsy,' and finally, 'The kitten turns into a lion, the wolf into a house pet.'"

George was so engrossed in his own story that he failed to notice Mark go pale.

"On behalf of my own Master, I felt I had to set out to try to help *his* Master. I have found my way here, but in truth, once I left the Nedjaz I heard not another word of either Malcom or this Gypsy."

"Esmarelda."

"Esmarelda, is it? So this is all true? And you have met this Gypsy?"

Now it was Mark's turn to tell his tale. He outlined the story of Malcom and Esmarelda with reasonable accuracy, but left out anything that might reflect badly on either himself or the Master Seer. And when it came to the part about Audy, Mark said that it was the *Gypsy* who had turned Malcom into a cat, and that she had then taken him to Resthaven to keep as a pet. Mark explained that when he had gone to rescue his Master, Esmarelda had tampered with his satchel so that the cat would be lost in the Alternate World. Then, still not satisfied, she stole the satchel so that Malcom could never be returned.

The story fit perfectly with Artie delaMar's tale. Too perfectly. George knew that Artie's tale was as false as his name. He also knew that Esma must not have intended to abandon the cat in the Alternate World, since she was now going to such great lengths to rescue it. George wondered what Mark knew of the place called The Lost Unicorn. 'What is going on here? Probably the apprentice himself did away with Malcom for his own selfish reasons. Could the cat really house the being of the Master Seer? Is such a thing possible, and if so, does Esma know of it? Surely she couldn't have had a hand in such maliciousness! How has Esma's Tarot card come to be on the Master Seer's mantle? According to her, the Master Seer stole both the card and the cat—but it must have been *Mark* and not Malcom.'

George picked up his fiddle and played some folk melodies to avoid having to make any further conversation with his host. He stared at the Tarot card. 'In the Devil's house the lies come easily to the tongue, and suspicions whisper incessantly at the ear. I should make away with the card myself and spare Esma the trouble of coming back for it. I hate the thought of her returning to this torment, whatever her role in it may be. Of course, I'll likely miss her again and she'll come back anyway and, not finding the card, possibly go off someplace where I'll never find her... No, tampering with Huliyana's satchel has gotten me into enough trouble; I'd better leave the Gypsy's Tarot card alone.' But he could not take his eyes from the visage of the Devil. As he peered into the gruesomely painted face, George felt his heart touch the soul of Malcom, and he knew the truth of the Master Seer. The palpable discomfort of Mark as he sat across from him at the table served to support George's conclusion. 'So, the Master Seer is changed into a cat; and the cat is taken to the Alternate World. A strange business, my pretty Gypsy, a strange business indeed.'

'He plays as if he is far away. And he stares at the card so. Does he know that it represents Malcom? His hair is so red, he could be the Devil himself.' A sudden wave of nausea overcame Mark. He muttered a garbled excuse to his guest as he rushed from the house and staggered, retching, across the lawn.

'It *is* him! No, it can't be—my dreams! It's not time yet— But what do I know? All of it, all of it, all of it could be his doing. This stranger—this Artie delaMar—how did he get here? His story is so convenient—could this be Malcom? Returned, restored, and already impersonating this fiddler in order to check up on me?' Mark was terrified. The idea that the Master Seer might have actually orchestrated *every* event—every occurrence including Mark's, Alvin's, and the Gypsy's actions and reactions—was insane. Yet here was the stranger, and Mark could not get rid of the thought that the red-haired fiddler might be Malcom.

'Should I just ask? Should I try a test of some kind? He is sitting there waiting for me! What am I going to do? What am I to do?!'

The music had stopped. Mark wondered what his guest was doing, but he was too sick to return to the house. Eventually, he found that he was so weak and exhausted that the fear had also been purged. Mark went back inside, ready to accept his Master's judgement. But the house was empty. Only the Fifteenth Key greeted him from its place of honor on the mantle.

Chapter 16

Johnny rode his bicycle along the ditchbank as he did every day after school. The excitement of the encounter with the crazy woman the day before came back to him as he neared the tree under which the Gypsy had been seen. He slowed down to look up and down the ditch, and even looped around to ride up the other side where the great tree stood. "Here, kitty, kitty; here, kitty, kitty," he called, remembering that the lady had been trying to catch a cat and put it in a bag. But there was no cat in sight and nothing to capture the youth's interest.

The next day, on his way to school, something caught Johnny's ever-roving eye. Stooping beside a thick hedge of juniper bordering the neighbor's yard, he lifted a lower branch and began to pull. He pulled and pulled, roughly untangling a net from the shrubbery. It took a long time to get the entire thing free, but Johnny persevered, only worrying about his tardiness after he had succeeded with his task. Then he hastily bunched the net into his book bag and pedaled off without giving his find a second thought.

"Who was that?"

"Robyn. She wants me to work again today."

"Again?"

"Well, you're working today, so I said yes. We can use the money; and if I come through for her maybe she'll give me a regular schedule—she seems to be getting busier and busier with these mysterious visitors."

"You're kidding! Is that why she needs you today?"

"Uh huh. She said her friend was back. Zeek, why are you giving me a hard time? I need a steady job; this could be it. It would be great to have a job I can walk to. It wouldn't matter so much that the pay is kind of low—we'd save all those car expenses."

"You're right, Faye, but do you really like working there?"

"C'mon, it's great! She gets the most amazing stuff. And the work is not that hard. Sometimes it's crazy, but sometimes I can just sit there and read."

"But what about the clientele? What about Robyn herself? She's a little unusual, wouldn't you say?"

"Well, we're a little unusual, too, wouldn't you say? I for one would rather sell magic potions than shoes or—insurance! Doesn't that make me just as weird as Robyn?"

"It would be hard to be as weird as Robyn, and you're much prettier. But don't pay any attention to me, babe—after all, I'm the one who gave up a good job as a programmer to come out here and build adobes."

"So you agree that I should try to get Robyn to give me a permanent job?"

"Hey, if you like it and you're good at it, go for it. I just don't want you to feel like you have to work there."

"Zeek, I love you. Who knows—maybe I'll learn something useful at the Lost Unicorn."

"Yeah, get someone to teach you a fame and fortune spell. That would come in handy."

"Now for *that* we have bath salts!"

"I'm not sure I like it, Esmarelda. It seems to me that any small animal could get in there and end up at the Master Seer's house."

The two women were standing in the kitchen looking out at the clay pot the Gypsy had placed near the back fence. Robyn had gotten up at dawn and watched Esmarelda carry it to its present location. She had mixed feelings about having the vessel from the other world in her yard. What if something went wrong? The Gypsy repeated her explanations and assurances.

"Only a creature from my world will dare enter the vessel. Take one of your own cats over there and see how she reacts, if you want. I guarantee she will run in the opposite direction. Only Audy should be attracted to the pot, and he *will* be drawn to it unless he's hopelessly lost. Whether Audy is caught or not, I will come back for the thing myself when the allotted time is up. If Audy has not been found by then, so be it, he will not be found. You see, there is a time limit. I won't let it stay here indefinitely."

"And what exactly is this time limit?"

"Let me see your Time Map."

Robyn handed Esmarelda a calendar and she paged through it. "Shortly after your New Years I will be back. Just a few days past, if my calculations are correct. Is that exact enough for you?"

"Well, I guess it has to be. You seem to know what you're doing. I'm sorry I'm giving you a hard time, it's just that—"

"No need to apologize, Robyn. I'm the one who's imposing." The Gypsy knew she ought to stay and look for the old satchel, but she was talking herself out of it. She could always come back; she would have to return anyway when it was time to do away with the vessel. Robyn's attitude combined with her own distaste for the Alternate World were serving to dissuade Esma from pursuing her mission right then. She needed to get away, from everything. She needed time to think about George Drumm.

"I really am glad to see you again, Esmarelda. Ramon should be getting up soon. Will you meet him? I've tried not to say too much, but I have told him a little bit about you. I had to tell someone."

"Oh, I don't know if it's good for me to come in contact with too many people in the Alternate World."

Robyn looked disappointed.

"I really think I should go right back."

Robyn sighed. "Are you going to go back to Resthaven?"

"No, I'm going to finish that tour of Sky. The Master Seer is waiting at his house for the return of the cat—"

"But why are you sending Audy back to *him*? I thought he was the one who stole Audy from you. This is what I don't understand, Esmarelda!"

Now it was the Gypsy's turn to be upset. "Please, Robyn! I've told you too much already. Call it a—debt. I know more about Audy than I did when I was last here. He—he's Malcom's—cat. Returning him to Malcom is my only hope of our settling accounts once and for all."

"Hey, who's here?!"

They heard Ramon's heavy steps in the second floor hallway.

"See you for New Year's, Robyn." Esmarelda touched Robyn's arm and with swift, silent steps retreated to the guest room. Ramon caught only a brief glimpse of a blue veil as he rounded the landing.

Robyn told Ramon that she had had another visit from the Gypsy. Ramon wasn't particularly interested. Robyn often had surprise visits from peculiar friends. After breakfast Ramon went out to work on his car. Robyn went to the guest room, but the Gypsy was gone. Outside, the clay pot sitting in the weeds by the chain link fence looked like it had been there forever.

Over the course of the succeeding weeks, the net was stored alternately in Johnny's desk at school and in his book bag, causing some dishevelment of his other belongings. The bag was often passed around among his friends at recess and a game was invented in which they took turns tying the net to their bicycles so that it could drag behind. They called this game "trolling for fish," and imagined themselves on great ocean-going fishing fleets catching immense specimens in their nets. In fact, not a one of the boys had ever seen the ocean, though their fathers would sometimes take them on long rides to high mountain lakes where they fished for rainbow trout.

Football season started and the boys lost interest in fishing. They turned their attention to painting black crescents under their eyes with grease and making shoulder and knee pads out of old socks. One day, Johnny's mother took him to the Goodwill Store and bought him a real football jersey. Riding to school on Monday, Johnny finally divested himself of the net, which was torn and had lost its unique spicy smell.

The over-stuffed book-bag was straining against the elastic cords that held it to the back of the bike; feeling it start to fall, Johnny stopped at the next corner. He leaned the bike against the low adobe wall of a small apartment complex and pulled the net from the book bag, tossing it over the wall along with some old school papers. His load lightened, the boy adjusted the book-bag on the bike and sped off once more.

That night a brisk wind blew. It swirled through the enclosed courtyard of the Del Rio apartments. The tattered magic satchel skidded along the ground, too heavy to become airborne. It skidded down some cement stairs leading to the building's cellar. There it lay until the manager of the complex tossed it into the cellar crawl space one day by way of cleaning up. He set out a fresh box of rat poison, swept up the leaves and dirt which had blown in, and nailed the sagging door shut, disregarding the gaping hole in the bottom of the door where some wooden slats had rotted away. The man looked at his work and shook his head; the wind blew hard in the dusty town and the children played rough. Every season the little courtyard looked more run down. He shrugged his shoulders and carried the bags of trash and leaves to the curb, which was lined with bulging boxes and bags in honor of garbage collection day. He nodded to Zeek, who was putting his bags out in front of the Del Sol across the street. A grey striped cat blinked at them from the drive.

The caravan rounded the foothills of Camelsback and sped onward toward the Fashlasi Plains. By dawn, the village of Andarra was nothing but a filament of wood smoke rising from the mountains behind them. Oskar's company made camp with resigned silence.

Prior to Esma's reappearance, everyone had been looking forward to the excursion into Camelsback. The women longed to acquire the fine linens they could trade in the cities, and the Elders eagerly anticipated a chance for prolonged meditation in the high places; one or two were even considering passing over. Tibareth and Huliyana had messages to leave and friends to ask about, for all Gypsy wise women at some time or other traveled to those mountains to meet and learn from the Magic Weavers.

But it was not to be this year—the visit to Andarra—or the year after, or the year after that—not for Oskar's people. Huliyana had explained it all to the company in a Time Dance. Around and around she had danced: Esma was with Ehrte three years and never did the clan come to Andarra during that Time. For the Esma who had just visited, that time was already passed; but for them, that time was still to come. Plans or no plans, the time ahead held no travel through the Camel Mountains. The die was cast. The Spiral wound out and out. The Gypsies would bypass Andarra. Another time would bring them back around. The Spiral wound out and out. Huliyana's dance brought the night swirling down. The Gypsies dreamed dizzying dreams.

"Have some tea. Have some biscuits." Tibareth was busily tending to her clanspeople. They were not used to traveling by night. They sat blinking exhaustedly in the morning light.

"Have some biscuits yourself!"

"What's wrong with you, Huliyana? You're usually the one who loves to be up all night."

"Yes; but not all night every night. I've barely slept since Esma's visit."

"You slept so well the night she left, you don't even remember giving your satchel to George."

"I did *not* give my satchel to George. Yes, we agreed that I would—but I never had the chance! He played that fiddle all night. By the goddess, I never spoke to him again after that horrible scene by the river. He *took* the satchel from me is all I can think, after purposely playing me to sleep. This is what keeps me awake at night. George *stole* that satchel. Now he may not succeed in finding Esma.

I never had a chance to show him the Knots or anything. You and your stubbornness over that fiddle! We could have done the thing right and helped the course of the lovers; instead I fear we have ruined their chances. What if Esma comes back without him and expects to find him with us? I can't bear the thought."

"Honestly, Huliyana! Here, have a biscuit. Don't you recognize perfection for what it is? George couldn't steal what was to be his anyway; it just *seems* like he did. And this is good because this way we have not given away something for nothing—which is what *you* would have had us do. No, we made an offer and George refused. So we didn't give him the satchel and its secrets. That is the Gypsies' way. Then we changed our minds. We decided we wanted him to have the satchel. Because we *want* him to have it, his having it is good, no matter how he obtained it. Since his having the satchel is right and as we wanted, the satchel will take him to where he needs to go. And since we didn't give away something for nothing, as Gypsies must never do—especially wise women and their secrets—our part in this is also right. You could not have been more clever, Huliyana. Falling asleep and letting George take the satchel was just the right thing to do—and I thought you were losing your touch! Here, have some tea." Tibareth leaned over and smiled with satisfaction. Huliyana was sound asleep.

Chapter 17

"Hi, can I help you?"

Faye had learned to give everyone a minute to adjust to the dark lighting of the store before speaking. Now, as the lanky, red-haired man began to focus on the treasures of the Lost Unicorn, she smiled at him from behind the counter.

The man did a double take and broke into a huge grin, which was soon replaced by a very confused expression. He stepped over to get a better look at Faye.

"You look like someone I know!"

Faye noticed an accent, Welsh, she thought. Strangely, he reminded her of someone too.

"You're a musician," Faye noted politely, nodding to the violin case under the man's arm. He seemed disoriented.

"Oh yes. Indeed I am. Do you know where I might get some work? I've just gotten to town, you see."

"Really? From where? What kind of stuff do you play?"

"Anything, anything you like. Yes, I can play any kind of stuff at all."

Faye laughed. The way he said 'stuff' like 'stoof' was cute. "Robyn's boyfriend, Ramon, is a musician. Maybe he can help you. Robyn's the owner. They're just out to lunch, should be back in half an hour if you want to wait."

"Thanks, don't mind if I do. There's plenty to keep me amused here, I see." George looked around at the array of occult wares. He could almost forget he was in the Alternate World except for the noisy reminder of vehicles roaring by outside. He felt he was so close to Esma now. This woman even looked like her; and here she was in the Lost Unicorn where Esma had said she was going. But that was weeks ago as best he could tell. Was there a chance Esma could still be here?

Some other customers came in and greeted Faye by name. 'She's definitely not Esma, but if you put kohl on her eyes and dressed her up, she could be Esma's fair-skinned twin. Have Faye and the Gypsy met? This gets more intriguing all the time!'

He had arrived almost on top of the magic vessel, and had located the Lost Unicorn without trouble. While George waited for the shop to open, he walked all around the neighborhood and, much to his delight, an orange-striped cat joined him. They were having such a good time kicking around the dusty town that George almost forgot about the Lost Unicorn. But when the sun grew high and hot, the cat sauntered over to a shady yard and plopped down, ready to sleep through the afternoon. A teenage girl appeared at the window of the house and whistled, then called, "Here, Skippy! How nice of you to visit. I have treats for you!" George took this as his cue to hurry back to the Lost Unicorn.

Now, finding Faye there, George was convinced that he should stay a while in the Alternate World. It was an omen, *another* omen. 'I've found the magic vessel. I've found out the secret of Malcom and Audy. I've even found a cat guide and a Gypsy look-alike. Perhaps *I* will be the one to rescue the Master Seer. Perhaps it is meant for me to be here to help Esma complete her mission. Then again, I may only be another curious Gypsy making up any excuse to follow a new adventure.'

George was excited to be in the Alternate World. And each trip in the magic satchel brought him closer to unraveling Esma's secret. It no longer upset him that he kept missing Resthaven; sooner or later he was bound to get there.

When Robyn and Ramon came back to the shop, George charmed them at once with his interesting brogue. He made up a vague explanation of his background, allowing his listeners to fill in the details, and used his own name. If Esma was nearby, he wanted her to know he had also found his way to the Lost Unicorn. Ramon took George over to Robyn's house and taught him some Spanish melodies. Ramon played the guitar. George thoroughly enjoyed the music—some of it was pure Traveler. By the time their session ended, Ramon thought he could get George a gig with a mariachi band and a room at his Uncle Sylviano's house.

It was surprisingly easy for George to adapt to life in the Alternate World. He had seen quite a bit of his own world, including the major museums of technology and the experimental communities which grew up around them. The Alternate World's appliances and vehicles were therefore not all new to George, although he had never seen such a variety of machines or a population so attached to them. The fiddler himself soon became enchanted with the electronically amplified and computer-aided music he heard emanating from devices that were themselves mysteries. While he thoroughly enjoyed performing with the mariachis, he also began to mingle in other musical circles.

Everyone found George refreshing, talented, and a quick learner. Ramon and his friends took endless delight in his unexpected facility with Spanish and Flamenco music. They called him *Jorge Rojas*, or the Latin Celt, and attributed his lack of familiarity with local custom and current technology to his being from some very remote northern island.

Of course there were those who secretly suspected that George's naivete was all faked to make him more popular with the women, for the ladies did take quite an interest in the tall redhead. But Robyn, after that first meeting, grew skeptical. She did not find George's sparse and ever changing history very convincing, and she pressed Ramon to press George for more details.

"I don't know what's with you anymore, Robby. George is a good dude. What does it matter if he doesn't want us to know everything about him? You know, we musicians have our—*pasts*," Ramon backed her against the wall and hissed in her ear

dramatically. "Maybe he was in *prison* over there; maybe he was in
the *IRA* . . ." Ramon started nibbling on Robyn's earlobe, distracting
her temporarily from the newcomer.

For his part, George paid little attention to those women who
flirted with him. Only Faye was of interest, because she looked so
much like Esma. And that first day, for just an instant, she had
looked at him with recognition in her eyes as well. 'Now here is
another puzzle of the Spiral Map. I know Faye is not my Esma, but
she must be connected to us. Otherwise, what would she be doing at
the Lost Unicorn?'

George would muse over these questions as he sat on the sagging
couch on Uncle Sylviano's sagging porch. Sylviano Gutierrez was
old by any world's standards. His house was blessedly uncluttered
with appliances, and he patiently explained to his guest anything that
George asked, showing no hint of surprise at any question. He asked
for no rent, and did not expect George to do chores, although George
helped out all that he could.

When, about a month after George's arrival, Faye reported to
Robyn that her neighbors needed a house sitter, George jumped at
the opportunity. Uncle Sylviano seemed neither disappointed nor
relieved at his guest's departure. George himself felt sadder about the
separation than the old Spaniard.

"Go, go. You have your own way to go. Whatever your
business, you'll finish it and be on your way again—if not now, then
later—and I could like you better by then. So go on now. Away with
you." He winked at George and waved him out. Ramon was waiting
outside in the pick-up.

"Your uncle's an interesting man."

"Oh, he's a character all right, that old *gitano!*"

George looked back at Sylviano on his porch. 'Here is yet another
mystery of the Spiral. One I will ponder for a long time, Uncle, a
long time.'

George was soon installed in a furnished two bedroom house that shared an alley with the Del Sol Apartments.

'The hand of fate again,' George thought. For it was here that he once more met up with the orange striped cat. He soon learned that this was Sylvestor and that the cat belonged to Faye—of all people—along with his grey twin, Felix. And, most importantly, it was here that George inherited a black cat and his pregnant female. The pair lived in the weeds by the alley in an arrangement that seemed to George highly unusual for cats.

George watched this domestic scene with interest: The black cat would not go away. The female, a rangy semi-Siamese, made every effort to demonstrate her disdain and sometimes took a swipe at him, but the black cat was not dissuaded. He lurked about day after day, bringing grasshoppers and birds to the portal of his mate's nest. George, as instructed by the owners of the house, put out water and table scraps for the pair. The male cat seemed much more tame than the expectant mother.

"Audy," George whispered, "Audy." The cat purred and came closer.

"Master Seer," George said, "Malcom." The cat appeared to have a mild seizure. It jerked and growled, jumping away sideways.

After that, the black cat stayed far away from George. George was able to keep track of the cat but wondered how he could snare the animal and take it to the backyard of the Lost Unicorn and Esma's magic vessel. Sometimes he wondered if he should even try.

'Maybe he doesn't want to be Malcom anymore. Maybe he wants to stay and be a father to those kittens. For the life of me, if the creature wanted to undo the spell, he'd find that magic vessel and nip into it in a minute. That's what I think. What on earth am I to do?'

George was troubled. He did not think he should abandon Audy. He was convinced that his getting the house and the cats to look after meant that he was intended to be Audy's protector. If he was not able to return the animal to its rightful world, at least he would be able to report the outcome of the poor creature's story to Esma.

And Esma was constantly on George's mind. Each day George

watched the comings and goings of Faye and Zeek. The two were so obviously in love, and Faye looked so much like Esma, that George could not help developing a strong attachment for their happy household. Each time he felt he must try again to reach Resthaven and to find Esma, he remembered the magic vessel waiting for Audy. Surely the Gypsy would come back to check on it, and then George would be there, and the two would be united, as were Faye and Zeek. It seemed there were many reasons for George to stay in the Alternate World, but he knew that the real reason he stayed was the kittens; like Malcom, he wanted to see the kittens.

There were only two: A Siamese mix like the mother, with a striking white spot on its otherwise sealpoint face; and a black and white splotched ball of fluff. They were both females. George was carefull to visit them when both parent cats were off hunting. He handled the kittens and spoke to them, looking for signs of anything—unusual. Now it was even harder for him to think of leaving. He had the house to mind, and the cats, Audy and the kittens; plus he was developing a good friendship with Sylvestor, who had picked out George as his preferred human—"We even look alike, don't we *Gato Rojo*?"—and then there was the band, which had picked up in popularity greatly since the addition of George's fiddle. George was becoming confused between his Alternate World responsibilities and his commitment to Esma. Everything served to hold him in Caliente a while longer.

The Prince of Canary paced impatiently. As the youngest of seven brothers he had always had to wait for everything, unless it was something unpleasant. He had received the smallest portion and the slightest praise. He was the brunt of all jokes, the scapegoat for all losses. And as his reward for such a belittled childhood, Derek—the youngest son of the mighty King Reginald of Upper Sky—had received the tiniest, remotest parcel of land in the province as his inheritance. Canary.

"Tiniest, remotest, *and most beautiful,*" Derek's betrothed was quick to remind him.

The Prince sighed. At least his father had not sold him short in the wife department. The Princess of Canary was a fine and handsome woman. 'Too bad so few people will ever lay eyes on her or her picture-perfect land.'

"I just wish a touring company would actually make it here! Beautiful can get so boring! We haven't had any decent entertainment for months. I know as well as any what a big place Sky is, but blast these weasely actors and clowns who can't be bothered to visit us here in Canary. Even the vagabond fiddler left us in the lurch—of all the insults! This Gypsy Queen or whatever it is had better show up, is all I can say. I'll take to the roads myself before I'll sit through another moronic concert put on by the school children . . ."

"Derek, you'll wear out the carpet . . . Oh, I think I hear her. Listen . . ."

"Aaaaaaaaaeeeeeeeeeyyyyyyyyyy" The sound of bells and trilling grew louder and reverberated against the palace walls. Esma leapt barefoot into the great chamber and slid on her knees to the feet of the Prince and Princess. Her veils fluttered about her and her black, tasseled braid flew behind.

"Greetings, Prince and Princess of Canary. I am the Gypsy Esma. I hope I have not frightened your Highnesses—I heard you were great devotees of the dance."

"Quite so! Quite so! And we are delighted that you have come. Such a preview! When will you perform for us?"

"Right now."

"Oh, but you can't. Not until we summon the others. Everyone must have a chance to be entertained."

"Very well, Princess. Tonight then."

"Yes, and tomorrow night and the next night as well."

Esma raised her eyebrows.

"Of course!" Derek was pleased with the Princess's thoughtfulness, and her interest in keeping her Prince entertained. Some new brides would be jealous of the mesmerizing Gypsy. "We'll need at least three performances in order for everyone in Canary to have a chance to attend. The people will need to take turns minding the shops and taking care of the children—"

"Oh, and you *will* give a special performance for the children, won't you?"

"I'll perform every night and every day for a week if that is your pleasure. And I'll tell fortunes in between," Esma offered magnanimously, unconcerned that she had no Tarot cards. She could still chart the stars and map palms.

"Marvelous, marvelous! You will stay here in the palace. Locklorie! Lockloren!"

Two attendants came forward. The blue wigged gentleman presented Esma with a velvet sack of coins and helped her to her feet. "For all your trouble in traveling to Canary," he murmured. Esma nodded solemnly, laughing inside. It had only taken her a few hours in the darkness of her satchel to travel from Caliente in the Alternate World all the way to Canary in the remotest corner of Sky. She curtsied to the royal couple and allowed the yellow wigged lady servant to lead her to her rooms. For all of the remainder of her stay in Canary, the colorful couple of Locklorie and Lockloren looked after the Gypsy's every need.

Chapter 18

Just when the mother cat was growing appreciative of her attentive mate, and spoiled by a continuous supply of birds and mice, Audy became erratic. He no longer seemed interested in the kittens. His own appetite waned, and his hunting successes dropped off considerably. George battled his own depression and watched the cats moodily as winter storm clouds brewed.

Sylvestor hovered near George at all times now, and took to urgently complaining as if sounding an alarm. Faye took him to the vet one day and brought him back to George, acknowledging the sympatico which superseded ownership. "There's nothing wrong with him. Not health-wise anyway. I guess he's just got a lot to say these days."

George invited Faye in for some lemonade but she declined. She and Zeek had always been friendly enough, but not very sociable. She stood and talked to George by his back door.

"Well, it's good of you to have Sylvestor here checked out. Did you know we have some kittens in the alley?"

"No, but I bet it's that Siamese cat."

"Yes, and the father is the black cat."

"What black cat?"

"You haven't seen him? He's been around all this time."

"Maybe Felix has kept him away; that cat torments all of the animals. The fact is, we've just been so busy lately we can hardly keep track of ourselves, let alone the cats."

"Oh, you two seem to do pretty well. Zeek is a lucky fellow, if you don't mind my saying so."

"I'd say we're mutually lucky." There was an awkward silence.

"So, I'll assume you're taking care of Sylvestor from now on. He and Felix aren't getting along. I can't really expect Sylvestor to keep coming home just so Felix can beat up on him—and we couldn't afford the vet bills if the two ever really went at it." Faye squeezed Sylvestor and rubbed her cheek against his soft fur. "Zeek and I really miss you, you crazy cat."

"Don't worry, I'll take care of him. He's a fine animal."

"Well, I'm glad to know he has a good home, anyway. I hope he stops that awful wailing—for the whole neighborhood's sake."

Faye gave Sylvestor one last hug and excused herself. Being around George made her uncomfortable.

Two days later, Audy committed suicide. George could describe it no other way. It was mid-day and everyone was off at work. George was sleeping late after a performance out of town and a long drive back to Caliente with Ramon. Sylvestor's crying brought George outside in time to see Audy leap from the roof of Faye and Zeek's apartment. If the cat was chasing a bird, George did not see it; nor did he hear any flapping of wings, but only the soft thud of the cat's body hitting the ground. The sound sent Sylvestor up a nearby tree and Audy's mate racing down the alley. (She would not return.) George hurriedly unlatched his back gate and rushed to where Audy lay. Two kittens mewed plaintively; they had witnessed the entire episode.

The cat had been close to starvation. George felt no heartbeat under the protruding ribs. He took the lifeless body and laid it in the grass next to his back door. He spent the day cleaning up the house. Periodically he went outside to put his hand on the black fur and in front of the cat's partially opened mouth; there were no signs of life. Sylvestor stalked about silently. He took a lizard to the hungry kittens but they wanted no part of it, preferring the milk George finally brought over. When it was fully dark, George took Audy's body to the back of the Lost Unicorn and placed it in the magic vessel. The cat's black fur met the depths of the black clay. George felt cool air rushing down and around his hands and withdrew them quickly. He fled the yard silently.

"OK, baby, I have an idea." Ramon had heard about enough of the Gypsy, the cat—and the magic pot in the back lot, which he was certain had been there ever since he could remember. "Why don't you go out there with some of your own magic and deactivate that pot—smash it! Why wait for her? And if you ask me, you should get rid of that bracelet. What do you want to be wearing someone else's name for anyway? Get rid of that thing and you'll lighten your load for sure."

Ramon waited for Robyn's indignant, misunderstood fury.

"You know, Ramon, you have just given me some really good advice. I needed that. Thank you."

Ramon went for the bottle of tequila. Things were more serious than he'd thought.

"I saw a man put a cat into that vessel last night. The cat had to have been the Gypsy's Audy, and the man looked an awful lot like George Drumm."

"Not this again!"

"Ramon, you take everything at face value; but, I tell you, there's more to George Drumm than meets the eye. I've said it right along and now I'm certain."

"Certain of what?"

"That George is not who he says he is. If you want to know what I think, I think that George is really that Master Seer who's been giving Esmarelda such a hard time. He came to get the cat himself, and last night he finally succeeded."

"Yeah, well, that's all very interesting. How about I ask George about the Master Seer when I see him at practice tonight?"

"*If* you see him—I bet we never see him again."

"You are one wacky lady, Robyn, but I tell you what: If I find out that George Drumm has split town today, I'll believe every word you say about your magic friends from now on. But do me a favor and get rid of that bracelet—I'll get you one with your own name on it."

"OK, Ramon. I'll send the bracelet back to the Master Seer and then I'll smash that clay pot. Since the job is done, there's no use letting it sit there any longer. Hey, maybe you should lay off the tequila; don't you have things to do today?"

Mark entered the laboratory and found the cold, gaunt figure of the Master Seer lying on the long table. He was not even surprised; the image had filled his dreams for the past two nights. Like the dream image, the deceased Malcom was wrapped in his favorite white sorcerer's robe, ready for burial. Bitterly, Mark proceeded with the disposal of the corpse just as it had been rehearsed in his dreams. He dug the shallow grave on the north slope, under the raspberry brambles, and laid the white-on-white corpse directly onto the damp earth. He said no prayers or incantations as he pushed the earth back into the grave. In the dreams he had laid no marker on the fresh soil, but Mark now added his own touch. He placed the Gypsy's Tarot card on the mound. The Fifteenth Key lay face up with a stone on each corner to hold it in place.

'Let her make no mistake that it is him and not me.' Mark had no doubt that the Gypsy would be back. He felt a kinship to her. They two were now the Master Seer's legacy, as they had once been his victims. 'It is time to leave this all behind now. I've buried the Master Seer with my own hands. I won't let him torment me another day. I wonder if Esmarelda can feel herself set free even now . . .'

Mark returned to the house one last time to gather his few belongings. He was not prepared for what greeted him. A scrawny, miserable, blue-eyed, black cat was winding around the legs of the table mewing pathetically, so weak it could barely keep from toppling over.

"What next? What next? Is that you Master? Is that you, Audy?"

The cat did not acknowledge either name and recoiled from Mark without recognition. Only when Mark offered food would the animal approach him and tolerate his touch. It ate the mash of bread and eggs ravenously.

Mark sat down weeping and laughing. Where a moment ago he had felt so betrayed, he now felt vindicated.

"Humility is indeed a powerful force is it not, cat? Here our great Master Seer thought himself immortal, and so Death was called to humble him. And humbled he is, for he lies with the worms and ants. But a cat—a lowly cat—speaks to Death and says: 'I don't ask to live forever, good sir, or to be constantly reborn. Give me but *nine* lives. Yes, nine lives will do just fine.' And it seems such a reasonable request—for nine cat lives represent a mere blink in Time for our friend Death—yes, it seems such a reasonable request—next to the posing of a pompous magician—that it is granted!

"And so you have a life or two left, do you, Moonshine? Well I'm glad of that! None of this was your fault. You were a helpless victim of circumstance—not many trespassers have to suffer such severe punishment for so little a crime. Here, let me make it up to you. I'll take you along with me and try to give you a better life this go-round.

"I bet the Gypsy would be happy to know that you survived."

Mark scribbled a note to Esmarelda while he waited for the cat to finish eating. He included only the barest facts about Malcom's transformation and his own impersonations, but described his dreams as if they were the true events. He hinted at the location of Malcom's grave, and ended with: "but the cat came back."

The cat, his belly finally full, allowed Mark to place him in a basket lined with cloth. He dozed contentedly as Mark strode off to wind his way out through the maze. The basket hanging from the crook of Mark's arm swayed gently. "Let's go find Alvin," Mark said to his new companion. "Won't he be surprised!"

∞

Esma dreamt she was falling. As she fell, she turned into a cat. She fell for a long time. Birds flew by but she could not catch them; as they flew, she fell. She fell for so long she turned back into herself. Then she began falling faster. She became afraid. She felt certain that when she landed she would die, if she did not die beforehand. She was falling so fast she thought she would explode. She was falling so fast...

Esma woke up. She was in her downy soft bed in the Canary Palace. She lit a candle, opened the drawer of the elegant nightstand, and took out her crystal ball. For the briefest instant she thought she saw the image of her missing Tarot card; then there was nothing but blackness for a long time. Just when she was about to put the crystal away, a bright blue cat's eye winked out at her.

'Malcom, Audy—something is happening. A bad situation is becoming worse. Should I go to the Master Seer's? Should I return to Caliente? No, there is nothing I can do. The allotted time is not up yet—and I have commitments here in Canary in the meanwhile. I must trust that the answers will be revealed in good time.'

Esma rolled over and went back to sleep, willing—for once—to wait for events to take their course.

"She's been here and gone? Just like that? Oh, for the love of—Sylvestor, tell me this isn't so! How could I let this happen? I'm done in! She's been here and *gone!*"

George stood peering through the darkness at the broken remains of the magic vessel. Not even twenty-four hours had passed since he put Audy's body into the clay pot and here it was, already destroyed. He clapped his hands for Sylvestor to follow and went back out to the street instead of going over to Ramon and Robyn's for rehearsal.

The smashing of the vessel was like the breaking of a spell. There was no question in George's mind that he should now leave at once. All this time he had instinctively avoided asking about the Gypsy, even though he felt certain that Robyn must have had dealings with her through the Lost Unicorn. George had no intention of giving himself away at this late date. If the Gypsy had been there, and he had missed her, then that was that.

"I should have left yesterday—as soon as my part was through—right after I put Audy in the magic vessel," he said to Sylvestor, picking up the cat. "This Alternate World is no place for Esma and me. How ridiculous to think that we could actually find each other *here*. I'm supposed to be waiting for her in Resthaven this very minute—I should have been there right along.

"You're about to take your first ride in a magic satchel, *gato*. Think Resthaven, lad. We've got to get to Resthaven this time, and hope that it's not already too late. We've got to catch up with Esma before she sets off to find Oskar's caravan! Now wait for me, I'll be right back."

George tossed Sylvestor into the house. Then he went to find the kittens. They were still in the alley and hungrier than ever. "Come along little ones, I have a wonderful home arranged for you. Just make sure to treat that Felix with due respect—he's the boss cat and don't you forget it. Yes, and here he is now ..." George had taken the kittens across the alley and over to Faye and Zeek's door. Felix, ever on the prowl, arched his back and hissed at George's approach.

"Shut up, Felix, I'll be out of your hair in a minute." George put the two small cats down right under Felix's nose and waited to make sure the adult cat did not attack the kittens. Felix stopped complaining and busied himself sniffing and examining the two newcomers. The kittens huddled together and did not try to run away; instead they inched closer to Felix, adopting him at once as their surrogate mother.

"Now that's a pretty scene," George whispered. He returned to the house, feeling for the magic satchel wadded up inside his coat. "Let's go, Sylvestor," he called as he opened the door. "It's time to ride the Spiral ..."

Chapter 19

"Now this, I believe, is Resthaven!" George held Sylvestor in one hand and Huliyana's magic satchel in the other as he surveyed the sleepy town. "I wonder where the Gypsy lives? Let's nip into town and ask after her, shall we?"

At last back in his own world, George felt his spirits lifting. The air smelled fresh again; the songs of the birds and insects were no longer drowned out by the noisy inventions of the Alternate World. His time in Caliente already seemed like a dream, the anxious dream of a man who has slept too long.

Insects buzzed in the air. Castanets clicked. The Gypsy was a swirl of radiant shapes, a kaleidoscope without color. Her dance was a dance of moving shadows and splinters of light. The air smelled of clover and . . . clove, of wheatgrass and . . . ginger. Malcom hid in the lush growth and spied on the Gypsy's dance. Like a cat, he stalked her . . .

Now it was Resthaven and it was Audy stalking the Gypsy. He sprang to the window ledge through the marigolds . . .

"Oh my god! Oh you stupid thing! Are you all right?" Faye plucked the black and white kitten from the floor. It had leapt to the window sill as if prepared to take flight, and had slammed squarely into the pane of glass.

"Where did you think you were going? It's a good thing you're so small and light or you could have really hurt yourself." Faye cuddled the kitten and the kitten loved her back, the spill already forgotten. "What got into you, anyway? A minute ago you were sound asleep."

The baker's helper kneaded his dough in front of the tiny window as he did every morning, watching the purple shadows give way to the pinks and golds and greens of Resthaven's carefully manicured lawns.

"Better open up early," he called out, watching the shadowy figure of a man approaching. "Stranger's coming into town. He'll be hungry."

Mr. Spense came to look over Carl's shoulder. The sun was starting to catch George's red hair, and he was now near enough that the men could see the fiddle case in his hand and the cat trotting behind.

"We get all kinds here in Resthaven, don't we?" Mr. Spense chuckled as he went to unlock the door. "Bake extra, son, we'll do great business today with everyone stopping by to ask about the newcomer."

The baker stepped outside to intercept the stranger. Looking back at his tidy shop, he nodded with satisfaction. His children had given him some trouble over taking a building on the very outskirts of Resthaven. "A bakery is supposed to be in the center of town," they'd said, "in the marketplace with all the other shops." But Mr. Spense liked the quiet of his little establishment on the fringe of town, and as he predicted, he did a booming business each day with the picnickers and hikers setting out for the countryside or returning from a long day in the woods. And anyone looking for gossip knew that if they came by for a scone or some tea cakes, Mr. Spense and his wife Judy would gladly fill them in on who had gone off horseback riding with whom, or who had bought a special cake for what occasion.

"Say there, lad, that's a fine cat you have. Care to stop for a fresh hot loaf? They've just come out of the oven."

"Now there's an offer we can't refuse! George Drumm's the name, and this here's Sylvestor." George reached out to shake the baker's hand.

"Martin Spense. Pleased to meet you both. Fine morning, tisn't it? But then every morning is a fine morning in Resthaven." He led George inside. Sylvestor followed and was soon prowling for mice. "Carl, bring us a loaf of cinnamon bread!"

Carl did so at once, eager to get a close look at the stranger. The cat followed him back to the baking area and set to work amid the bags of flour and sugar.

"On holiday or business?" The baker asked as he and George leaned against the glass counter drinking strong black coffee with sweet bread.

"Since my business is making merry, you could say both," George answered, nodding to the fiddle he'd set down by the door. "Fact is," he lowered his voice conspiratorially, "I'm looking for someone. A Gypsy. I've heard there's a certain Gypsy woman living here in Resthaven. Do you know of her?"

"*Was* a Gypsy woman living here, you mean. Hasn't been seen for a time, though. Some say she was never a Gypsy at all but a sorceress, and that she flew away on the Eve of Wicken's Moon. No one dares go too near her house. It stands empty now. All overgrown with vines on the outside, and on the inside spider's webs and what else I don't care to know."

"Where is this house?"

"Why, if you've just come up the Green Ribbon Road, you must have passed it. You can see the roof and chimney from the road if you look up; there's a little break in the evergreens on the east side that leads to the place. Oh, that house has been a mystery since long before the Gypsy came. She's been the only one brave enough to live there for some years. That's why folks say she's a sorceress. But what's all this to you? What business do you have with the Gypsy?"

"I'm her husband and I can guarantee that, if we are speaking of the same woman, she is no sorceress—though she enchanted me well enough!"

Mr. Spense gulped in surprise and burned his tongue on the coffee. As he spluttered and cursed, George went on: "Did you ever see this Gypsy? Was she about so tall? With black hair and black eyes? Did she dress in silks and flowing veils; did you find her as beautiful as a precious jewel? Did she say her name?"

"Slow down, boy, slow down! The Gypsy's husband! Who would have guessed? Now let me think—Judy heard her speak her name once. She didn't come into town much, you know, and everyone just knew her as The Gypsy. Those who went to her house to have their fortunes told did speak of her dark beauty, but then I thought that was true of all Gypsies—that's what Judy tells me, anyway. Let's see, what was that name? Something unusual—what was it? Estelle? No, not quite—Stella? Zelda? Imelda? That's closer—"

"Esmarelda?"

"Yes, yes! That's it. Esmarelda."

"Then I've found her!"

"But you haven't, son. I told you she's not here any longer."

"Ach!" George shook his head and rolled his eyes. "It is all my fault. I promised I'd come for her, but I'm so late! She must have gotten tired of waiting and gone off to look for me. Now my only course can be to go to her house and hope she'll return. If one of us will just stay put we'll eventually be reunited. Oh, this is all too much for me! Forgive me but I must go find this house at once and assure myself it is really Esmarelda's house. Haunted or no, it is as close to my darling wife as I can get for now."

"So, where have you been all this time? How did you and your wife come to be separated? That is, if you don't mind my asking." Mr. Spense hated to sound so nosy, but he owed it to his customers to learn as much as he could, and here the fellow was rushing off so fast.

"I've been to the Alternate World, Mr. Spense, the Alternate

World. A man can forget who he is there, what he is—he can lose all sense of Time. But it's a long story." George put a silver coin on the counter. "Sylvestor! Sylvestor! Where are you?"

"He's in here." Carl came around the corner holding two dead mice by their tails. "I gave him some milk for his hard work."

Sylvestor padded proudly over to George, licking his chops, and George picked up the cat and then his fiddle.

"Thanks to you both! That was the best breakfast we've had—ever! I promise I'll come back and play for you sometime."

With that, the stranger was out the door and on his way back down the Green Ribbon Road.

"The Alternate World? Wherever is that?" Mr. Spense turned the Kennedy half dollar over in his hand and then bit down on it before passing it over for Carl's inspection. "Oh, won't Judy be sorry for sleeping in today!"

Faye hurried down narrow cobblestone streets, which twisted and turned, glistening wetly in the lamp-lit darkness. She knew, as dreamers do, that she was being followed. Alone in the winding streets, she was trapped by fear. Up one street and down another she ran, making no progress. Finally, panicking, she ran into a jewelry shop. A man held up a bracelet.

"Dance for me! Dance for me!" he demanded, advancing menacingly. Faye tried to scream.

They were on a balcony now, a second floor landing. "Dance for me! Dance for me!" The man came closer. Faye felt the railing pressing into her back. There was no place left to run. She tried again to scream but could make no sound.

"Meeeeooooowwww." The bracelet clattered to the ground. Faye twisted away. Her pursuer toppled over the railing and fell heavily to the floor below. Faye, relieved, realized she was holding a cat in her arms. But it was heavy, too heavy, she was having trouble breathing.

"Oh, it's you, little one." Faye woke up. Dash was sitting on her chest kneading the blankets. She gently brushed the kitten aside and rolled over, throwing an arm across Zeek's back.

"Say good bye to this cat, Faye, because I don't think we'll ever see her again once we let her out the door."

Zeek stood poised to let the complaining animal outside while Faye hovered nearby.

"Well, what are we going to do? I don't know about you, but I'm not going to be able to stand it much longer. She just won't let up. Dot goes outside all the time and always comes back."

"That's because she's always with Felix. I've never seen two cats get along like that, have you?"

"No, but it's awfully cute. I can't believe Felix has decided to be so nice to these kittens after the way he treated his own brother!"

Dash mewed pitifully as the conversation proceeded without the door being opened. Zeek and Faye looked down at her.

"She's reminding me of Sylvestor now. I wonder where he and George went?"

"Could be anywhere. A couple of vagabonds, those two. Well, what do you say, Faye? Does she go out?"

"I adore this kitten, and I really think she likes us too, so we'll just have to trust each other. Let her out and let's see what happens. We can watch to see where she goes."

"We can try. OK, Dash, out you go." Zeek opened the door and, true to her name, the black and white kitten streaked out. Faye and Zeek followed, but the cat had already disappeared from sight.

Three days after New Years the Gypsy arrived in Caliente. It was dark, of course, and bitter cold. There was no light in the Lost Unicorn and Robyn's house was dark as well. Esma easily found a key under Robyn's doormat—for some customs know no boundaries—and let herself into the house. In the dark, she felt her way to the guest room behind the stairs; the candle and matches

Robyn had given her on her last visit were still by the bed. Esma lit
the candle and crawled under the covers. Robyn's two cats joined
her. The house was cold, and to the Gypsy the night seemed endless.
Where was Robyn? What had happened to Audy? After her
prolonged stay in Canary, being back in the Alternate World was like
a nightmare.

In the morning, Esma went outside and found the remnants of the
magic vessel. She walked thoughtfully back to the house and entered
the kitchen through the back door just as Faye was letting herself in
through the front.

"Here, kitty, kitty, kitties! Here, kitty, kitties! Here— What's
that? Oh shit! Oh god! Oh, it's you! Oh god, you scared the shit out
of me! Esmarelda, right? Jeez, I'm sorry—Robyn told me to expect
you but I forgot. Wow, that freaked me—god, I'm still shaking."

The Gypsy stood wide-eyed, as startled as her visitor. Half of
what the woman said was incomprehensible.

"So you found Robyn's key. Robyn said you're welcome to stay
as long as you like. I wish you would stay. Then you could take care
of the place. Because, man, I've got my hands full! I've got the Lost
Unicorn, which opens in fifteen minutes, by the way. I've got my
neighbor's place, because that sleazy musician split when he was
supposed to be house sitting. I've got this place and *her* cats, *plus* the
two kittens that showed up on *our* doorstep and are into
everything—it's really getting to be a bit much! Jeez it's cold in here!
You know how to turn on the heat?"

Esma, bewildered, watched Faye adjust the thermostat. "Where's
Robyn?"

"On her honeymoon! She and Ramon got married on New Years
Eve. Too bad you missed it. Robyn was hoping you might come back
early."

"It is a shame that I missed it, but I had another wedding to go to,
and Robyn never even hinted that she was planning this . . ."

"Oh, believe me, it was totally unplanned! Shit! I've got to get
out of here and get the store opened. Listen, you make yourself at

home and come on over when you're settled. I have a message for you from Robyn but I haven't got time now." Faye rushed out.

The Gypsy sat down and waited politely for an hour to pass before going over to the Lost Unicorn to get Robyn's message. She was sorry she could not have danced for Robyn and Ramon's wedding as she had for Marion and Derek's. The Prince and Princess of Canary had made the handsomest couple Esma had ever seen, and their public wedding ceremony was appropriately lavish. They had begged her to stay on indefinitely and take some students, but of course she had had to decline.

'If I ever get through with this business, I'll take George with me and the people of Canary will be doubly entertained. Oh, George, where are you? Sometimes I have this feeling I could bump into you at any moment, and then sometimes I worry that I'll never see you again.'

Esma brought out her crystal ball and sent all of her thoughts to George. But the crystal showed her only the places she herself had been: the Lost Unicorn, Sky, the Master Seer's house, Resthaven. The Gypsy sighed. She held the crystal to her heart before putting it away. "Wherever you are, George Drumm, my heart will find your heart."

"There you are. Hi, I'm Faye. Sorry I was so out of it earlier." The young woman extended her hand. She was dressed in blue jeans and a pink and gold patterned blouse. Her dark curly hair was swept up from the sides of her face and caught loosely in two large orange combs. 'This one has Gypsy blood in her veins,' Esma thought.

"I'm anxious to see Robyn's message. Although I appreciate your predicament, I'm afraid I won't be able to stay to help out."

"I kind of figured that. You seem to be on the move all the time. Anyway, Robyn wouldn't write the message down. She made me memorize it. Don't ask me why."

"Oh, I understand. It's the Gypsy way. I'm ready."

"OK, here goes: 'Esmarelda. The Master Seer was here. He took the cat. I sent your bracelet back and smashed the vessel. I hope I see you again so I can explain.'"

"The Master Seer was *here*. How would Robyn know?"

"Don't ask me. I don't understand a word of it."

"That's all right. Thank you, Faye. If I understand Robyn's message correctly, I think I must go now."

"Don't you want to leave a message for Robyn? In case you don't make it back?"

"Very well. Tell Robyn that I congratulate her on her marriage; and that I am still looking for the lost satchel. Tell her that even if I do not come back I will—phone her." The Gypsy chuckled at her secret joke and went out, leaving Faye to repeat the message over and over to herself, as well as every other detail of Esmarelda's visit. She wanted to be able to give Robyn—and Zeek—a full report.

"What say you?" Hulyiana and Tibareth stood on the crossroads with the Journeywoman. The caravan moved on ahead of them.

"Something that has been lost is returned. Someone you have missed will soon come to you." She tossed a stone into the air and watched it fall and roll. "You are on the correct path. Patience will take you to your meeting place." She walked off. Tibareth scratched a tiny figure eight into the stone and left it in the road where it had fallen. Then the two women ran to catch up to the caravan, giggling, seemingly untouched by the years.

There was no magic left in the place. The bracelet, which Esma had found lying on the laboratory table, no longer had her name inscribed on it; the silver bangles were blank. The shrubs of the maze had withered and no longer hid the spiraling paths from view. If not for all of this, she would never have believed that the Master Seer was dead.

Esma stood over Malcom's grave, holding the Tarot card in one hand and Mark's letter in the other. Something still did not make sense. It was Robyn's message. She had said: 'The Master Seer was here. He took the cat.' But if he *was* the cat, how could that be? "Mark knew from his dreams—as I did from mine—that the cat would be harmed and as a result the Master Seer would die. He had no way of returning to the Alternate World to prevent this, or to fetch the cat. But Robyn must have seen someone put the cat into the magic vessel or she wouldn't have destroyed it. Who could have done that besides Mark, or myself?" The Gypsy turned the Tarot card over and over. It was sun faded and warped. Esma imagined how this card would no longer match the rest of the deck, and was reminded of her instructions from Huliyana and Tibareth.

"Obviously, as all of the mysteries are not yet solved, neither are all of my tasks complete. I still have the old satchel to find. It does not appear to be here as I had hoped, so it must still be in Caliente. Oh, must I go back, Huliyana?" Esma twirled around and asked her question to the wind.

Silence. There were no more secret voices in the air. "I am on my own now," Esma said, at first tentatively but then a second time with conviction: "I am on my own now." Gradually the truth sank in: the Master Seer's spell was finally broken.

The Gypsy skipped down to the river, leaving Malcom behind. "Away, Away!" she sang to herself, "Away to Resthaven." She could almost smell the bakery and hear the hikers yodeling to each other through the woods. But it was no use. The lost satchel was certainly not in Resthaven, and she would have no rest until she found it.

"Very well, away to the Lost Unicorn—again. Since I did not really set my mind to finding the thing on my last visits, I owe it one more try. I will just go and stay at Robyn's and look for it every day until I find it. Yes, Huliyana—yes, Tibareth—yes, Red Mountain Witch—I will go find the wretched old satchel. I may be free of the

Master Seer, but I suppose I shall never be free of the meddling crones of this world. No doubt I'm destined to be one myself."

Esma put the best face possible on having to go back to the Lost Unicorn. She had come so far, now was not the time to give up. Yet she felt much resistance to the idea of returning to Caliente, and attributed this to her general dislike of the Alternate World. Her heart seemed to call her to Resthaven, but she chided herself: "It's foolish, this longing for 'home.' I'm a Gypsy; the house should mean nothing to me." She took a deep breath and steadied her thoughts.

"Away, away! Again, again! To the Lost Unicorn—the magic satchel to reclaim!"

Resthaven would have to wait.

Chapter 20

"She's back."

"Who?"

"Esmarelda."

"Really? So soon?"

"Yeah. She left me a note this time so I wouldn't freak out."

Zeek took the scrap of paper. It read: "Faye, I'm back. I'll feed the cats. E"

"So, did you see her?"

"Yeah. She came over to the store and asked if she could borrow some of my clothes. She said she came back because she needed to look for something she lost in the neighborhood, and she needs some practical clothes to wear."

"What'd she lose?"

"A satchel—remember the message she gave me for Robyn? The 'lost satchel.' I think she meant a purse. She's kind of old fashioned—or something."

"Maybe she's just broke. I mean, why can't she buy her own jeans? Why does she keep coming back here? You better watch out, Faye, this Esmarelda character may be casing the Lost Unicorn."

"You mean you think she's here to rip the place off? C'mon, Zeek—I know it all sounds strange but, well, you just have to meet her. Robyn trusts her and I have to admit, so do I. Anyway, she's not completely broke because she wears a bunch of jewelry, and it looks like good stuff, too. When she asked for the clothes she said that she didn't want to spend any time shopping because she really just wanted to find this thing and get going—"

"Going to where? Where *does* she go in her fancy clothes?"

"She's a Gypsy. She just travels around. Really, Zeek, it's no big deal. I'll just loan her a pair of jeans and a sweat shirt."

"Suit yourself. I guess Robyn would want you to help her out as much as you can—I just hope you two don't end up getting burned by this chick."

"You know, that's what Robyn kept telling Ramon about that George Drumm. I didn't really ever like him that much myself; but the Gypsy's different."

"What was wrong with George? I hope you're not mad now that he took Sylvestor—don't forget, you yourself told him it was all right. I thought George was a pretty nice guy—maybe not very responsible, but what do you expect from a musician?"

"I don't know; I can't explain it. I guess it's just that he always looked at me kind of funny..."

A good many people had taken to walking on the Green Ribbon Road of late, claiming to enjoy the exercise. They generally walked just to where the Gypsy's house stood hidden behind the pine trees, paused for a moment or longer listening to the strains of George's fiddle, and then turned around and walked back to town. A few brave souls actually strolled onto the path through the pines and skirted around the house as if heading to the pond. But George, watching from the upstairs window, noticed that the interlopers always turned back in hurried, secretive gaits.

"It's the fiddle," one might say the next morning to the knot of people in Mr. Spense's bakery. "It's the eeriest thing I've ever heard. So mournful. You can hear him crying out for his poor Gypsy girl. It gives me the shivers through and through. And her probably drowned in that pond—committed suicide thinking he'd abandoned her. Has anyone mentioned the clothes to him?"

"Well, he must have found them. No one ever took them away as far as I know. Do you really think she's drowned?"

"Now leave off about that nastiness, won't you?" Judy would interrupt at this point. "The lad doesn't think she's dead—and a loved one knows things like that, if you ask me. Besides, Gypsy girls don't commit suicide. No sir. They're resilient, crafty things, those Gypsy women. We have them in here from time to time. Really, can any of you who had a palm read by our Gypsy Esmarelda honestly tell me that she seemed the suicidal type?"

At this the crowd would grow silent and disgruntled. Judy usually egged on the gossip, yet here she was, taking everyone to task. She couldn't really explain it herself, except that she loved the romance of George coming to reclaim his bride. She couldn't bear the thought of love being foiled by foolish tragedy. If they didn't speak of it, perhaps it wouldn't prove true.

As for George, when he was not playing his fiddle or poking through the Gypsy's herbs and potions and charts, he spent most of his time at the pond. This is where he felt closest to Esma. He had indeed found her clothes—the second set—faded from sun and rain; and when he washed his own clothes he carefully laid them beside hers and imagined the two of them frolicking together in the dark water.

Sylvestor went everywhere, as he had in Caliente, and especially liked to visit his friends at the bakery. On George's periodic excursions into town Sylvestor always led the way. He would run ahead to make sure the shops were not busy, for George didn't want to be too social in Resthaven or risk drawing suspicion to himself—or Esma—by speaking too freely. Sylvestor always let George know that the coast was clear by circling around his legs two times before trotting over to the shop of choice. The only crowded place the cat allowed his companion was the pub, for it was here that George played for tips and bottles of grog.

Those who knew his story would shake their heads and wonder that the same man who played with such anguish behind the dark windows of the Gypsy's house could also play with such ribald gusto. The red-haired stranger played and ate and drank and laughed at the barkeep's jokes, but never spoke more than a few words to anyone.

While those of a morbid bent continued to speculate about the Gypsy's demise, many more Resthaveners found themselves adding a candle to their household offering—or knocking on wood, or crossing their fingers, or picking an Elder Blossom—for Esmarelda's safe return. And many a long married couple found they held each other at night with renewed appreciation as they envisioned the passionate embraces of the dashing George Drumm and his exotic Gypsy wife—if ever they would be reunited.

"I followed Dash today."

"Really? Where does she go?"

"Everywhere. She went all the way down to the end of the alley snooping in everyone's tool sheds. Then I lost her for a while. Then I saw her near the porch and went out and followed her up the driveway and watched her run across the street."

"You're kidding? That skittish thing?"

"She did. She crossed the street and ran over into the Del Rio compound. I was afraid if I followed her she'd get scared and run off even further, so I just left her alone. She showed up at the door with Dot and Felix right at five o'clock."

"Well, that's good. It's hard to believe that Dash and Dot are from the same litter, isn't it? They don't look alike, and they sure don't act alike. Dot only goes where Felix goes, and if he strays too far she comes right back to the porch. Have you seen her do that? It's like she hates to explore."

"Yeah, she doesn't like to get her fur dirty. And she's not very social either. It's a wonder she tolerates any of us!"

"We certainly have a temperamental menagerie here, my dear." Zeek kicked off his shoes and started dragging a string across the floor, trying to lure sleeping cats into action. Dot and Felix came lunging out from under the bed to Faye and Zeek's delight. But Dash, curled up in exhaustion behind the couch, was lost in half-human dreams: A woman called to her from a distant place. There was something she had to find, but a great spider's web blocked the path. Glistening spirals of silk stretched across a doorway behind which darkness loomed.

As the steam cleared, Esma watched her reflection emerge in the bathroom mirror. She looked ghoulish with her wet black hair plastered against her cheeks, and the skin around her eyes purplish from so many years of wearing the dark kohl that even a good scrubbing would not remove it's stains. She dried herself, braided her hair tightly, and put on Faye's clothes. The hot shower had been pleasant. Now the Gypsy's thoughts turned back to her mission: to find the old satchel. She put on a jacket she found hanging in the hallway, and a pair of Robyn's too-big boots over her own daintily embroidered slippers, and walked outside. "Where is the satchel?" she asked her talisman. The pendant swung around and around, giving no clear direction.

Esma went back inside and got out her crystal ball. "Where is the satchel?" she asked, trying to recall every detail of the satchel's texture and smell. The crystal showed her only blackness.

She went outside again. The Gypsy picked up a handful of dirt from the ground and tossed it up into the air as she had seen the Journeywomen do. "Where is the satchel?" The sand and dust blew back into her eyes.

She walked around the neighborhood in a spiral until she had covered several miles and her feet ached from the oversized boots. Then she trudged back to Robyn's house. Nowhere had she sensed the presence of the magic satchel. She had been having trouble concentrating—she wanted, needed, desperately to find the bag, but her thoughts drifted so. The day had been a total failure.

Esma put the tattered Tarot card on the kitchen table and sat down in front of it. "Where is the satchel, Malcom?" The Gypsy rested her head in her hands and wept. Malcom was dead. For the first time she felt pity for him. *"We* are the lost ones, aren't we, Master Seer? You—you are lost in the underworld. Why were you so anxious to learn those dark secrets? Are there not enough mysteries in living without our needing the mysteries of death to amuse us? But then, look at me. Here I am, dallying in the Alternate World as if my own world were not enough. And then there's George, unhappy with the Time in which he should properly stay. How indeed are we to find anything, when we ourselves are lost?"

But the Gypsy was actually encouraged in the midst of her despair. Here was another view of things. Instead of thinking of the satchel as being lost, she would think of it as being where it belonged. And she would imagine herself as misplaced in relation to the satchel. She spent the evening focusing on this new approach.

'If only I had a guide to help me find my way,' she thought, remembering times when a bird or animal had come to her aid as she traveled through strange lands. But over the course of the next few days, no creature of the Alternate World came to the Gypsy's assistance, or so she thought.

For a small animal, Dash had huge dreams. They were Magicians' dreams, full of rushing winds and bursts of light. The winds carried Dash down dark and descending passageways; the bursts of light shot out blindingly from an otherwise opaquely black, bottomless well. These were dreams so vast that Felix, having allowed the kittens to curl up with him for warmth, would shudder and awake with a start. Then he would stalk off, fur bristling, with Dot trotting behind. Dot could only doze. She was always on guard against the heavy mantle of sleep which would smother her in those same dark dreams engulfing her sister.

So spurned by her fellow felines, Dash lavished her attentions on the humans of the household, especially Faye, who alternately delighted in the kitten's fluffy affections and worried over the animal's survival. She did not understand that it was the dreams which sent Dash exploring so daringly. She only knew that if Dash was gone for half a day or more, it meant she would have to search for the kitten and try to retrieve her from whatever labyrinthine place she had managed to discover.

One day Dash dreamt not of spiraling downward but of climbing, climbing and flying. She climbed a tall tree. The sky blazed blue. There was Dot winking blue eyes from a warm perch on the roof. Dash scampered over to her and beyond to stand blinded by sunlight on the very edge of the roof's overhang. She seemed to sway in the brisk winter breeze. She seemed dazed and ready to topple over . . .

"Get away from there! Get away from there, you stupid cat! What are you doing? Wake up, you idiot!" Faye frantically scraped a handful of gravel from the driveway and threw it toward the roof. The wind carried the small stones away without effect, but Dash did regain her senses and retreat from her precarious position. She followed Dot down the tree and the two galloped over to Faye, tails in the air.

"What am I going to do with you two?" Faye asked as she picked them both up and nuzzled the furry armful. "It's a good thing you're so dainty, Dot, because your sister here is going to use up her nine lives early and will need to borrow some of yours!"

"Hi! We're home! Who's here? Faye?"

"No, it's Esma—"

"Esmarelda?! You look just like Faye in those clothes!"

"Hi. I'm Ramon." Ramon stuck out his hand thinking, '*This* is the exotic Gypsy?' "You do look a lot like Faye."

"I am wearing her clothes. She was nice enough to lend them to me." Esma spoke casually but her mind was racing as she glanced at herself in the hallway mirror. 'I was so careful not to bump into myself in the Past, I never considered my Future self.'

"Robyn, I've been looking for the old magic satchel that I lost the day Audy got away from me. But I'm giving up. I've tried everything and I haven't a clue. Really, I was just waiting here to see you so I could ask you about that message."

Esma led Robyn and Ramon into the kitchen and put up some water to boil for tea, as if she were at home and they were the guests. Ramon watched and listened to the two women quizzically. The honeymoon had made him fully appreciate Robyn's tendency to act as a magnet for the eccentric. They had met the oddest assortment of characters during their travels . . . Ramon doubted that the average tourist was likely to bump into even one shaman in the course of a two week vacation, but Robyn had actually met three in one day; and later in the same week they were invited to dinner by a self-professed spirit guide. After that, Ramon listened a little bit more attentively to Robyn's stories, and even had her re-tell some of her tales about Mr. Too and Madame Violetta.

"I saw a man put the black cat into the vessel with my own eyes," Robyn was saying. "And this man happened to be a stranger who had come to the Lost Unicorn just within the past couple of months. He insinuated himself in our lives in every way—playing music with Ramon and his friends, house sitting for Faye's neighbors . . ."

"Who was this man? He must have had a name? What did he look like?"

"His name was George Drumm—"

"George Drumm? George? He's been living *here*? Ayyyyy-ah!" Esma let out a little whoop. Her eyes were dancing and her face was flushed.

"I think this means George is not the Master Seer." Ramon said to Robyn as the Gypsy bounced up and down, laughing and murmuring exclamations to herself.

"I guess not."

The Gypsy regained her composure. "No, George isn't the Master Seer, but it's not a bad guess. He is from my world. We've, uh, gotten separated." Robyn and Ramon grinned at each other. They were catching on. "Now all I have to do is figure out where George has gone from here—and I already have a very good idea.

The first thing Esma heard when she awoke and crawled out of her satchel was the music of George's fiddle. An orange cat came over to greet her as she paused, wondering what to do next, how to announce her arrival. For all of her anxious hopes, Esma had not expected to find George so soon. Now that they were virtually reunited, she was momentarily stricken with doubt.

'Come now, isn't his being here proof enough that we are meant to be together? What am I waiting for?' She took deep breaths of the warm night air. 'My own world, my own Time, my own love—at last I truly know what it is to be home. And the house is the very least of it—I haven't missed the house itself at all. When my heart called me to Resthaven, it was telling me something quite different; but I wasn't listening. I wonder if George is listening.

"George, won't you come to the Deep Well with me?" She whispered almost inaudibly.

George came to the window at once. "Gypsy, is that you?"

The night became quiet, all of its creatures awaiting her reply. George knew then that she really was there. He bounded down the stairs and out the kitchen door.

Esma shook her tambourine and let out a long Gypsy trill. Her laughter and the clinking of jewelry rang through the woods as she raced to the pond. George loped behind. "Hah hah! Hah hah! Esma, Esma, Esma! Where have you been? I've been waiting for you!"

At the clearing, she turned and let him catch up to her. They threw their arms around each other and wept and laughed with joy.

"I want to swim," Esma said, leading George to the water's edge. "I'm grimy from the Alternate World."

"By all means." George helped the giggling Esma off with her clothes. "The Alternate World is indeed a grimy place."

"Yes, and I'd like to know what you were doing there. You have a lot of explaining to do, George Drumm." Esma waded slowly into the cool water, allowing George a long moonlit look.

"And I have a few questions for you as well. But I was hoping not to spend all night talking this time." George took off his own clothes and waded in after her. "I'm here to stay, Esma. And I'll make my explanations in the morning, thank you, I have other things on my mind just now." They paddled about in the water, watching each other's radiant faces.

"It doesn't bother you that you will be cheating the Spiral by staying with me in this Time?"

"But I'm not cheating the Spiral, I'm fulfilling it's necessary course. I love you, Magic Dancer, and the course of love *is* the path of the Spiral. There's no turning back now."

"Spoken like a true Gypsy."

"As I should be. The good folk of Resthaven already know me as your husband."

"Then it is time for me to make an honest man of you." Esma swam over and wrapped herself around him. They floated, entwined together, until George felt Esma shiver. Then he carried her out of the water and back to the house with her cloak wrapped around them both.

As George held her in the softness of the old bed with its down comforter, Esma felt herself in a dream. It was a familiar dream: She was reclining on a cloud with her bearded lover, floating above the mountains which bordered a dusty town in the Alternate World. "I love you, George. Tell me this is not a dream."

"It is *all* a dream, Gypsy, I am more convinced of that now than ever."

"But whose dream is it?"

"Ours. At last."

Dash returned to the courtyard of the Del Rio Apartments, no longer able to tell the difference between waking and dreaming. So many voices called to her. So many wills demanded expression through the kitten's miserable little body. She was no longer herself. She was neither cat nor human. She was neither of the Alternate World nor any other. She was the Spiral, the All—the Vortex, the Nothingness. Here were the threads of Life and Death entwined together into a Knot which could never be untied.

Dash slithered through the hole in the rotten wooden door. She was in the cellar now. The voices grew louder. The shadows loomed larger. Here was the Master Seer at once plummeting toward death and demanding resurrection. Here was the Gypsy beckoning to whomever could hear: "Help me, help me; be my guide." Only Dash could hear. She leapt up into a crawlspace full of rubble and utility lines and started to nose her way toward the satchel.

Then, so faintly—so softly, so far away—the whisper of the Red Mountain Witch herself: "Come to me home. Come to me home. So long lost—come to me home." Dash pawed at the tangled fibrous mass. The smell of herbs wafted up at her from far inside the bag. The kitten squirmed through a rip in the side of the satchel and followed her twitching nose from Knot to Knot. And there in the murky darkness, the satchel itself spoke to her in the language of the Spiral:

Away Away
Around Around
In and In and In
Out and Out and Out
Find A Way Home
Find A Way Away

The chant was taken up by the other voices. The Master Seer, the Gypsy, and the Red Mountain Witch joined in the satchel's refrain.

Away Away
Around Around

Find A Way Home
Find A Way Away

Now Huliyana, Tibareth, the Journeywomen, and all of the
Gypsy Elders were also present in a humming, whistling, jingling
chorus.

In and In and In
Out and Out and Out
Away Away
Around Around
Find A Way Home
Find A Way Away
A Way to Take Me Home

Dash bit down on a Knot. It alone held steady as all else became
a swirling sea. The spirit of Malcom slid away from her like the skin
of a snake. The Red Mountain Witch retreated back to her distant,
dimensionless place. The Gypsies fell silent. Huliyana and Tibareth
skipped down a winding cart path waving gayly to Esma before they
too disappeared. Only one voice remained.

"Dash!" Faye called. "Dash, where are you? Come home, little
one. Come home!"

Chapter 21

"What's the matter, Faye?" Robyn asked with concern; Faye looked depressed.

"My kitten, Dash, is missing. I think she's really gone. I haven't seen her since Friday."

"You've had a lot of trouble with that little thing, haven't you?"

"It seems like she gets into more trouble every day. We haven't had them for very long but, you know, I've really fallen in love with those kittens—and especially Dash. Zeek calls her the kamakazi cat because she seems so bent on self-destruction. He's been telling me right along not to get too attached to her, but I have anyway. I can't believe I'm being such a baby about this—she'll probably never come back and I should just make myself get over it." Faye was close to tears. "This is stupid, but I just hate the thought of Dash being hurt. What if she's been hit by a car or something? Even Felix and Dot seem to know something's wrong."

"Faye, do you want to take the day off?"

"No, I'll pull myself together. I'm sorry. There's not really much more I can do. We've looked and looked."

"Maybe there is something else you can try. Have you ever used a talisman?"

"Like for good luck?"

"No, to answer questions."

"Uh, no."

Robyn took a pendant from the display case. It was a pale amethyst crystal mounted on a copper disc and strung on a purple silk cord.

"You hold the talisman so that it can swing free." Robyn held the knotted cord. "Now, first establish Yes and No—do this someplace where you can concentrate, not like I'm doing here. This is just so you can get the idea. Anyway, keep your hand steady so the talisman is hanging perfectly still. Then ask: 'Talisman, show me No.'"

Faye watched as the necklace began to swing slightly from left to right.

"Then you steady it again and ask to see Yes. It should swing forward and back. You can test the Yes and No on questions that you know the answer to already. See, the whole idea is to ask yes and no questions and let the talisman answer by the direction it swings."

Faye was dubious. Obviously one's subconscious controlled the motion of the so-called talisman. She was glad Zeek wasn't there, he'd be laughing his head off. "That's it?"

"That's it. Use it to direct you to Dash. You can ask: Is Dash in this house? Is Dash in this neighborhood? Is Dash hurt? Whatever you want. Here, borrow this for a while. Wear it for a day to charge it with your energy before you use it. Give it a try, Faye. You may not admit it, but you're a very intuitive person."

Faye took the pendant from Robyn and put it on. She had admired that particular piece since her first day at the Lost Unicorn. "Thanks Robyn. I'll let you know how I do."

"That's quite a load you carry around." George was watching Esma collect her sword, hand shaped pouch, tambourine, and assorted jewelry, all of which were still scattered in the grass by the pond. They had brought a blanket out along with the fruit and bread they planned to eat for breakfast. "You're really quite a slim thing without all that costume."

"And with it?"

"A bit sharp and lumpy in places."

Esma laughed. "But you were not deterred."

"Never. From the moment I saw you emerge from your magic

satchel, I knew I had found the yummiest creature on the face of the earth."

"Yummiest?"

"Sorry, it may take me a while to loose my Alternate World slang."

"Well, speaking of the Alternate World, who should start first and where? "

"Let's see. We can alternate! You ask me a question and then I'll ask you a question. Eventually we'll get both stories told."

"Very well. What happened to Audy in the Alternate World?"

"A leading question, that—the answer is: he became a father." George handed Esma an orange and launched into the tale of Audy and the kittens. Every detail raised another question. Back and forth they asked and explained, until there were no more questions and their two stories melded into one.

"So, this is Faye's cat?" Esma mused, stroking Sylvestor. Neither she nor George had said right out what they had both noticed—the striking physical similarity between Faye and Esma.

"No, Felix is Faye's cat, and now the kittens. Sylvestor has always been my cat. He was just waiting for me to come and get him. Faye understood that."

"Yes, I believe it. You two are a matched set."

"I thought that was *we* two. Look at how late it's getting. Let me take you into town. We can play and dance at the pub and get a good meal there."

"Into Resthaven? In the first place, I've never danced in Resthaven or gone to the pub. The people here know me as a fortune teller only, and one who keeps to herself at that."

"Ah, but since I have come they've learned that you were really awaiting the return of your true love. It would only be fitting for you to dance again, now that we are reunited."

"Perhaps tomorrow night. Tonight I want to eat my meal with you alone and sleep out here under the stars. Let's go get some food from the house, and your fiddle, and the quilt—we can build a little fire by the rocks over there."

"Spoken like a true Gypsy!"

In Faye's dream she was in an underground labyrinth looking for something. As she wound deeper and deeper into the subterranean chambers, she became more and more afraid. The feeling of death engulfed her. Zeek would be looking for her. He would be worried. He would think she had died. Now Faye was the one who was lost. She anxiously tried to find her way out of the maze; that which she sought was not there.

"Here, you can have this back now."

"Did you use it?"

"I tried, Robyn, but I got conflicting messages. I enjoyed wearing it, anyway. Maybe I'll buy it for myself when I can afford to. But Dash has been gone a week now. I think I should just give up."

"You're not really letting go of her, I can tell. What did the talisman say?"

Faye sighed heavily. "Well, I went to each of the places I've seen Dash exploring and asked if she was there—the little sheds and things in peoples' yards on the alley—and the answer was always No. The only place which wasn't a definitive No was the Del Rio compound across the street. I watched Dash go over there once and disappear into the courtyard. So I went into the courtyard and asked—luckily no one was around—and instead of getting a No or a Yes, the talisman just went around in circles. At first it seemed like it would be Yes, but it started going around. I asked a bunch more questions like: Is Dash alive? Is Dash hurt? Is Dash dead? But all I got was the circles."

"That's interesting. Circles like that mean, obviously, that the answer is unclear. I think I'll try, if you don't mind." Robyn took the pendant from Faye and put it around her own neck.

"Actually I'd appreciate it. You're right, I haven't let go of Dash. I keep thinking of her so much, I feel like she must be around, maybe she's even trying to get back to me. And I've been having these dreams about looking for her. Then when I wake up, I'm left with this feeling that no matter how much I search, I won't find her—*she* has to find her way back to *me*."

Robyn stared at Faye. Ever since that night last week, she could not look at her without seeing Esmarelda. Now she even heard Esmarelda. Hadn't the Gypsy spoken exactly the same way about her own lost cat, Audy?

"Now, let me see if I've got this right. First we find your clan and return the satchel and Tarot card to Huliyana and Tibareth. Now, where do you suppose they'll be?"

"I'd try around Andarra. If they're not there now, they'll have visited at some point and we can get an idea of their itinerary. We could even leave a message."

"All right. So first we head toward Andarra. That's good because it will bring us near the Ethalees. Mrs. delaTorre did ask me for some of their goods, and I thought once we had finished your chores, we could go back to the Travelers. I'd like to see Rudy again, and thank his mother for sending me to the Gypsies."

"Yes, I owe her some thanks for that too, don't I? So you're suggesting that after the Hedzaj, we visit the Ethalees, and then set out for the Bay of Khios. You are intrepid, aren't you? That's a long journey."

"No longer than the one I've already taken. With you along, I'll enjoy every minute."

"I have an idea." Esma brought George a mug of hot coffee from the pot brewing over the fire. They had been camping by the pond ever since their first day together and continued to postpone their trip into town. "Once we're all the way out there with the delaTorre clan,

we might as well go on to Omanipinamo and sail back to Sumweir
Island so you can see your mother again. I would very much like to
meet her."

"You would spend one hundred days at sea with me? I don't think
you know what you're suggesting. Have you ever been on a ship?"

"I've learned all about it from your music. It's just an idea. We'll
have plenty of time to make up our minds—or perhaps come up with
another route."

"You're not suggesting . . ."

"Well, it is something to think about. We've both proven that we
know our way around a magic satchel."

"I surely would like to see Mum again and tell her all that's
happened to me. She's a feisty sort, but I know she'll be worrying."

"Now there's no need for that. We can start right away to get a
message to her. We'll send it through the Wanderer grapevine."

"And when do we start a'wandering ourselves, Esma, my love?"

"I was supposed to have found the old satchel. Don't you think I
should try again to find it? I had a dream last night that we left here
and then had to come back to get the satchel. But we couldn't get
back. We walked and walked but never made any progress, and the
whole while the satchel was here. We had had it but left it behind.
There's a way from here to Andarra that takes us right by Red
Mountain. If we had the satchel we could return it quickly and I
would feel much better about seeing Tibareth and Huliyana again."

"Personally, I'm dreading seeing those two. What do you think
they'll do to me for stealing Huliyana's satchel?"

"Nothing. They wouldn't dare. You followed the Spiral's course,
remember?"

"Yes, love's course. Esma, tell me your dream again." She did.
"If the Gypsies taught me anything, it's to pay attention to dreams.
Your dream seems to be saying that the satchel will come to us if we
don't abandon it. Let's just stay here and see if we can bring it back.
Don't you have some special magic for such things?"

Esma nodded. "You know, I do. You just gave me the idea.

We'll dream it back. But it would be easier if we moved back into the house. We'll need to burn candles all night and sleep on dream pillows. It's time to make that trip into town, too, I'll need some supplies."

They heard the mewing as soon as they entered the house. Sylvestor ran over to the cellar door and let out a long anxious cry.

"Now, how on earth...?"

"That door's been closed tight forever! I never used the cellar, did you?"

"Not since I've been here."

Esma lit a candle as George worked on the door. It was swollen from age, and even after the latches were undone it refused to open. George threw his full weight against it and it swung open. Sylvestor ran down the stairs into the darkness and George and Esma followed with the candle. Sylvestor led them right to the satchel, lying filthy and threadbare on the cold floor. A small animal writhed and cried within. George scooped up the dirty bundle and they hurried upstairs.

In the Gypsy's drawing room, Dash emerged from the old magic satchel. She was a pathetic sight, half starved and shivering with cold and fear. Esma fell in love with the kitten at once and ran to get it some food.

"I guess we don't need that trip into town after all. Here is the satchel just as you said. We can leave tomorrow as far as I'm concerned." The Gypsy fed Dash pieces of bread soaked in sour milk. "The four of us."

George and Sylvestor watched the Gypsy with the kitten.

"You know who that is, don't you?" George finally asked.

"This cat? I wasn't even thinking about where it came from. It's just some stray kitten from the Alternate World that wandered into the satchel, I suppose."

"It's not just any kitten Esma. I recognize it. So does Sylvestor. It's one of *Audy's* kittens."

"Of course! Who else could have found the satchel! Thank you, thank you, little one. I'll take good care of you from now on." Esma looked up with delight but George was frowning at her. She had never seen him look so displeased.

"You can't keep it. I want you to take it back to Faye. I gave the kittens to her in exchange for taking Sylvestor away—an honest Gypsy's exchange, and because I just felt she should have them. I can't explain it, Esma, but I don't feel right about keeping this one. I bet Faye is missing her even now."

"Take it back? You want me to go back to the Alternate World? Now? I should have the kitten. It's Audy's offspring, after all—it's Malcom's offspring, too, in a way. It doesn't belong in the Alternate World and neither do I, not for another minute!"

Esma clutched the kitten to her heart. George picked up his fiddle and jammed his hat on his head. "I'm going into town."

"Is Dash in the Alternate World?" Robyn asked. The talisman swung from left to right.

"Is Dash in the Gypsy's world?" The pendant swung away from Robyn and then toward her.

"Has Dash returned the lost satchel to Esmarelda? Does Esmarelda have Dash now?" Twice more the motion was forward and back.

"Thank you, talisman." Robyn returned the necklace to its display case and then locked the store up for the night. She was glad Ramon was out of town. She had work to do.

"Robyn, what are you doing here?"

"I came to tell you that we want Dash back."

"Dash?"

"The kitten."

"But it's my kitten. It's Audy's kitten. Why can't I have it?"

"It's Faye's kitten. Faye saved that kitten's life. It's Faye's kitten."

"How did she save it's life?"

"She took the poor thing in in the first place when it was barely weaned. She pried her out of the engine of a pick-up truck. She kept her from falling off the roof."

Esma woke up. Falling off the roof? That was how Audy died. She rolled over and found herself alone in the bed. George had been spending all of his time playing at the pub or roaming around by the pond. He had barely spoken to Esma since they had found the kitten. Just when all of their preliminary tasks were completed and they should have been setting out on their journey, their plans for traveling were in limbo. They were furious with each other.

"Dash! Dash! Here, Dash!" Esma got up and went looking for the cause of all this dissension. The kitten was squatting by the closed cellar door, crying plaintively. Not even she had been friendly to Esma since the argument with George. The more the Gypsy tried to win her affections, the less interested the kitten was. After her first ravenous mouthfuls, she barely ate; and she slept by the cellar door no matter how much tempting bedding Esma put down elsewhere.

"Dash?"

The animal looked up and mouthed a silent meow.

"Do you want to go back to Faye?"

"Eeeeeeee-Yowwwwww." This time her answer was far from silent.

"I guess there's no arguing with that." The Gypsy looked down at the kitten, scrawny and trembling, and was reminded of Mark's message: *'The cat came back.'* A shiver went up her spine.

"And back to the Alternate World *you* go, little one. You have done your part and deserve to be returned to your home, as your father was to his." Esma gathered up her cloak and satchel and dressed hurriedly. She did not consult her charts or take her pack. It only took her a minute to get ready. "Let's go," she said, wrapping the kitten up loosely in a gauzy veil, which she then tied to her belt. The Gypsy ran out and down the path to the pond. George was curled up in a blanket on the grass.

"I'm going to return Dash." Esma whispered in his ear. He moaned and rolled over. "Why don't you go and keep the bed warm for me. I won't be long."

George sat up and peered through the darkness at Esma. He heard the kitten mewing.

"I'm just going to drop off the kitten and then I'll be right back. I'm sorry I tried to keep her. I'm sorry I made you so mad." Esma put her face in George's beard. "I don't know what got into me. It's just that when I realized it was one of *his* kittens, I felt I had to keep it."

"It's all right, darling. I'm sorry, too. I'm sorry you have to go back to the Alternate World, but it is the right thing. I should have given you some time before demanding that you do this. Hurry home, my love." He gave her a long, tender kiss and then got up and headed toward the house, leaving the Gypsy to prepare herself for the Spiral.

"Robyn, it's me."

"Must you always show up in the middle of the night?"

"Sorry, it's the way the satchel works. Listen, this is absolutely my last trip back here. I've brought this kitten back and I just need to know where Faye lives so I can return it to her."

"So you got my message!"

"I got everyone's message. It just took me a while. Please, Robyn, George is waiting for me."

"So, you found him, too. Why didn't you tell me about George from the beginning?"

"Please, Robyn!"

"But I'll never see you again, and there's still so much you haven't explained."

"If you can get a message to me, you can be sure I can get one to you. As for explanations, my friend, there is no explaining the path of the Spiral, one is hard pressed even to describe it. It's late, Robyn, and cold. Please direct me, us, to Faye's house." The kitten cried softly.

"It's right around the corner. Here, I'll throw a coat on and walk over there with you."

The two women stood at the end of the driveway of the Del Sol apartments. "That's their place straight ahead, number six." Robyn pointed. "Look, there's Felix and Dot, Dash's sister." The cats stood in the light from the porch as if waiting for someone.

"Well then..." Esma released Dash from her veil and watched her run to the door, where she was greeted curiously by Dot and Felix. Felix immediately let out a long cry. Robyn and Esma saw a light go on in the apartment, and then Faye came out onto the porch wearing a bathrobe.

"Felix? Is that you? Come on in." Faye held the door open and Felix trotted in, but Dot and Dash scampered off under a car. "Oh my god! Dash? Zeek! Zeek!" She went back inside, leaving the door open. Felix ran back out. Zeek emerged with Faye a minute later. He too wore just a robe; his hair and beard were wild from sleep. This was Esma's first glimpse of Zeek. She watched as he and Faye worked together to lure Dash out from under the car. When they finally had her, they held her between them in a gentle hug as Dot and Felix wound around their feet. Esma could just make out their excited voices.

"The crazy cat came back. You knew she would, didn't you, Faye?"

"I just knew I couldn't give up on her. Hey, it's freezing out here! And Dash is half starved. Let's all get inside."

"He looks like George!" Esma exhaled in disbelief.

"What?" Robyn was shivering in her slippers and light jacket.

"Oh dear, we better get you indoors too." As Faye, Zeek and their three cats disappeared into the apartment, the Gypsy hurried Robyn back to her house.

"Move over." Esma crawled into bed next to George. Sylvestor made a nest for himself in her soft clothes, which lay piled on the floor.

"Ummm. That didn't take long. Did the kitten get back all right?"

"Just fine. I'm glad I went back. It was good to see Robyn one last time."

"Ummm. She's quite a character."

"Aren't we all?"

"Ummm."

"So, will you take me into town tomorrow night so we can play and dance at the pub? It's time for us to get to work..."

"Ummm. Come here."

"...and take to the road."

"Ummm. You smell good."

"And I thought of another place we must go: Canary. I promised I'd be back to see Derek and Marion."

"Ummm. Add it to the itinerary. But don't forget the first stop."

"Andarra? No, I guess the first stop will have to be Red Mountain."

"No, darling. You're thinking too hard. The first stop for this caravan is right here—I call it Bliss."

"Do you believe in magic, Zeek?" Felix, sharing a pillow with Faye, seemed to be purring secrets into her ear.

Zeek was wiggling his toes under the blankets, braving the sharp claws of Dot and Dash. "I used not to believe in anything, Faye. But then I fell in love with you and, most amazingly, you fell in love with me."

"So?"

"*So?* So, now I believe in everything."

"Including magic?"

"Especially magic."

Spiral Map of Time Trilogy Book 1

The adventure begins . . .
THE TIME DANCER
A Novel of Gypsy Magic
by Zelda Leah Gatuskin

Can one really navigate the vast sea of Time? Celtic fiddler George Drumm is intrigued by symbols etched on the cairns of his remote Sumweir Isle home by ancient Wanderer tribes. The closed double spiral is said to depict the alternating timelines of two parallel worlds. When George learns that there are still Wanderer peoples crisscrossing the great continent, he sets out to find them and learn their secrets.

Across the ocean, George soon finds the Wanderers and woos them with his music. He travels with one group after another, at last joining a Gypsy caravan far inland. When time-dancing Gypsy Esmarelda drops in on them from the Future, romance blossoms. But the couple is out of sync in Time. Esmarelda is on a mission to rescue her cat Audy, presumably stolen by her nemesis, Malcom the Master Seer. Her quest takes her, and then George, to the parallel, frighteningly un-magical Alternate World. But in the dusty town of Caliente, New Mexico, the lovers find a friend in Robyn, proprietor of The Lost Unicorn metaphysical shop.

As Esmarelda and George leapfrog across the Spiral Map of Time in search of lost cats, missing satchels and each other, they share glimpses of their enchanted universe with Robyn, and confirm what she has always suspected: There *is* a world of Magic just the other side of our dreams.

Spiral Map of Time Trilogy Book 2

The magic dance continues . . .
THE TWO MAGICIANS
From Nowhere to Forever
by Zelda Leah Gatuskin

Esmarelda and George Drumm, with Sylvestor the cat, have their hands (and paws) full when they attempt to find the Red Mountain Witch and return her magic satchel. Drawn into the dangerous doings of the Goathorns Coven, which collects and corrects lost charms and broken spells in their mystical domain, the couple fears the Witches will force George to make up his ten-years leap in Time.

In the Alternate World, the Summer Solstice Harmony Convention in Piper Canyon, now in its fifth year, has been increasing the leakage between parallel timelines. The New Age gathering in the Rockies happens to be a mere spiral-turn away from Goathorns Peak, a.k.a. The Top of The World, where the Spiral Map of Time reverses direction, Future meets Past, and the mundane world turns into a world of magic.

With Robyn and her belly dance troupe joining the Harmony Convention on one side, and the time-traveling Gypsies approaching on the other, the Minder of the Knot and the Loophole must work valiantly to restore order and prevent Time from unraveling. Before he is done, Brooks the Minder will expose the dark history of the five sisters of the Goathorns Coven, the recent transgressions of their shape-shifting Familiars, the secret lives of two Master Seers, and his own deepest desires.

Spiral Map of Time Trilogy Book 3

History repeats itself . . .
THE TEN YEARS
Double or Nothing
by Zelda Leah Gatuskin

Both Past and Future are catching up to Esmarelda and George Drumm, who have taken liberties with Time in order to stay together. Now, fleeing the Goathorn Mountains after their escapades with the two magicians, they find that their lives have been turned upside-down.

Across the Spiral in Caliente, New Mexico, Robyn's universe is also shaken. Her metaphysical shop, The Lost Unicorn, is still serving as a way station between worlds, and the mammoth cottonwood tree in back has become an actual portal. Mr. Brooks, the Emissary, and others she thought she would never see again after last year's Harmony Convention debacle, resurface.

At The Top Of The World, Weaver Oshi contemplates the tangled threads of Fate that have brought together more than one pair of Time-crossed lovers. When all of the Witches', Gypsies' and New Agers' magic has played out, where—and when—will everyone end up?

Here is the passionate, mind-blowing, music-and-dance-filled resolution to the Time Dancer's conundrum.